Finding Fiona

Finding Fiona

Donna Fasano

Contents

.

What reviewers are saying about Donna Fasano

"...has plenty of wit and fun, and more heart than the usual run of chick-lit. It's got mystery, humor, romance, and friendship." ~E. Lewis, Librarian, for **Finding Fiona** (Women's Fiction)

"...tons of emotions up and down and an ending I didn't expect." ~L. Ryan, Kindle customer, for **Finding Fiona** (Women's Fiction)

"The pleasure of Fasano's style lies in the scrumptious descriptions... and her characters' sincere, mature desire to make things work." ~Publishers Weekly for **Following His Heart** (Contemporary Romance)

"...funny and realistic." ~Wilmington News Journal for **The Merry-Go-Round** (Romantic Comedy / Women's Fiction)

"...an utterly charming romantic comedy that pulled me in right from the start." ~ Karen McQuestion, author of A Scattered Life for **The Merry-Go-Round** (Romantic Comedy / Women's Fiction)

"...heart-wrenching, sweet, touching, and requires a box of tissues. In this story, life isn't always perfect, but happy endings are still possible." ~USA TODAY for **An Almost Perfect Christmas** (Sweet Romance)

"...a unique, captivating, emotional tale that will keep you thoroughly enthralled until the very end." ~Books and Pals Review Blog for **Two Hearts in Winter** (Contemporary Romance)

"...realistic, intelligent, and heartwarming." ~Books and Pals Review Blog for **Her Fake Romance** (Contemporary Romance)

Chapter One

Just Another Day

Before the duffel bag even had a chance to thump to the floor, Fiona said, "Pick that up, Sam."

Her son tossed her an eye-roll that had taken him every one of his fifteen years of life to perfect. He bent, grabbed the canvas strap, slung it over his shoulder, and took the stairs two at a time.

"And put that sweaty uniform directly into the washer." Fiona hated shouting, but Sam would surely claim not to have heard her if she didn't.

She dropped her keys on the lowboy by the front door, and saw that her daughter had finally gotten herself from the van to the house. "Your dad will be home any minute. Set the table for dinner."

"It's Sam's turn," Cassie reminded her.

Fiona wanted to groan. Sam had hit puberty as if it had been the proverbial brick wall. He couldn't remember a damn thing lately. Forgot homework assignments, books, practice times, phone messages, you name it. He could go from being jovial to surly with nary a lick of warning. Getting him to complete any task was enough to wear a person's nerves raw. However, Fiona knew it was a battle she had to wage or else Cassie would begin to complain about the unfairness of the Rowland house, and then her firstborn would quickly move to the unfairness of the world in general. No one could work a whine like a seventeen-year-old female.

"Okay, okay. I'll get him to do it. How about pulling the laundry out of the dryer and—"

"Can't," Cassie chimed. "Gotta get online and do some research. I'm supposed to bring maps of Ancient Egypt to study group tonight for our World History project."

"That's fine. Just fine." Fiona set down her purse and started toward the back of the house, muttering, "I'll gather up the laundry. I'll wash the laundry. I'll fold the laundry and I'll put away the damn laundry." No one could hear her grumbling. No one was interested, either.

Even though she found herself complaining every now and then about how little help she received from her family, she couldn't help but feel pleased that her children's lives were so full. The private schools they attended offered grueling college preparatory curriculums and extracurricular activities abounded. Both of them had to do some hopping in order to keep pace with the schedules they'd set for themselves; and, heaven knew, Fiona danced as fast as she could, as well.

She sighed as she entered the kitchen. The rich scent of rump roast and onions hung heavy in the air. Tuesdays called for an easy Crock-Pot recipe. Most days, Fiona was so busy she didn't know if she was up or down, coming or going. Tuesday shifted life into overdrive. All because she stubbornly refused to give up these sit-down family meals.

This was the one night she felt as if she, Stan, and the kids were a cohesive unit. A loving, caring, nurturing family rather than a pack of gypsies scattered across the countryside. And she'd have her one night of family togetherness, damn it, even if it meant smacking knots on the heads of each and every member of the Rowland household.

Fortunately, measures that drastic were rarely necessary. She opened the fridge and pulled out the salad fixings, grinning all the while. She didn't mind admitting that she possessed quite a flair for threatening.

Once the lettuce had been washed and torn, the tomatoes chopped, and the cucumber sliced, Fiona picked up the bowl and deposited it on the dining room table on her way to the stairs.

"Hey," she called toward the upper regions of the house. "Dinner in ten minutes. Sam, get down here and set the table." Then she went back through the kitchen and down the stairs into the basement to take care of the laundry. Out of the dryer, into the basket. Out of the washer, into the dryer. Out of the hamper, into the washer. A ritual filled with such fun and excitement it endangered the soundness of her mind.

Once both machines were whirring, she trudged back up the steps with an overflowing basket of clean clothes and set it in the family room. The folding would have to wait until later, while she relaxed in front of the television.

Sailing back through the kitchen and dining

room to the base of the stairs—she didn't need a fancy pedometer; she fulfilled the suggested daily requirement of ten thousand steps just keeping this bunch moving—she shouted, "*Sam! Now!*" She gritted her teeth when the faint strains of video games drifted from above. Sam should be in the kitchen helping out, not killing rogue warriors. "Don't make me come up there."

Evidently, she'd mustered the right amount of menace in her tone because the beeps and explosions ceased and she heard Sam's footsteps clomping down the hall. Why did teenage boys have to walk like Frankenstein's monster?

By the time she'd goaded Sam into completing the simple task of placing plates, glasses, and cutlery on the table, Fiona was sorry she hadn't opted for takeout pizza. Cassie only made matters worse when she breezed into the room ready to nitpick.

"You've got the fork on the wrong side, dweeb," she sneered at her brother.

Fiona wanted to ask her daughter when she'd turned into a Martha Stewart clone, but she squelched the comment.

The fuse on her sanity was shortened even more when everyone was ready to sit down to eat, but

Stanley had failed to arrive home. He knew how important these family dinners were to her, and timing was everything on Tuesdays. He worked late most days, then he went out several nights a week to shoot pool, play poker, or teach his accounting class at the local community college. He also made himself available for tutoring those students who were gearing up to take the certification test. Stan had a lot of interests, and Fiona didn't mind. But he certainly should be able to arrive on time for one measly meal together each week. That wasn't too much to ask.

"Let's sit down and get started," she told the kids. "Dad's probably on his way."

As he held out his plate to be served, Sam launched into a litany, detailing the high points of his day. "And Mr. Richards got pissy today—"

"Sam." Fiona arched her eyebrows, the spoonful of green beans she held hovering over her son's plate. "We do not use the word pissy in polite conversation."

Without missing a beat, he continued, "Sharon and Isabelle were whispering and passing notes, and Mr. Richards got all jacked up about it and gave us all extra homework." Fiona served herself some beans. "'*All jacked up*,' huh? I've never heard that phrase before."

Cassie chimed in, "It means he got pissy."

Her kids shared a laugh, and she couldn't help but chuckle herself. This kind of camaraderie was exactly why Fiona willingly endured a bit more stress on Tuesdays. And her husband was missing it.

The idiot.

Sam went on to tell them about practice. He'd made the cross-country track team and he was doing all he could to prove himself to his teammates.

Two red spots brightened his cheeks. "Dave says Isabelle wants me to ask her to the dance."

Surprise made Fiona want to whoop right out loud, but she contained herself. Effusive maternal reaction could instantly ruin a pubescent boy's whole mood. But this news delighted her. She and Stan had recently talked about how their son seemed to be bebopping through his early teens, seemingly content with sports, video games, and his buddies. Before this evening, Sam had never mentioned a girl by name before. If he talked about girls, he usually lumped the females of the species together as a group, typically followed with some disparaging remark. Seems his world was changing, and he was even willing to talk about it. Yes, her boy's spirits were high today, despite the extra homework his teacher had assigned.

"You going to ask her?" Cassie queried carefully.

Fiona noticed that her daughter kept her eyes downcast, her tone curious but nonthreatening. It seemed that Cassie, too, sensed the importance of this moment for Sam.

He shrugged, dipping his head; however, Fiona could tell the prospect of a first date excited him.

Her gaze darted toward the front door, and the hope of hearing Stan's car pull into the driveway preoccupied her. Dark clouds rolled over her mood.

"You okay, Mom?" Cassie stabbed a tomato wedge.

Fiona nodded. "I'm fine, sweetie. But I am going to refill my drink." She reached for her nearly full water glass. "While I'm in the kitchen, I'll give your dad a buzz. Make sure he's on his way."

Fiona snatched up her cell phone from the counter and tried to let go of her anger. Stan missing dinner didn't necessarily mean he was being insensitive, or absentminded. An accident could have stalled traffic. He could be sitting on

I-95 or 202 with the thousands of other people who commuted into and out of Wilmington every day for work. Or car trouble could have left him stranded on one of the narrow, winding roads leading home to Hockessin.

Guilt swam around in her stomach as she remembered thinking ill of him this morning when she'd arrived home from the morning car pool run and found his lunch still sitting on the counter where she'd set it out for him. She'd mentally deemed him an idiot then, too, but a flash of glee had burst through her as she'd placed the brown bag back in the fridge; the thought of not having to make his lunch tomorrow morning had her grinning like a fool herself. God, how she hated the monotonous chore of making that ham and Swiss on rye every day.

She shouldn't be so tough on Stanley. He worked hard. Handling other people's money was a nerve-racking job, and his accounting class demanded a great deal of time and attention, too.

When his cell phone went directly to voice mail, she left a message that they'd started dinner without him and that she hoped he was on his way home. Then she called his office number. Again, she reached a voice mail system, and she left a duplicate message, this one snippier than she intended.

She ended the call and set her phone on the counter as an odd, whispery voice soughed through her head. Stan hadn't missed a family dinner since—she thought back over the months—well, since last spring. Like every other CPA, her husband's world turned nightmarish during tax season.

Some odd and nebulous gut feeling had her pulling the junk drawer open. She fished out the worn and tattered address book. She really should buy a new one and transfer the numbers and addresses before this one fell completely apart. What she should do is transfer everything into her cell, but who had the time or the energy for that?

She found the number she wanted, that of the only colleague of Stan's she knew. George Harrigan had moved into the office next to Stan's when the man started working for the accounting firm about seven years ago. Stanley and George had hit it off instantly, not just forming a work relationship, but becoming buddies, as well. Fiona had invited George and his wife, Connie, to dinner once, but as it turned out, Fiona and Connie hadn't found a single common thread on which to base a friendship.

Connie had been an up-and-coming exec with a local banking company at the time. With no children of her own, the woman simply couldn't relate to Fiona. In fact, she'd made it pretty clear that she couldn't fathom Fiona's stay-at-home-mom lifestyle.

George answered mid-ring, identifying himself straightaway.

"Hi, George. Fiona Rowland here." They exchanged some quick pleasantries, and then Fiona asked, "Have you seen Stan around today? I expected him home by now, and he's not answering his phone."

"I passed him in the hall this morning. I haven't had a chance to sit and talk with him in weeks, though. We're all overworked lately with these new clients coming on board." He huffed out a sigh. "The job security's worth it, I guess."

The tone of his voice implied that the jury was actually still out on that issue.

"He's probably just running late," George continued. "Don't be too hard on the poor guy when he does get there."

"I won't. Thanks, George. Good talking to you."

Another pang of guilt shot through her as she set her cell phone on the counter. Stan hadn't told her that anything was going on at work. After topping off her glass from the pitcher of filtered water in the fridge, she went back to join the kids.

"I left a message." She slid into her chair at the table and tucked her napkin onto her lap. "He's on his way, I'm sure."

Sam and Cassie didn't appear in the least concerned, and Fiona fleetingly wondered why she struggled to keep Tuesdays sacred.

"Did you bake the cookies for the sale?" Cassie asked.

Fiona nodded. "All twelve dozen."

She'd been a little miffed when not one but two of the other mothers on the fundraising committee had called to remind Fiona of the sale. Both women had maintained that their day jobs would keep them from doing any of the baking, but they had the gall to insist that store-bought cookies wouldn't do.

The bake sale would benefit a good cause. Fiona had focused on the new laptops that would be purchased for the computer lab as she'd mixed the second double batch of cookie dough late this afternoon. She hadn't minded, really. Baking was one of her passions.

Her daughter's eyes grew large and she rested her elbow on the corner of the table. "I got so mad at Emily today. Even though she knows how much I like Johnny Williams, she flirted with him after school." Cassie's tone conveyed that she clearly thought her friend had committed a sacrilege.

St. Anne's was an all-girls school, but no amount of regulation and supervision on the part of the nuns could keep the randy neighborhood boys from sniffing around after hours.

"Honey, I really can't see Emily doing that to you."

"Mom, she leaned up to the fence and practically put her boobs right in his face."

Sam snorted, and Fiona directed a silent warning his way as she speared a piece of juicy beef.

Fiona thought of the chaste, Peter Pan-collared blouses the girls were required to wear. "Those uniforms don't afford the opportunity of showing much in the way of cleavage," she reminded her daughter.

"As soon as the bell rings, some of the girls have

started unfastening the first couple buttons of their blouses."

Surprise made her jaw muscles loosen. "On school grounds? While they wait for their rides? And this is okay with Sister Bernadette?"

"She's such an old bat."

"Cassie," Fiona admonished. "You love Sister."

"Yeah, well." Her daughter wobbled her head acerbically in response. "Emily was the first one to get away with it, Mom. She complained to Sister Bernadette last week that it was too hot, and Sister never said a word to her. Now lots of girls are doin' it."

The melodrama in the teen's tone made it sound as if Emily had been standing in the school yard half-naked.

Cassie muttered, "But if I tried it the old bat would give me two demerits, I just know it."

Her daughter's friendship with Emily reminded Fiona of her own high school best friend. Thoughts of Diane Fleming flashed through her mind. Lord, but the two of them had been complete opposites. Just like Cassie and Emily were now. As different as night and day. Yet something special seemed to connect them. Cassie might be irritated with Emily at the moment, but in a snap the girls would iron out their differences and come out of the dispute smiling.

Cassie and Emily always ironed out their differences.

An odd sadness swept through Fiona. Di had been her best friend for years, yet it seemed that one day Fiona had turned around and Di was gone from her life.

"Mom."

Sam's voice enticed her back to the present.

"It's six twenty."

"Oh, my." She tossed her napkin onto the table. "Cassie, you're supposed to be at the library at six forty-five, right?" She looked at her son. "And your Scout meeting starts at seven."

"If you'd buy me a car," Cassie said, "your driving would be cut in half."

"You already know your father and I are not going to buy you a car. You may earn a car."

"But—"

"Cassie, we don't have time for this conversation now." She stood. "You rinse the dishes and put them in the dishwasher. I'll put the food away."

Sam pushed back from the table and started helping. Even with Cassie's moping, the air took on a sudden static.

Fiona took the bowl of green beans from her son. "Sam, you get that uniform out of that duffel bag. If it's not down in the laundry room, it won't be washed and ready for tomorrow."

Fiona stood in the empty dining room and took a moment to just breathe. Cassie had the water running at the kitchen sink, and Sam clunked up the stairs. Fiona juggled the platter of beef, the bowl of beans, and the potatoes—and she was off.

Later that evening, she went up the stairs with a glass of merlot in hand. She loved this time of night. The errands had been run, the chores were finished, the kids were settled, the house was quiet, and she could change into her soft jersey pj's and slip between the sheets with a good book. She could count this as another successful day. The only thing keeping it from being perfect was that Stan had missed spending time with the kids at dinner.

On her way down the hall, she stopped to look in on Sam.

"Don't stay up too late," she warned.

"I won't."

"You finish all your homework?"

His eyes didn't budge from the TV screen. "All done."

"Okay." She looked at him in silence, unable to believe he was already as tall as his father. Nearly all grown up. "Turn that off soon."

Impatience flashed in his grayish blue eyes. "All right, already."

Fiona chuckled. "You know my primary objective is to annoy you, right?"

He shook his head, offered her a half smile, then gazed back at the video game as he murmured, "'Night, Mom. Love you."

"Right back at you. Good night, honey."

The door of Cassie's bedroom was closed, so Fiona knocked softly.

"*Entrez!*" French was one of Cassie's favorite subjects.

"Hey, there." Fiona offered her daughter a smile when she twisted around in her desk chair. "I was going to bed and wanted to say good night. But I just realized I didn't ask how study group went. Is everything all lined up for the project?"

Cassie sighed, the impatience in her expression making Fiona feel she was looking in a mirror. It was peculiar how her daughter had taken after her, from the golden-brown hair and the hazel eyes to the slightly upturned nose and long fingers. Sam, on the other hand, had inherited his father's auburn hair, thick and burnished, and his expressive steel-blue eyes.

"Emily didn't bring her stuff, as usual," Cassie said. "I'm searching for her information now. But we'll be ready."

"Hon, I wanted to talk to you about Emily."

Fiona remembered how her own self-esteem had been affected by having a best friend who'd been more physically developed than she. Fiona had spent years feeling inadequate. She didn't like the thought of Cassie viewing herself as somehow lacking simply because her hormones hadn't fully kicked in yet. Seemed a mother-daughter discussion might be called for.

Excitement danced in Cassie's eyes. "Oh, everything's okay, Mom. We talked after study group. Emily said that after I left school today, Johnny was asking her about me." Cassie grinned. "Way cool, huh?"

It took Fiona a fraction of a second to realize her daughter wasn't in need of a bolstering lecture on her sense of self-worth. "Yes, sweetie," she said softly. "That is way cool. 'Night."

"Love you, Mom."

"Love you, too."

Alone in her room, Fiona set her wineglass on the nightstand, moved the pillow shams to the chair, pulled down the spread, and folded it neatly at the foot of the bed. She tugged down the bed linens, made herself comfortable, tucked the blankets around her, and then reached for the new paperback she'd just bought, a cozy murder mystery sporting a calico cat on the cover. She was reading page one when Sam arrived at her door.

"I forgot about these." He came to the side of the bed and thrust several papers at her. "Coach said the school's insurance company needs signatures from both parents. You need to get Dad to sign 'em when he gets home."

"His poker games usually run pretty late, but I'll try to wait up for him."

Oh, there'd be no trying about it. Fiona planned to wait up, all right. She wanted to know why Stan had missed their family dinner. If he didn't have a good excuse, he was in for an earful, new clients joining the firm or not.

"You both need to sign," her son repeated. "Or I don't get to run in the next meet."

"I understand."

Alone once again, Fiona took a deep drink of her

wine, set the glass aside, snuggled down into the pillow, and opened the novel. She yawned. Every night of the week, it seemed, she went to bed exhausted, but Tuesdays were especially grueling.

The words on the page quickly began to blur.

Fiona awoke with a slow, deep inhalation. Stretching her legs, she opened her eyes and blinked several times. She felt as if she'd only closed them for a few minutes, yet sunlight poured through the window. Adrenaline shot through her as her gaze zipped to the clock. Damn.

Throwing back the covers, she sat up on the edge of the mattress. Everyone was going to be late.

"Stan! Cassie! Sam!" she called. "Get up. We've overslept."

She was out of bed and at the bedroom door, intending to rouse the kids, when her steps slowed. The room felt oddly empty. She whirled around on her heel.

Stanley's side of the bed hadn't been slept in. The insurance papers that Sam needed to have signed still sat on the pillow, undisturbed. Her stomach went queasy.

Finding Fiona

Something was wrong. Something was terribly wrong.

Chapter Two

You Call Your Life Normal?

Fiona pulled open the door, which had Delaware State Police, Troop 1 emblazoned in gold block letters across the plate glass. What kind of wife was she that her husband could go missing and she'd spent the entire evening fuming at him? She fought back the wave of panic threatening to swallow her whole, just as she had earlier this morning. Surrendering to hysteria then wouldn't have done any good. That had been the first decision she'd made while standing at the threshold of her bedroom staring at Stanley's side of their king-size bed.

Upsetting the kids hadn't been an option, so she'd done her best to act as normal as possible. She'd hustled Cassie and Sam out of their beds and then raced back to her room to dress. She'd called Stan's cell phone, but she hung up after four rings. Vacillating between fear and panic, she couldn't find the words for a message. To save Sam from catching any grief from his coach, Fiona had scrawled Stanley's name at the bottom of the insurance form. Then she'd hurried downstairs to throw together some breakfast, although she didn't know why she'd bothered. Cassie had turned her nose up at the microwavable sausage, saying she refused to go to school with pig flesh in her teeth. Fiona had slapped some turkey breast on rye for their lunches. Stan's brown bag from the day before sat on the shelf in the fridge, and Fiona had nearly lost her rickety grip on control.

Where the hell was he? What could have happened? Why wasn't he answering his cell? Why hadn't he called?

That final question haunted her. Stanley would have called her if he could have.

If he could have.

Shoving the ill omen from her mind, Fiona approached the counter. A young woman—scantily clad and clearly hung-over—was handcuffed to one of the metal benches that ran along one wall of the small foyer area. A bleary-eyed man perched on the edge of a chair nearby, his knee bouncing like a jackhammer. A uniformed officer sat at a desk behind a thick wall of plate glass, his head dipped, his attention riveted to the stack of papers in front of him.

The man didn't look up. "Help you?"

"I need to talk to someone—" Fiona's stomach somersaulted as she leaned closer to the small semicircle opening in the glass "—a-about a missing person."

"Hold a sec." He reached for the phone at his elbow. His gaze swung away from the papers only long enough for him to jab three digits. "DeSalvo," was all he said before slamming down the receiver.

The uniformed officer made eye contact with her for the first time. "Someone will be right out, ma'am."

"Thank you."

Not thirty seconds later, a young man strode toward them from the hallway leading toward the back of the building. Certain this was not the person called to help her, Fiona stepped away from the counter and shifted her body a quarter turn.

"Good morning. Can I help you?"

Startled that he'd addressed her, Fiona just stared.

A vibrant energy danced in the young man's dark brown eyes.

"Don't let DeSalvo's baby face fool you." The officer behind the plate glass snickered. "I can vouch that he is out of high school." His pause was brief. "Barely."

DeSalvo grinned. "Jealousy doesn't sound good on you, Joe."

The wisecracking officer tossed DeSalvo a look of mild cynicism, and Fiona got the impression that, had there been fewer people to overhear, he'd have happily delivered a crass rejoinder.

DeSalvo turned his attention back to Fiona. "Detective Chad DeSalvo." He offered his hand and she automatically took it. His grip was firm enough to offer assurance.

"Fiona Rowland."

"Is there something I can do for you, Ms. Rowland?"

"Mrs. It's Mrs. Rowland."

The moment had arrived. She had to spit out her reason for coming here. Panic seized her in an icy grip. "I need someone to find my husband."

He instantly sobered. "I'm sorry, Mrs. Rowland."

Fiona couldn't tell if he was offering condolences because Stan was missing or if he was apologizing for his jovial behavior in the midst of her crisis.

"Let's go someplace where we can talk."

She followed him down the hallway, the heels of her loafers clicking on the shiny marble floor.

"Have a seat," he told her, ushering her into his small office. "Can I get you some coffee? Or juice? A bottle of water?"

"Nothing, thanks. I'm fine." Fiona eased down onto the cracked Naugahyde-covered cushion, set her purse on her lap, and rested her elbows on the cold metal arms of the chair.

"Sorry about the conditions. I just transferred over to this division and I haven't had a chance to requisition some decent furniture."

The sparse office had that gone-to-seed look. About a hundred years ago, the walls had been painted a dove-gray. Smudge marks and nail holes dotted them now. A chipped gunmetal desk took up the majority of the cramped space. An ancient looking chair, yet another shade of gray, was situated behind it. A stunted steel trash can sat within easy reach. The file cabinets didn't come close to being a matched set, but someone had attempted to make them appear so by slapping on paint the same gray color as the walls. The airy potted fern sitting on the deep windowsill presented the only splash of color in the room. It couldn't begin to break the monochromatic monotony.

DeSalvo moved around the desk and sat. "Now, Mrs. Rowland, why don't you tell me what's happening with your husband?"

Anxiety had her feeling green about the gills. There was something she had to get off her chest before she said another word. If she didn't, she just knew she'd regret it.

"Detective," she began, haltingly, "I don't mean to insult you. Honestly, I don't. But... is there someone I can talk to who has some... well, some experience in locating missing people?"

Oh, Lord. Even spoken softly there was no way that could come off sounding anything but offensive.

Her brows furrowed. "It's just that, I'm in trouble here and, well—"

"Mrs. Rowland, let me assure you, I have plenty of experience. Believe me, I'm not as young as I look." There was weariness in his expression, as if he'd been forced to give this assertion too many times.

"But the officer out front said you were barely out of—"

"High school," he finished for her. Absently, he picked up the pen sitting on his desktop. "And there is a hint of truth in that. But I haven't actually been attending school. I've been working. Juvie drug division."

Those late night police shows helped her to put the pieces together. "You're a narc."

"Was, actually. I was a narcotics officer." He ran the backs of his fingers down his jaw. "This youthful face kept me in the schools long after my colleagues were forced out. But it does get tiresome, assuring people that I'm old enough to buy myself a beer."

"Sorry." She pinched her bottom lip between her teeth, trying to work up some sympathy for him. But there certainly were worse problems for a person to contend with. Hers, for one. Stanley's, for another.

Detective DeSalvo tossed the pen aside. "Now, Mrs. Rowland, why don't you tell me about your husband?"

She clutched her purse to her stomach. "Stanley

didn't come home for dinner last night. In fact, he didn't come home at all."

"I see. When's the last time you saw him?"

The question took her aback, and she found herself scrambling for an answer. "I'm not sure," she murmured, but when she saw the detective's dark brows draw together, she immediately regretted having spoken without thinking through her answer.

"Let's work backward. Mr. Rowland didn't make it home last night, and he wasn't there for dinner. I'm assuming he works. Did you see him yesterday morning?"

"I didn't." She felt as if some kind of terrible confession had been forced out of her.

"Okay. Let's back up to Monday evening. Did you see him then?"

"He didn't come home from work Monday. But that's not unusual. He tutors his accounting students on Mondays and Thursdays. I was late coming in from my Women's League meeting, so I slipped into bed without turning on the light." She swallowed, trying to remember if she'd felt him by her side Monday night. Could Stan have been missing longer than she'd thought?

Thankfully, her memory kicked in, assuaging her guilt almost instantly.

"But he had to have come home sometime that night. Yesterday morning, the coffee was made when I got up. It was still warm when I poured myself a quick cup." Her throat constricted. "I just assumed we hadn't crossed paths. I made his lunch and left it on the counter, as I normally do." She drew in a ragged breath. "I was annoyed when I returned home from taking the kids to school, and found his lunch still on the counter. I'd gone to the trouble to make it and I—" nerves had her swallowing jerkily again "—and I thought he'd forgotten it."

"Is it possible he left the house before you? Was his car at the house when you left?"

Fiona blinked. "I hadn't thought of that." Now she felt badly about being annoyed with Stan over the forgotten lunch. He could have left the house before she'd even made it. "I didn't see his car, no. But, then, I wouldn't. He keeps the Volvo in the garage. I never bother pulling in the van. There's room for two vehicles, but I've always got something to unload. Groceries, sports equipment, school projects. Parking in the driveway's just easier." Feeling she was babbling, she clamped her mouth shut. She lifted her gaze to the detective's. "I don't know if he left the house before me or if he was still there when I left the house yesterday morning. I just assumed he was there. I called out a goodbye. Even reminded him that it was Tuesday."

"There's something special about Tuesday?"

"Family night. It's the one evening we all sit together to eat dinner. So we can keep in touch. Talk. Catch up with what everyone's been doing. But we usually end up stuffing our faces and then rushing out for the evening activities."

The detective was quiet a moment. Then he asked, "Not seeing your husband in the evenings or mornings... is that normal?"

Fiona bristled at the subtle disapproving innuendo. "I was exhausted Monday night. I ran the kids to their activities, stopped at the store, and barely made it to my meeting on time. As I said, I got in late. It is normal that Stan and I miss each other most evenings. He has tutoring and teaching and poker nights. I have Women's League and my book club and school meetings, and I'm forever running the kids all over the country. And mornings are hectic in my house, too, Detective. I'm busy getting the kids ready—making breakfast, packing lunches, not to mention finding favorite sweaters, missing uniforms, books, homework papers, you name it. I drive my children to school. Separate schools. If you have children, then you know how weekday mornings can be."

"I don't have children, Mrs. Rowland."

His reply made her too aware of the entreaty in her tone. Her chin tipped up. "Then I guess you wouldn't know. But I can assure you that getting two teens to school on time involves a great deal of chaos."

Suddenly, she was acutely aware of how he must have felt a moment ago when she'd forced him to make his own earnest declaration regarding his age and experience. Just as she'd offered him a look to reflect that there were worse problems than being carded in bars, his steady gaze suggested that he had doubts about a mother's morning rush hour.

"So, Mrs. Rowland—" DeSalvo's words were measured "—can you pinpoint for me exactly when it was that you did see your husband last?"

Fiona's mind raced. She rubbed her fingers across her forehead as she thought back. "I didn't actually see him Monday morning," she said. "But he was in the shower when I went into the bathroom to brush my teeth. The kids and I had to leave early that morning to pick up Emily—she's my daughter's friend." As an afterthought, she murmured, "Emily needs a ride to school on Mondays."

"Did the two of you exchange words?"

"My mouth was full of toothpaste, Detective. The shower was running. But Stan was behind the curtain, I'm sure." She paused. "Although Cassie has been known to use our shower if Sam is taking too long. They share the hallway bathroom."

DeSalvo's dark eyes bored into her.

"When did you actually see your husband, Mrs. Rowland? When did you actually talk to him?"

Fiona moistened her lips. "That would have been Sunday evening. He and Sam were watching a football game on ESPN. I was on my way upstairs and Stanley asked me to make him some popcorn. I—I," she stammered, then stopped. "I told him no."

The urge to avert her gaze was strong, but she resisted. "Sam is your son?"

"Yes."

"How old is he?"

"Fifteen."

The detective picked up the pen again, slid a yellow legal pad in front of him and jotted down

Stanley's name, as well as Sam's and Sam's age. He wrote "car: Volvo" under her husband's name.

"And the daughter you mentioned? Cassie?"

"Yes. Cassie's her name. She's seventeen."

DeSalvo put down the pen, propped his index fingers together, and touched the tips of them to his chin. "So, let me see if I have the situation straight. You haven't seen your husband since Sunday night, but you didn't become concerned until he didn't show up for dinner on Tuesday evening."

My God, what kind of wife am I? A lump of emotion threatened to close her throat.

"Now, just hold on a second." She straightened in her chair. "I told you that Stanley was in the shower Monday morning."

"You said that could have been Cassie. Could she also have made the coffee?"

Fiona went still, but then had to offer a dejected nod. She'd told Cassie she didn't like her drinking coffee in the morning, but her daughter sometimes imbibed anyway, creeping down the stairs early before Fiona could stop her. But then Fiona brightened. "Stan was at work yesterday."

"You did talk to him, then."

"No. But when he didn't show up for dinner last

night, I called his cell phone and his office line. When he didn't answer either one, I called George Harrigan. He works with my husband. George said he'd seen Stan yesterday at the office."

DeSalvo's head bobbed. "If that's true, then your husband's been missing barely twenty-four hours."

Something in his voice made her heart flutter. "You're not going to wait to file a report, are you? You need to start looking now. I'm telling you something has happened to Stan. He wouldn't stay out all night without calling me. He just wouldn't."

"Mrs. Rowland, couples argue all the time."

The detective folded his hands, his tone taking on a well-practiced quality meant to calm. It annoyed Fiona.

"Maybe the two of you had words earlier on Sunday," the man continued. "Maybe you had a little spat. Maybe you were angry enough over it that you refused to fix him that popcorn during the football game. Maybe that was the breaking point and Mr. Rowland just needed to get away for a while. Whatever this is all about, I have a sneaking suspicion that your husband will show up soon and—"

"Stanley and I were not having a little spat." Even though she was trying to keep her wits about her, it seemed that her voice insisted upon raising a few octaves. "We did not argue on Sunday. I wasn't angry about anything. I didn't fix him the popcorn because my husband likes to crunch on those little kernels that are always left in the bottom of the bowl. He chipped a tooth on one last week, which resulted in a six hundred dollar visit to the dentist. I told him if he wanted any more popcorn he'd be fixing it himself."

She felt her face and neck flush with heat. One hand clenched the arm of the chair, the other held her purse in a death grip. "Something's happened to Stanley. And whatever it is can't be good. Are you going to help me or not?"

DeSalvo stared at her a moment. Then he swung his chair around to the file cabinet, jerked open a drawer, and fished out a form.

"Let's file an official report," he said, "so we can start looking for your husband."

While she answered the detective's elementary questions, Fiona was filled with a murky dread. Could it really be true that she and Stan hadn't exchanged words since Sunday evening? And the last thing they had discussed was a damn bag of popcorn?

Chapter Three

In the Blink of an Eye

The lights flickered on automatically the instant Di opened the door of her office. A nifty convenience. She juggled her suede satchel, several overstuffed manila files that wouldn't fit inside, and her customary "tall" mountain chai. None of that snooty "double latte, half caff" crap for her. A plain cup of hot, spicy tea revved her engine just fine.

Her team wouldn't start their workday for another thirty minutes, which would give her plenty of time to go over both the Harding and Fisher proposals before the day's meetings began. She'd already read the files. Understood clearly what her customers were looking for. And the signboards were mind-blowing; she didn't mind saying so herself. Di glanced at the posters sitting in the far corner of her office. She was ready for both presentations, but a final recheck this morning wouldn't hurt. Landing these two accounts would launch her already-bursting-at-the-seams third quarter reports over the top.

It never occurred to her to bemoan her excessive work hours. Single and childless, she was unencumbered by a life outside her job. In other words, she was a slave of Roche Advertising—her job was her life—and she loved every minute of it. Her dogged attitude had long ago earned her the privilege of four walls and a door as opposed to a flimsy little cubicle out there in the open. But it was her merciless approach to business that had won her the title of Vice President of the East Coast Marketing Division and all the perks that came with the job, including a personal assistant, a coveted corner office overlooking the Delaware River to the east and Philadelphia's fabulous Old City to the south, as well as a few other niceties she'd succeeded in negotiating. Securing two more juicy accounts in this squeaky tight economy just might carry her up another floor in the Roche building.

She slid her tote onto the credenza and dumped the files on her desk. Then she shoved open the vertical blinds and popped the lid off the tea. She inhaled the steamy scents of exotic spices and flipped on her computer's monitor while she sipped. Di settled into her chair and reached for the Harding file.

A stickler for punctuality, Michael Fielding of Harding Associates would arrive early, so she'd sent the members of her team a memo yesterday reminding them to be prompt for the nine-thirty meeting. Her assistant would see to the light refreshments. Sandy realized the importance of these meetings so she wouldn't need a reminder about picking up the muffin trays, coffee, and tea that had been ordered. All the bases were covered.

Di barely had time to glance at the contents of the file before a flashing icon on the computer screen alerted her that she had email. Morning mail was rare for her because the last thing she did before leaving the office was clear out her mailbox. Evidently, someone had been at work later than she was last night, or had arrived earlier this morning. Talk about dedication! She clicked the link and saw that the message was from Roche3. The top dog.

The bold caps snapped her to attention, just as they were meant to.

READ ATTACHED AND SEE ME ASAP—HAL

Harold Lewis Robert Roche III was her richer-than-God, ugly-as-sin boss. A man so wealthy that he'd successfully married not one, not two, but three model-stunning women. Not all at the same time, of course. By Di's calculations, each Mrs. Roche lasted an average of 4.5 years, and it was always Hal who did the leaving... or rather the tossing out.

A bitty slip of a man, Hal had a balding pate and a mouth full of crooked, horsy teeth. His smile frightened young children and the most hardened of executives alike. Not that he smiled all that often, thank God. He was an assertive, no-nonsense kind of guy. One would think that going through life with an Airedale face would subdue a person's personality, agitate insecurities, if nothing else. But not Hal. Oh, no. The man had scads of confidence. The kind of confidence only old money—and loads of it—could buy.

The post made Di break out in a cold sweat. This

was freakishly abnormal. When Hal wanted a meeting, the summons always came from his secretary.

The cursor seemed sluggish as she moved it to the paperclip icon. One click opened the attached document.

To: Hal Roche
From: David Swanson
RE: Proposal For Reorganization
H,
Seems to me splitting marketing into E and W Coast divisions is not only pointless, but puts unnecessary strain on company budget. Substantially diminishes bottom line profits. Cutting Diane Fleming's position, and that of her personal assistant, would be cost effective. I was once part of the East Coast team. Am confident I could manage what would become "Roche National Marketing Division." Eliminating Fleming and her assistant would save 500K in salary, medical bennies, T&E, etc. (Forgive my forwardness, but am amazed you authorized a $10,000 annual wardrobe budget. Am appalled that a Roche employee would have the audacity to ask.) As you know, "the merge" is my forte. Am sure uniting the teams as one will be a smooth process. I realize the new responsibility would entail

coast-to-coast travel. No problem as I spend a great deal of time in the East visiting family that remained behind when I relocated to CA division. Would be a great move for Roche Advertising. Let me know what you think. DS

Holy shit! Di sank back in her chair, numbness pervading her arms, her fingers, her brain. With her hands limp in her lap, she looked out over the Delaware River, where sunlight glistened on the blue-green water. People were boarding for one of the paddleboat tours down at the marina. A ferry scudded across the water on its way to New Jersey. Daily life went on; the world continued to spin. But her skin flamed, her pulse pounding in her neck so violently she feared her veins would burst.

In her head, she heard her yoga instructor's quiet voice. *Inhale, 2, 3, 4. Exhale, 2, 3, 4.* Di hadn't suffered an anxiety attack in years.

David Swanson. That son of a bitch, bastard, asshole!

He was proposing that Hal do away with her and Sandy. *Inhale, 2, 3, 4. Exhale, 2, 3, 4.*

Who the hell did he think he was? He was trying to get her fired. And the son of a bitch had the nerve to mention her wardrobe allowance.

Last year, Di had come up with an ingenious

plan. She'd gone to Hal and explained how she would forgo a raise if he would consider giving her a stipend for clothing. A woman had to look professional when wooing clients.

She blinked. No one knew about that arrangement except Hal. And Sandy. Di chewed her lip. She may have mentioned it to some of the women who worked for her. *Bragged*, a voice in her head intoned. She remembered just recently showing off a new Ferragamo handbag and a flashy pair of Stuart Weitzman sling-backs, crowing that they were "compliments of Hal." A big mistake.

Okay, so boasting had been a blunder on her part, but she'd thought her team members trustworthy. And now she was learning that one of them had knifed her in the back.

Son of a bitch! That bastard had wormed his way right into her team. He'd schmoozed and inveigled until one of her people had defected.

But hadn't she done her share of schmoozing a time or two... or forty-seven?

Hell, yes. A person had to have balls of steel to work in the cutthroat world of advertising. And since she had no balls to work with, she had to run harder, act tougher, and scheme faster than any man in the league.

Swanson had hated it when she'd stolen the East Coast vice presidency right out from under him. He may have had more seniority when the job opened up, but she'd had more cunning. She'd been quite clever in winning the position, and he'd never forgiven her for it. A couple years later, he was offered the West Coast title when it had become available. He'd accepted, but he had been incredibly outspoken about loathing the idea of moving across the country. Tough for him was how she'd felt about it.

She and David had been forced to attend the same quarterly meetings, and he'd treated her fine after a while. So, with all being fair in love and war and all that, Di had thought he'd gotten over himself. In fact, the last time they'd met he'd even spoken fondly about West Coast living.

The phone rang. She flinched before snatching up the receiver.

"Mr. Roche has been expecting you upstairs, Ms. Fleming," Hal's secretary said.

"I'm on my way."

The elevator ride was miserably short. Hal's office occupied the entire tenth floor. He had his own conference room, workout room, massage area, steam sauna, dressing room, and bathroom.

No one ever referred to the spacious maze as Hal's office. Everyone merely called it "upstairs."

The doors slid open and Di stepped into the reception area. Hal's secretary refused to meet her gaze.

"You can go on in." The woman tugged open a desk drawer, rummaging with the intensity of someone who'd lost her life savings.

Oh, this was bad. Very bad.

The door to Hal's office opened before she touched the knob.

"Come in, Di." Hal smiled. "Come right on in."

. . .said the spider to the fly.

He motioned for her to sit and then he rounded his massive cherry desk. The high-back leather chair seemed to swallow her whole. He did that on purpose, she suspected. Forced people to sit in oversized furniture that made them feel small and insignificant.

"Let's get right down to business," he said. "You've read David's proposal, I'm sure. Tell me what you think?"

He was smiling way too much. Every time she spied those teeth, she had to fight back the compulsion to whinny.

"It'll never work." She cringed at the defensive

aggression in her voice. She tried again. "What I mean is that it's pretty common knowledge that Roche clients on the East and West Coasts have vastly different needs, Hal. I'm sure David would agree." Just uttering that asshole's name made her fume. "Besides, he has a tendency to hire people who can't find their butt crack with both hands."

Hal's smile slipped.

Oh, dear. She'd crossed the line of professionalism.

"David's a good man. He's got a good heart. He's given me a lot of years of dedicated service."

Di was happy she was wearing her Prada crocodile platforms. The bullshit was getting high. When did "heart" ever come into play in business? And what about her years of service? She chomped down on her tongue, leaving the questions unasked.

"When we were golfing last weekend, he never uttered a single criticism about you or your team."

Hal's guilt tactics fell on deaf ears. That West Coast weasel might not have denigrated her then, but he was trying to get her axed now.

"You were in California?"

"David flew in for the weekend. He visited his

mother. You do know she's in a nursing home here in Center City?"

Di ignored the question. She would not feel sorry for Swanson. At least he had a mother to visit. Her mind raced.

"Look, Hal," she began, "you have to admit that I can work rings around David Swanson. I proved that when he was a member of the East Coast team. That's why you gave me the vice presidency when it opened up. I agree that having one person head both divisions would save the company money. But I'm sure that I'm the best choice to run the show."

Again he smiled, and Di wondered if he ate oats for breakfast or if he just grazed out on the square.

He reached over and plucked a piece of paper off the top of a pile. "I'm not so sure about that," he told her, offering her the official form.

She noticed her signature at the bottom of the page. Identified it as her "get this crap off my desk" scrawl. Her gaze zipped to the header and date to find out exactly what she was reading.

"You were the one who dubbed David the merging marvel, remember? You'll see it right there on that recommendation you wrote up for him when he was up for the West Coast position."

Di tried to control her gag reflex. Her own words were being used against her? Her only thought at the time she'd written the recommendation was to get Swanson out of her hair. After she'd stolen the East Coast vice presidency from him, he'd become a stinker to work with. He'd dragged down the morale of her entire team.

"That West Coast office was in a shambles when I sent him out there." Hal rested his elbows on the desk. "He brought together three different groups and managed to meld them into one terrific division."

She went still, imagining her career at Roche spiraling right down the toilet. It seemed clear that Hal had made up his mind about this before she'd ever arrived upstairs. But she had to give it one last shot.

"But I'm footloose and fancy free," she blurted. Screw cliché. She was in trouble here. "Flying back and forth across the country wouldn't be a problem for me, Hal. David's got a wife and kids in California. And an ailing mother."

God, talk about slinging bullshit. But she'd never experienced this kind of desperation.

"Which is exactly why I can't let David go. He

has a family depending on his paycheck. You're free of family obligations."

Deep sympathy softened his smile, and unwittingly, Di lifted one platformed foot and hoofed the carpet.

"One good thing," he pointed out, "you're not being terminated. Your position is being phased out, which makes you eligible for a nice juicy severance package." He paused a moment. "Sandy Fields, unfortunately, hasn't reached a level to qualify."

Di's head started to pound.

"You're bright, Di. Talented. And we both know you have the ability to land on your feet no matter what's thrown at you. You'll be fine."

That was it? Her chance to argue was over?

"I'll send someone from HR to your office this morning to discuss your package." He stood and rounded his desk. "You'll do the decent thing and let Sandy go, won't you?"

"But—but," she stammered, "I'm meeting Michael Fielding this morning. My team is ready. I've spent hours preparing. And the Fisher presentation this afternoon—"

"I don't want you to worry."

He took her by the elbow, helped her to stand,

guided her toward the door, and she followed like a docile lamb.

"All that will be taken care of."

By David Swanson. Hal didn't have to say it. Di's gut told her the truth.

That son of a bitch, bastard, asshole.

Hal opened the door and Di noticed that his receptionist wasn't at her desk. The uniformed guard who had materialized near the elevator looked uneasy. He was the same gregarious man who often walked her to her car when she worked until midnight.

She fixed round eyes on Hal.

"I'm sure you understand, Di," he whispered. "This is necessary."

He shooed her out the door like a young child who had become irritating.

So this was to be the culmination of her illustrious career at Roche Advertising: a royal screwing, confiscation of keys, deleting of passwords, punctuated by a security escort out of the building.

Di sat in the dark sipping her favorite single malt Scotch, short and neat. Her career at Roche was over, her reputation ripped to shreds, her career ruined. Hal saw to that by having her paraded through the halls towed by a security guard while she hauled a cardboard box full of personal belongings. When she passed the glass walled conference room, Michael Fielding and Hal and every single member of her team turned to stare, the presentation she'd worked so hard to perfect grinding to a halt.

But the absolute worst of it had been the few moments she'd spent with Sandy. The woman had become more than just her personal assistant. She'd become her friend. Firing her had been difficult, especially when all Di could offer her was a measly two weeks' pay. They'd both gotten weepy, but Julie from HR had interrupted them with a knock on Di's door. After giving Di a quick hug, Sandy had left to clean out her desk.

Sometimes life just sucked.

Di gulped back the last swallow of liquor, the after-burn deliciously smooth and smoky. Disgrace tasted best ingested in the dark. She'd pulled the blinds when she arrived home. That had been hours ago.

No good ever came from wallowing in self-pity, girl.

Viv's voice might be rising from the great

beyond, but Di thought it couldn't have been louder or clearer had the woman been standing before her in the flesh.

Get off your skinny butt and do something constructive.

Di's scornful chuckle echoed across the silent room as she set the highball glass on the end table. She reached up and snapped on the lamp, turning her face from the bright light.

The living room was in almost as much of a mess as her life.

Her jacket lay across the back of one chair where she'd tossed it. The sexy red suit she'd worn especially for today's presentations was wadded in a heap on the floor. Two days' worth of scattered mail just about hid the top of the coffee table. She'd been so focused on winning those accounts that she'd done nothing but work. Thank goodness she hadn't thrown out the paper. She needed to scan the want ads.

She twisted her lips. Want ads were so yesterday. She needed to check LinkedIn. Better yet, she needed to reach out to a headhunter. She'd been contacted by a couple over the years. Hmmm. LinkedIn and corporate headhunters. Sounded like a loose semblance of a plan. Ah, wouldn't Aunt Viv be proud?

Julie from HR had brought some good news, at least. Di would be socking away eighteen months' salary from her severance package, and her health insurance would be paid for a full year. However, it really wouldn't be wise to rest on her laurels.

Reaching for the folded newspaper, she realized instantly that the one on top wasn't the Philadelphia news at all, but the local paper from her hometown in Delaware. Why she continued to subscribe was beyond her. For nostalgia's sake, she guessed. Memories of more innocent and easier days.

She shook her head. Innocent, maybe. But easier?

Di tossed the paper onto the table and bent to retrieve the Inquirer, but a picture on the front of the Hockessin Post stopped her cold. The fold cut the man's face in half, but his eyes looked familiar. She picked up the Post again, deliberately shaking out the newsprint.

Why, it was Fiona's Studly. But the vague smile on Di's mouth waned when she read the caption.

Local Man Missing.

There was little in the way of facts in the too

short article, and the piece ended with a general call to the community at large for information.

Poor Fiona. She must be sick with worry. And the kids... Di mentally calculated the years. Cassie had to be in high school by now. And Di had never even met Fiona's son.

Di placed the newspaper on the table, continuing to stare at Stanley Rowland's face. God, all of that seemed like a whole other life right now. Some foreign existence in a distant land. She still regretted the way she and Fiona had parted all those years ago. Hated how she'd treated her "best-est friend in the whole wide world."

Without even realizing what she was doing, Di went to her bedroom and pulled her suitcase from the closet, childhood memories dancing in her head like so many pink-clad ballerinas. She and Fiona hiking through the small patch of woods near their homes in search of butterflies. She and Fiona giggling under the blankets with flashlights long after ol' Grumpy Ass, Fiona's father, had yelled at them to go to sleep. She and Fiona munching on peanut butter sandwiches Fiona had made for them because Viv's kitchen cupboards were bare, and if Grumpy Ass had ever discovered that the girls had spent all those nights alone in the trailer, he'd have forbidden his daughter from staying over with Di.

Fiona had made Di's childhood bearable more times than could be counted.

The clicking of the suitcase zipper had Di blinking her way out of the past. She pushed the lid open and then moved to the dresser, satisfied with her instinctive intention to go to her friend in her time of trouble. That Fiona needed her, she had no doubt.

As she folded a pair of jeans into neat thirds, the doorbell buzzed. She wasn't expecting anyone. She tucked the blue jeans into the suitcase, checked the sash of her robe, and went to the front door. She peered through the peephole. What was Cliff doing here?

The dead bolt clunked hollowly. "Hey, Cliff..." Her bewildered greeting died when she saw the condition of his face. "What the hell happened to you? You look like you ran into the side of a bus."

Cliff Bowers was a member of her team. She'd caught his surprised expression when she'd passed the conference room earlier today.

Di stepped back so he could come inside, and as he slipped through the doorway she got a better look at the bluish lump in the middle of his forehead. Dried blood laced a cut on his lip.

"It was a baseball bat," he told her. "And it ran into me."

"What?"

He tugged at the sheer curtain covering the narrow sidelight that ran the full length of the door, staring out into the night.

"Listen, Di, I came to warn you." He straightened and turned to face her. "Things got flaming crazy after you left today. The team went into a complete panic."

Surprise arched Di's eyebrows, but she'd be lying if she said this news didn't give her a small sense of satisfaction. She hoped the East Coast team fell apart without her. Hoped Hal would come to regret phasing her out and crowning Swanson king.

"Things were shaky before we even saw you this morning," he continued. "Several of us were worried when you didn't show for the presentation. Then we grew suspicious when Roxanne seemed too eager to take over. She went to your office and got the boards and the handouts. She was strutting around the conference room like she was privy to some earth-shattering secret."

So Roxie had been the one who had ratted to David about her clothing allowance. Obviously, the slut had joined forces with Swanson.

"Then Hal arrived." Cliff checked the street again. "He told us about the reorganization. That your job had been phased out. And that David would be taking over." He shook his head. "Before anyone could take a breath, two factions formed. Those for you and those against you. It was nuts. And it all happened so fast."

He scrubbed his jaw with his fingers, wincing when he accidentally hit the cut on his lip. "I told Hal I didn't think this was a good idea. But Roxanne immediately recommended that Hal sack me, too. She told them all we'd been sleeping together."

"But it's been over between us for a while." Di pressed her fingertips to her lips. Then she murmured, "Consensual sex between co-workers can't possibly be a reason for legal termination, Cliff."

It seemed that he hadn't even heard her. "Needless to say, it didn't take long for the gossip to reach bookkeeping. Jonni Jean stormed onto the eighth floor. She slugged me right there in front of everyone." Evidently, the memory alone was enough to make him flinch.

Jonni Jean was Cliff's wife. They'd met when she took a job with the firm. They'd married six months later, when Jonni Jean discovered she was pregnant.

"I thought she'd calmed down by the time we arrived home. But I stepped out of the shower and heard her outside screaming like a wild woman, busting the windows out of my Grand Cherokee with a baseball bat. I threw on some clothes and went out there to calm her down." He reached up and fingered the bump on his head. "That wasn't a good idea."

"Jonni Jean did that to you? Damn, Cliff. You didn't hurt her, did you?"

He shook his head. "I did what any sane man would do. I ran."

He turned and looked outside again. Di noticed that his hair was still damp.

"Do you want some ice?" she asked. "That looks like it hurts."

Cliff just shook his head. "I can't stay. If Jonni Jean finds out I was here, she'll kill me." His green gaze was grave. "You need to get out of town for a while."

"Oh, Cliff—" she waved her hand "—Jonni Jean wouldn't hurt me."

"Listen to me." There was real fear in his eyes, and he looked as if he wanted to reach out and shake sense into her, but he didn't. "I'm serious. Jonni Jean comes from... well, from a long line of Appalachians."

Di had always thought Jonni Jean's Southern twang was cute.

"Mountain people don't get mad, Di. And they don't just get even. They want their pound of flesh and an extra hunk of meat for good measure."

Something icy slithered up Di's spine as she stared at Cliff's battered face.

"You've got to get out of here. Tonight."

She swallowed. "I am leaving Philly," she told him. "I'm going to see a friend in my hometown."

"Good." His shoulders relaxed a little. "That's good. I've got to go now. You be careful, you hear?"

Di nodded and held the door when he opened it. He slipped out into the night. She didn't watch him leave, didn't see where he went, but closed the door and secured the bolt.

When she was back in her bedroom, her packing took on a more frantic pace. Okay, so she now had more reason to leave the city than merely going home to Hockessin to help Fiona. But no one in Delaware need know about the horrific state of her life.

What Di intended to do was forget about her own trivial problems and focus on Fiona. The poor woman must be distraught in the face of what life had thrown at her. Di intended to be there for Fiona. And she would be a good and dependable friend this time around.

Chapter Four

Reunion

Grasping the thick stem at the base, Fiona yanked the weed until it came out of the ground, root and all. She flung it onto the growing pile behind her and sat back on her heels. Her front yard hadn't looked this good in years. She used to love gardening; however, becoming the mother of teens had somehow crowded out the hobby. Now, though, she needed to fill every waking moment or lose her mind altogether.

Four days since she'd reported Stan missing. Where the hell was he?

She heard Detective DeSalvo's car crunching up

the gravel lane before she saw it. She'd been waiting for him. So was a fresh pot of coffee. He'd made a habit of stopping by every morning since she'd filed the missing person's report. He was doing his best to keep her informed, and she was grateful. It hadn't taken her long to decide he was someone she could trust.

Fiona tugged off her gardening gloves and tossed them on the ground. A quick swipe removed the grass and soil from the knees of her jeans.

"Morning," he called as he made his way toward her.

She wanted to attack him for information, but she didn't. "Have time for coffee?"

The composure in her tone surprised her. Could a person actually get used to a constant state of sheer panic? She doubted it. Right now, she was feeling numb and tired.

He nodded. "A quick cup."

They headed toward the front door.

"Cassie and Sam home today?" he asked, following her toward the kitchen at the rear of the house.

"No, I made them go back to school. They weren't happy about it, but…"

They trekked the rest of the way to the kitchen

in silence. He pulled out a chair for himself while she washed her hands at the sink.

"I think it was a good idea. Them going back to school."

"As you said yesterday, this could go on for some time." The rich scent of coffee permeated the air as she poured. She carried two mugs to the table. "I need to get back some sense of normalcy for them."

It seemed an impossible task when the standard had turned topsy-turvy. She had to give it a try, anyway. However, the moment she'd arrived home from driving the kids to school this morning, she worried that she'd made a terrible mistake. It was easier to be strong when they were around. Alone in the house, she'd felt her fear pressing in on her. It had chased her from room to room and even outside where she began jerking at weeds like a fiend.

Fiona sat down and slid the plate of sticky buns toward DeSalvo. "Help yourself," she told him. "They're homemade."

He shook his head. "They look great, and I'm a sucker for anything with pecans, but I'm trying to watch the waistline."

She slid the plate back a few inches. "Cassie used the same excuse. Sam had a couple, though. I was hoping to sweeten the idea of going back to school." She'd also needed something to do at three a.m. She spooned sugar into her coffee and stirred it slowly. "How did your day go yesterday?" He'd told her that on Wednesday he'd visited Stan's office complex and interviewed his co-workers. Yesterday, he was supposed to visit some of the people on the list she'd provided—a couple of cousins, friends, students taking Stan's accounting class. Fiona had supplied the names of even the most casual of acquaintances in the hopes that someone knew something. *Anything.*

"I talked to your husband's poker buddies. And as you already know, he didn't show up for the game Tuesday night. He didn't—and hasn't—contacted any of them."

She knew all that. She'd spent the past two days phoning everyone and anyone she could think to call. No one had seen or heard from Stan. Not a single "John Doe" had turned up anywhere, not at any of the area hospitals, and thank God, not at the morgue. It was as if he'd vanished into thin air.

"None of the five guys I talked to could even make a guess where he might have gone or what might have happened." DeSalvo paused, lacing his fingers together. "He has no enemies that I could find. All his friends told me he's not the kind of guy who would skip town. The people at Fox and Associates said the same."

I told you so, she wanted to say.

"So where the hell is he?" The question rolled through her mind at least a thousand times a day, and she'd voiced it to the detective each and every time they met. Hopefully, one of these times he'd have an answer.

He leaned forward, resting his forearms on the edge of the table. "Mrs. Rowland, I'd like to discuss Sunday again. I want you to go over the events of the day for me."

"But... we already did this. You talked to the kids about—"

"Humor me, okay? If we go over it again, you might remember something. Something that could help."

"Okay." She relented, shrugging one shoulder. "Let's go over it again." She pushed the ceramic mug away from her. "Stan had to go into the office for a few hours on Saturday, which ate into his golf game, so he loaded up his clubs bright and early on Sunday morning and went to the driving range. None of which is out of the ordinary. Fox and Associates pays Stan well, but he earns every penny, believe me. He's expected to drop everything if a client calls with a problem—nights, weekends, whenever."

"Does that annoy you?"

She just looked at him. "I never thought about it. No. I guess not. It's his job."

"But doesn't it eat into family time? Put more pressure on you?"

"Put more pressure on me?" She shook her head, bewildered.

"To do for the kids. Take care of all their needs by yourself."

"Why should that annoy me? It's my job. Stan earns the money. I take care of the house and raise the kids." Having described their traditional lifestyle aloud, Fiona found it somehow archaic compared to how most people lived these days, with their dual incomes and sharing of parenting duties and household chores. Her cheeks heated. "My being a stay-at-home mom might sound freakish to you, Detective, but it's the way we've always done things." She lifted both shoulders a fraction. "It works for us."

After a moment, he asked, "What time did he arrive home?"

She sighed. This was such a waste of time. She'd already explained all this.

"He came in after I'd fixed lunch for Sam and Cassie. He made himself a sandwich, and he and Sam were going to cut the grass. We have a big yard, Detective. Sam rides the John Deere and Stan push-mows around the house, the bushes, the trees."

DeSalvo nodded. "That's new information."

"What? That we have a big yard?"

"That Sam uses a riding mower while your husband pushes one."

"And just how is that helpful to your investigation?"

"You never know." He sat back in the chair. "And where were you Sunday afternoon?"

The question irritated her. "You know where I was. At the mall. With Cassie. Looking for white blouses with a Peter Pan collar. We'd only found two when we went school shopping, and she needed a few more."

If he was aware of her irritation, he didn't let on.

He prompted, "And you returned home..."

"In time for dinner. I've already explained that. Just as I explained that I brought pizza home with me. Half pepperoni, half extra cheese. That Cassie ate hers in front of the TV, and Sam had his in his room, and Stan didn't have any at all because he was too busy in the den on the phone."

"You didn't say how you felt about your husband not having dinner with you."

She frowned. "How I felt? How should I have felt? I already told you that none of us ate together that night."

The detective shrugged. "You might have if Stan hadn't been too busy on the phone."

The emphasis he placed on the words *too busy* made her pause.

"I don't understand, Detective," she said. She realized suddenly that he hadn't touched the coffee she'd set in front of him. "What is it you want me to say?"

The doorbell rang just as realization struck. Anger shot through her.

"You want me to admit that I was angry with Stan. You're focusing your investigation on me." Whoever was at the door would have to wait. Agitation forced Fiona to her feet and she glared at DeSalvo. "You think I've done something wrong."

"I'm not focusing on any one person, Mrs. Rowland. I'm only trying to gather all the information. It's just like those pecan buns there.

You can't make them properly if you don't gather together all the ingredients. I'm just gathering ingredients."

His tone was so damn calm as he gazed up at her, it pissed her off all the more.

"I'm not forming any conclusions yet," he assured her. "It's too early for that."

"Don't you dare—" she slapped the tabletop "—waste another minute of your time questioning me about my relationship with Stan! It's ridiculous! My marriage is fine. My husband is a good man who provides for his family. To think that I would—"

The inference upset her to the point that she couldn't even finish the thought.

The doorbell rang a second time.

"It's ludicrous." She stood in silence, trying to regain her composure, but her anger refused to subside. "Why haven't you found him?" The question was most definitely an accusation. "Why haven't you found the Volvo? Or at least tracked down his cell phone records? Stan has to be *somewhere*. Not a stitch of his clothing is missing from our room. Not a razor. Not a toothbrush. Nothing. A man doesn't run off without clean underwear, Detective. Not Stan, at least. A person cannot simply fall off the face of the earth. He has to *be* somewhere. And as you've seen for yourself every morning this week, he isn't here."

The frustration was more than she could handle. Whoever was on the front step pressed the doorbell two times in quick succession.

"Excuse me," Fiona said, and then she stalked out of the kitchen.

The morning sunlight glared against the screen door, obscuring the face of the woman standing on the stoop. Fiona wished she'd had Stan install the No Solicitation sign as he'd wanted.

"I'm sorry," she called, still several feet from the door, "I'm very busy at the moment. I've got company."

"Too busy for a sugar fix?"

She knew that voice. Fiona stopped dead.

"I guess I could take my Krispy Kremes and come back another time."

"Di?" Fiona was uncertain if she'd actually spoken or not. She hurried to the door, twisted the handle and pushed open the screen. "Oh, my God. Is it you?"

"In the flesh." She stepped into the foyer.

The flat box Di carried got in the way of their hug, so Fiona snatched it from her friend and shoved it on top of the pile of mail that had been accumulating on the lowboy. Emotions raced through Fiona: joy, relief, giddy delight.

"I can't believe this." She smoothed her hand over Di's back and then pulled away far enough to look into her face. "What are you doing here? How've you been? God, you look good."

She looked great. But then Fiona wouldn't have expected less. Di's full lips glistened with color and her bright blue eyes had been expertly accentuated with just the right amount of liner and shadow. Fiona couldn't say if she'd even remembered to brush mascara on her lashes this morning. Di's white-blond hair was cut in ultrafashionable short, spiky layers. Fiona reached up and fingered the twisted knot at the back of her own head. Her shoulder-length hair was freshly washed, but would be a hopelessly wrinkled, mousy brown mess when she took it down later. Oh, well.

Di wore an orange twin set, the cardigan draped over her shapely shoulders, and a pair of form-fitting brown capris. Sassy-heeled bronze sandals completed the outfit. Fiona wore Levi's and a Habitat for Humanity T-shirt that, up until this instant, she'd been proud to own. The polish on Di's pedicured toes matched that on her manicured fingernails. Fiona couldn't say when her nails had last seen a file, let alone polish. She fought the urge to tuck her hands into the pockets of her jeans.

"You look good, too."

Fiona almost believed her, but then Di had always been a superb liar. When they'd been kids, Di could make up a story straight off the cuff that could mollify teachers, the rare police officer, even Fiona's raging father. As long as Fiona succeeded in keeping her mouth shut, the girls rarely saw trouble... even when that's exactly where their antics should have led them.

"Did you get into town this morning?" Fiona asked.

"Last night. But it was too late to come by, so I took a room at the Continental Suites."

"You should have rung the bell. I was probably awake."

Di sobered. "Honey, I read about Stan. In the paper. I came right away."

Fiona closed her eyes, fighting back tears. "It's been awful, Di."

A polite, masculine cough had Fiona turning to see the detective standing a few yards away.

"I should be going," he said. "I need to stop in at the station. Then I have some leads to follow up."

"Leads?" Di's tone was hopeful, her hand tightening on Fiona's forearm. "They've got leads?"

"Not that I know of," Fiona murmured.

The detective remained silent, an obvious question in his dark eyes.

"Detective DeSalvo, I'd like you to meet my friend, Diane Fleming. Di, this is the officer who's working to find Stan."

Di flashed a Hollywood smile and shook his hand. "What's this about leads?"

"Not for this case." He reached up and straightened the pen in his breast pocket. "I've got other cases I'm working on, as well." He looked at Fiona. "But we'll have something on your husband soon, Mrs. Rowland. Don't worry. We will find him."

The women watched him amble down the front walkway.

"Sounded like that could have been a promise," Di commented, "or a threat."

Di's curiosity was unmistakable, but Fiona didn't want to ruin the happiness that her friend's arrival had brought so she said nothing.

"Either way," Di added softly, "the man's got a great ass, that's for sure."

Fiona laughed. "Oh, Lord, it's good to have you here." Hugging Di's upper arm with both hands, she shook her head and turned her around. "Grab that box." She pointed to the doughnuts. "The coffee's fresh. Let's dig in."

"Krispy Kremes to the rescue."

They sat at the kitchen table most of the morning, gabbing like teenagers and eating like pigs. It took hours to catch up. They realized they hadn't seen one another for over eight years, the last time being a very brief encounter at Aunt Viv's funeral. Vivian Fleming had died right smack-dab in the middle of one of the most hectic times in Di's life. Di had been forced to trust the funeral director to make burial arrangements, and she'd hired a local lawyer to take care of the meager estate her aunt had left behind, all because Di had been working seventy hours a week in order to win the Lancing account, the biggest of her career up to that point, the one that had forced the "big boys" to notice there was more to her than shapely legs and cleavage. So although Fiona had attended the funeral, she and Di hadn't had a chance to spend any real time together. They'd made promises to keep in touch, but neither had been very good at keeping them. Di hadn't even been aware that Fiona's father had passed away three years ago.

Fiona told Di what she knew about Stan, which certainly wasn't much. She kept to the facts, shying away from emotion that was too dark and raw to face.

When Fiona learned that Di had come to stay for a while, she felt overwhelmed with gratitude. So much so that she wasn't able to speak right away. But she'd regained her composure and decided immediately that Di should move out of the hotel room and into the in-law suite that had been built over the garage for Fiona's father after he'd had his first heart attack.

They spent the afternoon pulling the sheets off the furniture, dusting, vacuuming, and airing out the apartment. It felt good for Fiona to have her hands and her mind occupied with something positive and pleasant for a change, but the fear in the pit of her gut never left her for a moment.

By mid-afternoon, the September sun blazed, heating the still air to sweltering. Di had long ago removed her cotton cardigan, the thin matching tank played up delicate shoulders and a rich tan that Di confessed was the result of standing in a booth and being sprayed down with bronzer rather than lying on some tropical sandy beach. The women stood in the shade of the big oak tree out near the driveway, both with car keys in hand.

"So we'll meet back here for dinner?" Fiona swatted at an irritating gnat.

Di nodded. "I'll gather my things and check out of the hotel. Shouldn't take long. I need to stop and pick up a few things at the store. I can't wait to see Cassie. She was just a baby the last time I saw her. And Sam." She shook her head. "It seems impossible that I've never met him."

"Don't expect too much from them," Fiona warned. "They're worried sick. And none of us have been sleeping very well. They're moody and—"

"It's okay. I'm only here to help. I don't want any of you treating me like company. I'm family. Well, as close to it as a person can get anyway, right?"

Fiona smiled. "Right."

Di had walked to her car and opened the door when Fiona called her name. "I'm glad you're here."

Di just looked at her for a moment before replying, "So am I."

Chapter Five

My Mother Did What?

"Coach wants to know when I'll be coming back to practice." Sam slouched in the chair, holding out his dessert plate to Fiona for a second helping of warm apple crisp. Normally, she'd have commented on his posture, but she was letting a lot of things slide lately.

The dinner invitation Fiona had offered Di this afternoon made her realize she hadn't been to the grocery store, nor had she cooked a hot meal for the kids since this ordeal began. She had no idea what or when Cassie and Sam had eaten Wednesday and Thursday. All she remembered was the silence. And the waiting. Waiting for the crunch of Stan's tires on the gravel drive. Waiting for the clink of his key in the dead bolt on the front door. Waiting for the phone to ring. She and Cassie and Sam had roamed the house like wraiths, the leaden quiet causing more anxiety than any of them could bear. That was the main reason she'd urged her kids to return to school this morning.

Di's arrival was a godsend for Fiona. A friendly nudge that had shaken her out of a fear-induced stupor. After the two of them had parted earlier today, Fiona had rushed through the Super Mart, tossing fresh fruit, veggies, meats, canned goods, and snacks into her cart. Then she'd whizzed to the schools to pick up her kids. She'd spent time in the kitchen preparing Sam's favorite meatloaf and the sour cream and chive mashed potatoes Cassie loved so much. And what better comfort food was there than spicy apple crisp topped with buttery oats, toasted walnuts and sweet coconut?

"Do you feel up to it?" Fiona scooped some soft vanilla ice cream on the cinnamon-scented fruit before handing the plate to her son.

He shrugged. "I guess." His gaze slid from hers as he mumbled, "But I dunno if I should."

"Of course, you should." Di set her spoon down on the table. "Sitting at home worrying isn't going to help anything. You and Cassie need to keep busy. Keep your minds occupied. Don't you think so, Fiona?"

When she'd introduced Diane to her kids, Fiona could tell they weren't quite sure what to think of the vivacious woman who had swooped down on them seemingly from nowhere. Over the years, she'd mentioned Di to them. Mostly at Christmas, when addressing cards would trigger her reminiscing. However, she guessed she hadn't clearly explained Di's energetic spirit. To be fully appreciated, that had to be witnessed, firsthand.

Cassie and Sam had been overly polite and way too quiet during dinner, and Fiona had seen the two of them exchange cautious glances several times when Di tried to engage them in conversation. As it turned out, Sam had talked a little, but pulling words from Cassie had been as difficult as extracting molars with a pair of pliers. Fiona hoped the kids would warm up to Di, because something had happened to her today: her panic had subsided just the tiniest bit. Oh, she was still scared witless every time she thought about Stan, which was with every other breath. But knowing she had the support of someone she could count on gave her a tremendous feeling of relief.

Keeping busy. Keeping the mind occupied. It had certainly helped Fiona today.

She nodded, looking from Sam to Cassie. "Di's right. You two should try to get back to your regular schedules. Cassie, you need to go to soccer practice and study group. And the advisor said you can't miss any meetings if you want to work on the school paper. Sam, you should go back to practice. Don't you have a meet soon?" Glancing at Di, Fiona explained, "Sam runs cross-country."

"But, Mom—" alarm edged Cassie's tone "—what about Dad? We can't just act like nothing's happened."

"That's not at all what I'm suggesting. We'll keep working with the police. You know I've been talking with Detective DeSalvo every day. They're using every resource possible to find your father."

"Where is he, Mom?" The ice cream on Sam's plate melted as it sat, forgotten. "What could have happened to him?"

Fiona reached out and covered her son's hand with her own. Her kids had asked that question of her almost as many times as she'd asked it herself. "I don't know, honey. I just don't know."

"He's dead, isn't he?" Cassie asked softly. "He's got to be dead."

"Don't talk like that." Hearing the sharpness in her tone, Fiona checked herself. "We can't think like that. We have to remain positive."

Heavy silence fell over the four of them.

Finally, Sam cleared his throat awkwardly. "What's gonna happen to us? If he never comes back, I mean."

"He's coming back, damn it." Fiona shoved her chair out and stood, tossing her napkin onto the table. "I don't want to hear any more of this pessimism." She stormed into the kitchen and began shuffling the pots and pans she'd used to cook dinner.

Her hands trembled and her stomach felt queasy. She shouldn't have snapped at Sam. He'd only voiced what everyone was thinking. She wasn't angry that he'd asked. She was frustrated by the lack of information.

Fiona heard Di's soft words of comfort, and guilt welled inside her. She should be the one reassuring her kids, but for all her talk of remaining optimistic, Fiona had to admit that she didn't feel hopeful for a positive outcome.

What was going to happen to them? That was a good question. What the hell were they going to do? How would she provide for her children? Pay the mortgage? The electric and cable and phone and water bills?

Panic nearly spun her thoughts into chaos, but she paced the kitchen, grappling with her terror until she had it under control. She could not dwell on these fatalistic thoughts. She'd told the kids that their father would be coming home. She had to believe it. Otherwise, she seriously doubted she could hold on to her sanity.

She stopped near the doorway when she overheard Cassie.

"...always been a great cook." Her daughter chuckled. "But don't tell her I said it. It could ruin my 'picky eater' reputation."

"Nothin' could ruin that," Sam said quietly.

"Shut up, you."

The warm and unmistakable camaraderie in her children's joking made Fiona smile. She had great kids. She would do whatever was necessary to keep them safe, to secure their future.

"For a while," Cassie told Di, "Mom talked about writing a cookbook. But she never did."

With her emotions securely contained, Fiona felt now was as good a time as any to rejoin them. She breezed into the dining room. "I never found the time, actually. It's still something I intend to do. Someday."

"That's good to know." Di poured more merlot into her wineglass. "Meatloaf is usually a ho-hum dish, Fiona, but yours is extraordinary. People would pay for that recipe. What's in it?"

"Oh, a little of this. A little of that."

"Tell her your secret ingredient, Mom."

"Cassie, a woman doesn't give away her—"

"Oatmeal," Sam and Cassie said in unison.

"*Oatmeal?*" Di was obviously surprised. Then she nodded. "It did have a different texture. Soft. Almost creamy."

Fiona clicked her tongue at Cassie and Sam. "Giving away family secrets. You two ought to be ashamed."

"But it's really good, Mom," Sam said. "Everything you cook is good."

"Yeah, yeah," her daughter teased. "Miss Perfect is what we should call her."

They were being so nice. Abnormally nice. Had

been so—to her and to each other—since their father went missing. Fiona swallowed back the lump threatening to form in her throat.

Anxiety swirled around her, taking her by surprise. How was she going to take care of her kids? Making a great meatloaf wasn't a skill that would be particularly helpful in the job market. Fiona shoved the dire thoughts out of her head.

"Yeah, well—" Di picked up her wineglass and reclined against the chair back, drama in every movement "—she wasn't always so perfect. I could tell you a story or two about your sweet mother."

Fiona held up her hand. "Hold on, now—"

"Oh, Di!" Cassie brightened, leaning forward. "You have to tell."

Sam nodded, grinning widely. He spooned a bite of apple crisp into his mouth.

"Hmm." Di's blue eyes narrowed as she deliberated. "One against. Three for." She lifted one shoulder. "You're outvoted, Fiona. Sorry." She sipped her wine and then set the stemmed glass on the table. "Well, there was the time in junior high when your mom and I were tennis partners during gym. She intentionally walloped the ball over the fence. The teacher was furious. I think she knew Fiona meant to do it. She told us to get the ball. We searched all over and finally found it. In the creek. Then we thought it would be neat—"

"*You* thought it would be neat," Fiona corrected.

"And you agreed so fast it made my head spin." She laughed, focusing on the teens once again. "We thought if we 'accidentally' fell in, that we'd be sent home to change. We were walkers, you know. Lived really close to the school. A free afternoon, we thought. How great would that be?"

Fiona took a drink from her wineglass.

"But that's not what happened." Di paused long enough to toss a mirthful glance Fiona's way. "We were sent to the Home Ec room, where we stood around in skimpy gym towels while our clothes were in the dryer. But Mrs. Martin didn't leave them in long enough, and we walked around all day in soggy underwear that smelled faintly of algae."

Sam snickered.

Cassie cringed. "Eeew."

Di launched into her next tale. "That same year, we arrived at school, and as usual, we met up in the girls' room. Some idiot had left her gym clothes there. Your mother filled up the sink and plunked everything in, sneakers and all."

"You wanted to shove them in the toilet," Fiona pointed out.

"Yeah, but Miss Prissy Pants wouldn't let me do that." Di combed her hair back with her fingers. "Later that day, the principal brought Brenda Shively around to all the classes and gave the biggest sob story about how Brenda was going to miss gym because her shoes and her uniform were wrecked. Your mother started blubbering like a baby, and everyone knew who did it."

"And you put on the most innocent face," Fiona accused Di. "Looking at me as if you were flabbergasted that I could do such a thing."

"I did. I was quite the actress, even back then."

"Poor Brenda Shively," Cassie said.

"Mom, you had a thing about water when you were a kid, huh?" Sam's pale blue eyes sparkled with mischief.

"You two should not be enjoying this so much." Fiona tried to affect an air of insult, but she couldn't keep from laughing.

"By the time we got into high school," Di said, "we'd pretty much perfected the prank."

Fiona shook her head. "Di, I don't think we should be telling—"

"Oh, yes, you should," Cassie said. "These stories are too good to go untold, Mom."

Di slid her dessert plate a few inches away from her. "There was a pizza place in town that started advertising home delivery. So on Friday nights, we would order pizza for one of your mom's neighbors. Then we'd climb out her bedroom window onto the roof and watch what would happen."

"Mom! You didn't!"

Fiona looked at her daughter and was forced to admit, "I did."

"I wish I'da thought of that one."

Pinning her son with a narrow-eyed gaze was all Fiona needed to do.

"I didn't say I'd do it." Sam shifted awkwardly. "Sheesh."

Di folded her napkin and placed it beside her dessert plate. "We hitchhiked to Wilmington for the first time when we were in tenth grade."

"Mom!" Evidently, Cassie was vacillating between utter astonishment and sheer delight.

Fiona could have smacked Di for divulging *that* bit of information.

"Oh, now, Fiona, don't glare at me. Your kids are

smart enough to realize it was a different time back in the day."

Fiona tilted her head and arched her eyebrows. "That's true. There weren't any criminals roaming the roads back then."

Di chuckled. "None that we found, anyway. Besides, we're talking about seeing Ian Anderson at the Grand Opera House. We'd have faced an army of criminals to—"

"Ian who?" Sam asked.

Di looked positively shocked. "Don't tell me you've never heard of Jethro Tull." She looked at Fiona. "What? Have you kept these kids locked in the basement?"

"What else did you do?" Sam asked.

"Well, we drag raced in my Aunt Viv's Oldsmobile—"

"On a deserted road of an old industrial park," Fiona quickly added.

Without pausing to breathe, Di said, "And we snuck a bottle of Tango into a football game once."

"Tango?" Cassie shook her head, not quite understanding why that would be a bad thing to do. "You mean that orange stuff the astronauts used to drink?"

"No, sweetie," Di explained. "I think the

company's out of business now, but Tango made premixed screwdrivers."

Cassie's jaw actually dropped open as she fixed rounded eyes on her mother. *"Liquor?"*

"Bought legally." Fiona stressed both words. God, she was never going to live this down. Maybe Di showing up out of the blue wasn't such a good thing after all. Fiona felt frantic to downplay the past. "The football game was in Maryland. The drinking age there was eighteen at the time, and Di had just had her birthday the week before."

What she chose to leave out was the fact that she'd still been seventeen. Underage drinking was a common occurrence among kids who had very little supervision. It was true then just as it was now.

"Yeah—" Di grinned wickedly "—the two of us spent a lot of time in Maryland, didn't we, Fiona?"

Sam and Cassie were laughing openly at her. Fiona wanted to slide right under the table. This wasn't funny. Di was putting ideas into her children's heads. Bad ideas that were going to haunt her in time, she just knew it.

Fiona began gathering up dishes and cutlery. "It's time we got cleaned up here." She stood and ordered the kids to help.

During the ten minutes it took to rinse the dishes, place them into the dishwasher, and wrap up the leftovers, Di had revealed two more stories from their past. Thank goodness these were a bit tamer.

One was a midnight excursion to Lum's Pond, where a group of girls and guys went swimming in their underwear. They'd had a blast until a ranger threatened to call the state police if they didn't leave the park.

The other was the time they'd climbed up onto the roof of the high school the final day of their senior year and tossed water balloons down on a group of teachers. They'd very nearly gotten caught, and if they had, they most probably would have been refused the privilege of participating in the graduation ceremony.

Sam closed the door of the dishwasher. "You really did have a thing about water, huh, Mom?"

He, Cassie, and Di laughed, while Fiona felt her face tighten with annoyance. No mother wanted her children to know of her childhood mistakes. It wasn't the revealing of her screw-ups that bothered her as much as the danger that her kids might get the impression that, because she'd pulled pranks and acted immaturely, they had a green light to do so, too. Di should have known better than to recount all that crap, entertaining or not.

"Since we're all cleaned up," Sam said, "do you mind if I go upstairs now?"

There was always a video game of some sort calling her son's name.

"Sure." Fiona hung the dishcloth on the hook.

"I'm going to go phone Emily." Cassie halted at the kitchen door, turning to face her mother. "If that's okay, I mean."

"Of course it's okay. Tell Emily I said hello."

Her daughter smiled and nodded before flouncing off toward the stairs. Normally, they weren't nearly this cooperative, or this polite. The straining situation had them acting out of character.

Immediately, Fiona confronted Di. "What were you thinking? I have to live with these children after you're gone. They're going to throw every one of those stories in my face—"

"Whoa, whoa, whoa." Di waved her hands, palms out. "I didn't mean to cause trouble. I was only trying to make them laugh. And you've got to admit, I did."

Fiona went silent. It was true. For a while there, the fear that had consumed her kids since their father disappeared had been lifted. She hadn't heard laughter in the house for days. Di had changed that.

"So what if I knocked you off your pedestal?" Di refilled both their wineglasses. "It was worth it to have them forget about their problems for a few minutes."

Sighing, Fiona released the pent-up tension that had her shoulders rigid. "I'm sorry, Di. You're right."

Di handed her her glass. "Of course I'm right. And you know full well that I withheld the juiciest stories. Like when we celebrated your eighteenth birthday with not one but two pitchers of Vicious Virgins and ended up puking our guts out by the roadside."

Fiona groaned. "I could never forget."

"Or the time we came up with the brilliant idea to use sandwich Baggies as condoms."

"Oh, God, I am so glad you were the guinea pig on that one." Fiona grew thoughtful. "We were horrible."

"Not horrible. Normal." Di leaned her hip against the edge of the counter. "We didn't have anyone except each other. There was nothing else for us to do but work it out for ourselves." She lifted her glass in a salute. "To working things out."

Touching her glass to Di's, Fiona smiled. The wine tasted good. Rich and full-bodied. A memory flickered in her mind. The last time she'd had merlot was the night she'd fallen asleep waiting for Stan.

"You know—" thick guilt grated in her whisper "—I think he was gone for two days before I noticed."

For a long moment, Di didn't speak. Her blue eyes were hooded. Her tone was gentle when she finally said, "Tonight shouldn't be about beating ourselves up, Fiona. Tonight is about getting reacquainted." She grinned. "And about getting a little tipsy. Everyone needs to let loose every now and again, right?"

Fiona agreed by taking another long sip from her glass. She looked over the crystal rim at her friend. "I know I've said this already... but thanks for coming." She paused. "It's really nice not feeling all alone."

Chapter Six

Knock, knock. Who's There?

"So DeSalvo is sure now that Stan's been gone since last Monday?" With her hair wrapped in a towel, Di poured herself a second cup of coffee from the carafe Fiona had brought to the apartment over the garage.

Fiona nodded, watching Di lift the lid off the sugar bowl and spoon a little into the cup. "We suspected it when we found out Cassie was the one who had made the coffee on Tuesday morning. And that she'd been using my shower. But we weren't positive until the detective was finally able to talk a judge into signing a warrant to confiscate

Stan's work computer to find out the last time he'd logged on."

"With all that's going on, I don't understand why Stan's boss wouldn't just hand over the computer."

"Jim Fox called me last Friday to explain." Fiona lifted one shoulder. "He wanted to help with the investigation all he could, but was afraid of invading Stan's privacy. He said his lawyer advised him not to relinquish anything until he was forced to. Personnel files, computers, whatever." Almost as an aside, she added, "Covering their butts, legally speaking."

But dead men can't sue anyone, she'd wanted to rail at him at the time.

Di stirred her coffee. "Sounds like a bunch of bullshit to me."

Fiona couldn't argue with that.

"What about the guy who said he saw Stan on Tuesday?" Di stretched out her shapely legs, crossing her ankles.

"George Harrigan. Detective DeSalvo was finally able to interview him yesterday. Apparently, George wasn't at Fox and Associates when he'd gone there to interview Stan's coworkers last week, and they played phone tag for several days.

Anyway, George admitted to lying to me about seeing Stan."

"What? Why would he do that?"

Fiona sighed. "George told DeSalvo it was a knee-jerk reaction, one buddy protecting another. He said I sounded 'testy' when I called on Tuesday and that he only meant to help Stan out. Once the words were out of his mouth, he couldn't take them back. DeSalvo said George was embarrassed by the admission. I guess that's why I haven't heard anything from him."

"Lying low, is he? Men can be so brainless."

Reaching up, Fiona lightly plucked at her chin. "George told DeSalvo that he doesn't see Stan much anymore. That he'd accepted a promotion six months ago and moved to a bigger office in another wing of the building." She glanced out the window. "Stan never said anything to me about that." Fiona looked back at Di. "If your best friend got a promotion, wouldn't you mention it to your wife?"

"I don't know." Di smoothed her thumb over the porcelain cup handle. "What else did the delicious detective tell you when he visited this morning?"

Di hadn't touched any of the food Fiona had

brought over on the breakfast tray, but she was sucking down her third cup of coffee.

"Well, until the police got their hands on Stan's computer, there was some confusion about the last day Stan had been in his office. There's no sign-in required at the agency, no time sheets are filled out, and the downsizing they went through last year means there's no middle management to supervise the coming and going of employees. They use the honor system."

"In the business world it's called getting the biggest bang for your buck."

"But now that DeSalvo has talked to everyone at Fox and discovered that Stan didn't log on to his computer at all last week, they've decided for certain that he's been missing since Monday."

Both women were quiet for a moment.

"The detective was confused all over again," Fiona admitted, "that I didn't report Stan missing until Wednesday. He made me go over the events of Sunday once more. I swear it makes me so—" Emotion swelled in her chest, cutting off her words, and tears blurred her vision. "He thinks I've done something to Stan," she whispered. "He hasn't come right out and said it, but he thinks it."

Di planted her feet on the floor and leaned

toward her. "To hell with him, Fiona. Let him think what he wants. He's an idiot. You have enough to be upset about without letting him get to you."

Fiona sniffed and Di handed her a tissue from the box on the side table. Her friend's vehemence made her smile, albeit ruefully. "You're the only woman I know who can call a man delicious and an idiot in the same conversation."

Di set her coffee cup on the tray, picked up a strawberry and popped it into her mouth. "Just because a man is a hottie doesn't mean he's got brains between his ears."

"I know DeSalvo is only doing his job. I just wish he wouldn't waste his energy on me."

When the detective had made her reexamine the events of Sunday evening—Stan's last night at home—Fiona's temper had revved like an engine in a foreign sports car, going from zero to sixty on the anger speedometer in about five seconds. But he hadn't balked at her tirade. Instead, he'd remained calm and professional. The man made her want to rip out her hair.

"Did they find anything else on Stan's computer that might help?" Di picked up a blueberry muffin and peeled back an edge of the paper cup it had been baked in.

Fiona shook her head. "Not really. All his emails were strictly business. His history showed no personal use of the internet. DeSalvo was amazed at the amount of hours Stan logged in. But I told him that last week."

"Vindication is a good thing." Di nibbled on the muffin, set it on the tray and nudged the whole thing away from her.

No wonder the woman stayed so thin. Fiona had wolfed down fruit, yogurt, and two muffins with her coffee, and she'd eaten another half of a muffin once she'd returned from driving the kids to school.

Di tugged the towel from her head and began finger-combing her damp, blond locks. "Let me take you away from all this," she said. "Let's go have a manicure. And then we'll go shopping."

Fiona heard a car rolling slowly up the driveway, and without thought, she went to the window.

"Who is it?" Di came up behind her.

"Don't know."

The powder-blue Duster was missing the front bumper, and both front and back fenders on the driver's side showed signs of rust. A vertical crack marred the passenger side of the front windshield.

The driver, a young, dark-haired woman, cut the engine, got out of the car, and stalked toward the front door.

"Avon Lady?" Di guessed, her tone quiet as if she feared the woman might overhear.

"Don't think so. No satchel."

"Ah, you're right. Jehovah's Witness?"

"Nope. No leaflets. And Jehovah would never approve of that short skirt."

Di tapped her on the shoulder. "Girl, you are quick."

They watched the young woman lumber up the front steps and ring the doorbell.

Fiona felt suddenly exhausted. "I'd better go see what she wants."

"I'll come along for company."

"I sure hope she's not selling something. I'm not in any mood to listen to a sales pitch."

Di chuckled softly. "And I'm in no mood to have my soul saved."

By the time they'd exited the apartment and rounded the garage, the young woman had given up using the bell and was now pounding on the door with the heel of her hand.

"Excuse me," Fiona called, continuing across the lawn. "Can I help you?"

She wasn't a woman at all, Fiona surmised. She was just a girl. Hardly more than a year or two older than Cassie, by the looks of her. She wasn't fashionably slim, but rather doesn't-get-enough-to-eat skinny. The dark smudges under her eyes accentuated her pallid complexion. Even her lips were pale. When she opened her mouth to speak, Fiona could see the shadow of a cavity between her two front teeth.

"I need to see Stanley. Mr. Rowland. Is he here?" The girl raised her hand to protect her eyes from the morning sunlight.

Behind Fiona, Di whispered, "Homely little thing, isn't she?"

Fiona wanted to shush her, but didn't. "No. He's not."

The girl came down the steps and onto the grass. "I went to study group last night and he wasn't there. The kids said he hasn't been there for a week. I've been sick. Haven't been to class. They said the dean told them another teacher would be filling in for Stanley—for Mr. Rowland. They said there was a story in the paper that he'd gone missing. I don't watch the local news. And Daddy won't get the newspaper. Says it's full of vile nonsense."

"You're taking my husband's accounting class?" Fiona asked.

She nodded. "I've always had a knack for numbers." She moved closer. "My name's Karen. I really need to talk to Stanley." She paused long enough to swallow, moisture welling in her sunken eyes. "I need to warn him. Is he really missing? Like... gone?"

Fiona ignored Karen's questions. "Warn him about what?"

Karen licked her bloodless lips, then words just burst forth from them. "Daddy said he's gonna kill Stanley. And Buck Snow is crazy enough to do it, too. He's as evil as the devil."

Buck Snow. Why did that name sound so familiar? But the answer was crowded out by another more urgent question.

"Why would your father want to hurt my husband?"

"He's going to kill 'im. Dead. Daddy's a hunter. He owns guns. Knows how to use them. He's also a boozer. And he's a mean drunk."

Like a flash of white lightning, it came to Fiona. More than once, she'd read Buck Snow's name in the Cops and Courts section of the digitized local news. The man was notorious, and Fiona had secretly chuckled at his outlandish troubles on many occasions while reading the online column.

Slowly, Fiona corrected herself. "Why would your father want to kill my husband?"

Karen's chin trembled and fat tears rolled down her cheeks. Her dull gaze slid from Fiona's as both her hands slid over her lower belly. "Daddy found out about the baby." Her shoulders sagged.

Fiona stood there, her mind reeling so fast she felt dizzy. The whole scene took on a surreal quality as the implication sank in. Her knees went wobbly and Di caught her by the arm. "Whoa, there. You okay?"

"Oh, God. No. No, I'm not okay." Fiona couldn't catch her breath. "Stan couldn't do this. Stan wouldn't do this."

"Here. Come over here." Di marched Fiona to the front porch steps. "Sit. Put your head down." She shoved her head between her knees. "Breathe." Then she barked, "How old are you, girl?"

Fiona stared at the wooden steps and heard Karen say, "Twenty-one," between sobs.

"I've got to go call Detective DeSalvo. He needs to know—"

Di placed a strong hand on Fiona's shoulder. "You're not going anywhere just yet. You need to calm down."

Twenty-one. Twenty-one. Stan was screwing a twenty-one-year-old?

It wasn't true. It just couldn't be true.

Karen started to wail. "Daddy's gonna go to prison. Who's gonna help pay the rent? I'm going to have to find a second job. How will I earn my certificate?" A muculent sob caught in her throat and she hiccupped. "I'm gonna be sick." Fiona looked up in time to see Di snatch Karen by the arm and haul her over to the stairs.

"Sit," Di ordered, shoving the girl down beside Fiona. "Get a grip. I do not clean up vomit."

Apparently, the sharp order was just what Karen needed to pull herself together. Her crying softened considerably.

Shock had Fiona's own stomach rumbling. She hoped her breakfast didn't come roiling up all over the lawn.

"Di, I really need to make a phone call."

"In a minute. You're white as a sheet, Fiona. I doubt you could stand on your own just yet."

She was shaky, that was true enough.

"Fiona, do you think Stan knew this Buck Snow had it out for him?" Di shifted her weight on her feet. "Maybe Stan's hiding somewhere. From Karen's father. And from you, for that matter. Maybe he knew the shit was going to hit the fan and he'd better make a quick exit—"

"But Stanley didn't know about the baby."

Fiona and Di turned to look at Karen.

Fresh tears spilled down her face. "I haven't had a chance to tell him." She looked out across the yard. "I've been so sick lately. And I didn't want to tell him on the phone. I knew he was going to be disappointed. Oh, God. Oh, God. This is all my fault. Stanley's dead. And Daddy's going to prison."

"Stop talking like that," Di retorted. "You don't know that for sure." Then her tone changed dramatically. "Do you?"

Karen held her stomach. "I really am gonna be sick."

"Maybe some saltine crackers would help settle her stomach." Without even thinking about it, Fiona reached over and stroked Karen's shoulder with the palm of her hand. "Let's go inside."

Di gave both Fiona and Karen a hand up the steps.

"When's the last time you ate?" Di asked Karen.

"Can't remember. Yesterday afternoon, maybe?" She shook her head, murmuring, "How can they call it morning sickness when I'm hovering over the pot at all hours of the day?"

Fiona cast a pitiful look at Di. She couldn't believe she was actually feeling sorry for this kid.

"I was going to have some Cheerios this morning, but the milk was sour."

Maternal instinct forced Fiona to slip an arm around Karen's bony shoulders as they traipsed through the house to the kitchen. She sensed the girl's appreciation immediately.

"I'm sorry to have to come here," Karen told her softly. "I never meant to make trouble for you. Or Stanley."

"It's going to be okay." Why those words didn't choke her, Fiona couldn't say. What the hell was she doing reassuring her husband's side piece? And how in the world could any of them believe that this was going to be okay?

Something didn't feel right about it, but everything was so hellishly wrong that Fiona couldn't think straight. While she whipped up a bowl of warm oatmeal and plunked two pieces of bread into the toaster, Di grilled Karen for more information.

As it turned out, Karen wasn't at all certain that an actual murder had taken place because she hadn't seen her father since early last week. Her frequent bouts of upchucking had raised his suspicions, and after slugging back a half bottle of Jack Daniel's on Sunday night, he'd launched into a drunken rant and accused her of being pregnant. When Karen had fessed up to her condition, he'd flown into a rage, demanding to know the name of the man "who knocked up my baby girl." He'd named off some of her old boyfriends and then he'd mentioned Stanley. ("That snooty college teacher" was the phrase he'd used, although why her father would think Stanley was snooty was beyond Karen, when he'd never even met the man.) Di had her hands full keeping Karen focused.

Buck Snow had acted surly and anxious all day Monday, and he'd continued to drink all that night. By Tuesday morning he'd grabbed up his shotgun and announced he was going hunting. Karen hadn't seen him since. She'd tried to call Stanley, but he hadn't answered his cell phone, and she'd been too ill last week to do anything other than cover her hours at the diner. If she wasn't waiting tables, she'd been either bent over the toilet or resting on the couch, feeling limp as a wet washrag. Although, *worshrag* was how she'd pronounced it.

As soon as she set the oatmeal and dry toast on the kitchen table in front of Karen, Fiona pulled out Detective DeSalvo's card and picked up the phone receiver, but she didn't immediately dial. Instead, she stared at the small black numbers.

She'd portrayed Stanley as a good father, provider, and husband. A reliable, upstanding man. She certainly didn't relish the idea of telling DeSalvo about Karen Snow and her "condition." But there was no getting around it. It had to be done. Never in a million years would she have suspected Stanley of something like this. Nerves quaked inside her, threatening her composure. She took a deep breath and tapped in the numbers.

"Mrs. Rowland?"

She had known her name would pop up on his caller ID, had known also that he'd be surprised to hear from her when they'd talked just that morning. But she hadn't prepared for having her vocal cords freeze.

"Is something wrong?"

His surprise turned to concern.

"Have you heard from him?"

"No. No," she was finally able to spit out. She cleared her throat and turned her back on Di and Karen Snow. "I've found someone you need to talk to. Or rather, she found me. A student of Stan's came to see me this morning. She's been..." anxiety forced Fiona to hesitate "...ill. She wasn't in class last week. Didn't find out about Stan until last night."

Plain old pride kept her from divulging, *she's claiming to be pregnant with my husband's baby.*

"You need to talk to her, Detective."

"She's there now?"

"Yes. Sitting right here at my kitchen table." Fiona turned to look at her guest.

Karen had taken a couple of bites of the toast and her color was returning. The young woman picked up her spoon and began shoveling oatmeal into her mouth, reminding Fiona of a starving puppy. Sympathy flooded through her. What the hell had her husband been thinking, to take advantage of this pitiful girl? She could tell by the intense look in Di's blue eyes that she was wondering the same thing. Fiona focused her attention back on the phone call.

"I'm swamped," DeSalvo told her. "I can't get back out there right now. Could you send her here?"

"Of course." Fiona felt a sudden desperation to hang up. She didn't want him asking any more questions. Let Karen Snow deliver all the pertinent information. Putting her hand over the phone, Fiona asked the girl, "Can you go to the police station to answer some questions?" When Karen nodded, Fiona told DeSalvo, "She'll be there soon." She placed the receiver into its cradle, relieved that she hadn't been forced to reveal what an utter hound dog her husband was turning out to be.

With a father like Buck Snow, Karen was well aware of the location of the police station. Conversation swiftly lulled. The walls of the spacious kitchen seemed to close in. Making small talk with a kid barely out of adolescence who claimed to be carrying Stan's child was difficult, if not impossible. Quite surprisingly, Fiona realized she wasn't angry with the girl. She was angry with Stan. Furious with him, actually. He was the adult. He was the one in the mentor role. He was her instructor, for crying out loud. He was the one who should have known better.

After Karen finished breakfast, Fiona plunked an apple into Karen's hand and walked her to the door, while Di remained in the kitchen.

Out on the porch, Karen's misery once again sparked Fiona's maternal instincts. But the scorned woman inside refused to allow her to act on the urge to reach out any more than she already had. The young woman looked her in the eye, and Fiona experienced a queasy feeling that the girl was about to plop another big, slimy fish into her lap. Fiona doubted she could take any more surprises. But then Karen's gaze shifted to her feet, her lanky hair falling across her face. She muttered a quick apology, turned on her heel, and tramped down the steps.

By the time Fiona returned to the kitchen she felt emotionally drained. She slumped down into a chair.

"Can you believe that child?" Di had cleared the table and was stacking the china into the dishwasher. "I just can't believe it. She's so young. Why, she's not that much older than…"

The rest of Di's sentence went unspoken, but having had the same thought, Fiona picked it up almost seamlessly.

"Cassie." Her voice sounded weary even to her

own ears. "And you're right. I can't believe it, either. But it would be pretty foolish to deny the truth when it's staring you right in the face." Fiona's thoughts were finally slowing. "It's odd. Strange, really. It took me three years to get pregnant with Cassie. The doctors ran tests on us both, and we were told that Stan had a low sperm count. It took months and months for me to conceive Sam."

Di shrugged. "You don't know how long Stan's been doing her, Fiona." Her eyes widened as she latched the dishwasher door. "I'm sorry, hon." She moved across the floor. Slid into a chair. "I should be more careful about what I say."

Fiona shook her head. "You're just voicing the facts. It is hard to believe that Stan would..." She heaved a sigh. "And that girl is so... young. You said it. She's a child, Di." She smoothed her palm over the oak tabletop. "Did you see her eyes? There wasn't an ounce of guile in that girl. She didn't want to come here. Didn't want to confess her secrets to us. All she was worried about was warning Stan."

After a moment, Di said, "She was so thin. Aunt Viv would have said, '*If that girl stood sideways and* stuck her tongue out, she'd have been mistaken for a zipper.'"

Di's rendition of her aunt's croaky "smoker's" voice was dead-on, and Fiona smiled, despite the bizarre situation.

Suddenly, Di sobered. "Did you ever suspect that he was fooling around?"

"Never." Fiona sighed. "Oh, I've seen the daytime talk shows. All of them claim that cheaters show signs. But I never saw any. Not one." She examined her blunt nails. "Never would I have imagined any of this. Stan vanishing. That child showing up. Pregnant." She shuddered involuntarily.

Di reached over and touched her forearm. "But I view this as good news."

Fiona looked at her as if she'd suddenly sprouted a second head.

"Don't you see? Now there's a reason for all of us to think that Stan's okay. That he's simply run off. Because he doesn't want to face the music."

"But he's not like that," Fiona insisted. "He's got too much—"

Strength of character, she was going to say. But she clamped her mouth shut. She'd thought she knew her husband, but she wasn't so sure anymore.

Fiona slid her hands into her lap. "We were so happy. We were young and in love and newly married. Full of dreams for the future. He was my champion. He took me out of that house of anger, and I loved him for it. Stan offered me stability and security, and a lightheartedness, a..." she struggled to find the perfect words "...a happiness that was really and truly complete. It was something I'd never experienced before." She combed her fingers through her hair, tucking it neatly behind her ear. "I have no idea what happened to us, Di. What happened to our marriage."

Fiona could hear the birds singing from the maple tree just outside the kitchen window. High, puffy clouds floated on the late-summer heat. She saw the second hand on the clock sweeping in a circle, time continuing to plow forward, just as if her life and her marriage hadn't been ripped to shreds.

She noticed toast crumbs on the table, but was too absorbed in her misery to care. "I can't remember the last time we talked about the future." The oak was cool against her elbows when she planted them on the table. "I can't remember the last time we talked. I mean really talked. Hell, I can't remember the last time we had sex." She shook her head. "It seems that we somehow got sidetracked onto different paths. Different... *lives.* He works such long hours. And then he spends time with his poker buddies and his pool team. He teaches. He tutors. I'm so wrapped up in the kids. In their education and their extracurricular activities. I have my book club and the fundraising committees and my Women's League."

She looked at Di, her eyes so dry they burned. "And now I find out..." Something ugly reared up inside her. "Why aren't I hurt, Di? I should feel hurt by what he's done. All I feel is anger. No, I'm... I'm furious. I've been raising his kids and keeping his house, and he's been out doinking a girl young enough to be his daughter."

One corner of Di's mouth twitched. She pursed her lips, but not before Fiona noticed.

"What?"

"Nothing," Di insisted, trying valiantly to keep a straight face. "It's nothing."

"What?" Fiona wasn't in the mood to coax out an answer.

"Okay." Di surrendered to a smile. "It's just..." A chuckle got the better of her. "*Doink?* Fiona, hon, you're over forty. I'd say it's okay for you to say fuck."

Single and childless, Di wouldn't have any idea of the lengths to which a mother went to exert control over herself, over her behavior and her language. The instant that baby popped out, something happened to a woman. She became something new, something different. She was converted into an instant role model who had to live like someone worth imitating. However, Fiona had to admit that, in this particular instance, Di was absolutely right. She needed a release, and she needed it now.

Closing her eyes tight, Fiona balled her hands into fists and expressed every drop of anger in her. "Oh, fuck!" She opened her eyes, her shoulders relaxing on a huge exhalation. "That felt so good."

Chapter Seven

More Reality

Di followed Fiona into the house and watched as her friend tossed her ring of keys onto the table by the door. The keys slid into the mound of mail, toppling it over. Dozens of envelopes and catalogs, postcards and grocery store advertisements fluttered to the floor. A Lillian Vernon catalog slapped Di on the ankle and she bent to retrieve it.

"I'll get that." Cassie rushed in from behind her, dropped the backpack she'd been carrying, took the catalog from Di's hand and began gathering up the other mail that had skittered across the smooth, tan quarry tile.

"Thanks, kiddo," Di murmured over her shoulder, then hurried to catch up with Fiona, who was breezing through the house, seemingly unaware or uncaring of the mess she'd made in the foyer.

Karen Snow's visit two days ago had affected Fiona. Taken the oomph out of her. Zapped her energy. She'd continued to take care of the kids—cooked their meals, washed their laundry, picked up after them, carted them to and from school and their activities. In fact, they were just arriving home from retrieving Cassie. Fiona had promised the kids pizza for dinner this evening, and after phoning in the order, Di was supposed to await the delivery with Cassie while Fiona drove back into Wilmington to pick up Sam, who had stayed at school to practice with his cross-country team. Just contemplating Fiona's schedule made Di want to kick off her shoes and take a nap. The woman was like the Energizer Bunny; she kept going.

This motherly devotion crap that plagued Fiona (not that Fiona saw it in that light, of course) completely baffled Di. It reminded her of Tammy, the Support Specialist at the marketing firm. That girl was dedicated to her dead-end, grunt-work job. She went from one office to another picking up files that needed copying, letters and packages that needed mailing, lists of personal errands that needed running. Like a mouse in an endless maze, she raced through those halls, always perky and upbeat and ready to satisfy everyone in every way possible. The reality was that, outside of the payroll department, no one at the firm could remember the girl's last name.

At least Tammy was rewarded for her efforts twice a month, even if all she received was a cheesy little paycheck. As far as Di had discerned after staying here for a little over a week, Fiona didn't get anything out of her devoted service as wife, mother, housekeeper, gardener, chief cook and bottle washer, chauffeur or any of the other hats she wore, either. Di had wondered more than once how Fiona remained so driven, so committed.

Over the past couple of days, however, as hard as Fiona tried to plaster on a smile for her children, Di could see that the discovery of Stan's indiscretion had squashed her spirit.

"Fiona, wait." Di touched her friend on the

shoulder and Fiona stopped, then turned to face her. "Are you okay?"

"Of course I'm okay. Why wouldn't I be okay?"

Di glanced back toward the foyer where Cassie was attempting to balance the mail on the table.

"Oh, that." Fiona waved off her concern. "It's nothing. Just a few envelopes on the floor. Cassie's getting it."

Fiona walked away and Di followed her into the kitchen. Fiona went directly to the dishwasher, opened the door, and began putting the clean dishes away.

"They're not just envelopes, Fiona. I saw bills scattered across the foyer." She rested her hand on the back of a kitchen chair. "I know you're going through a lot right now. I know you're worried. But you have to be practical. If you don't pay the electric bill, the lights will be shut off."

Fiona straightened, a drinking glass in each hand. Shadows haunted her hazel eyes. Di hadn't seen her this vulnerable since the first night she'd arrived and Fiona had guiltily confessed that her husband had been missing for days before she noticed.

"That's Stan's job." A frown bit into her brow and she spoke quietly. "He pays the bills, balances the checkbook, files the receipts." Gently, she set the glasses on the counter, her expression spectral. "If I go through the mail, it's like I'm admitting that he won't be coming home."

Di's heart pinched as tears filled Fiona's eyes and slid down her cheeks. "Besides, finances aren't my thing. Stan has told me so over the years." She waved her hand breezily and forced out a laugh, but the result sounded tragic.

"You know, early on I handled the checkbook. For the first few years we were married." Another harsh chuckle grated from her throat. "But I screwed up the account so badly that we actually had to change banks. Stan was furious."

Fear widened Fiona's eyes. "I haven't handled our finances for ages, Di. For ages. I have no idea what it costs to run this house. I don't know what we've got in savings. I don't even know what Stan's salary is." She swiped the moist tracks from her cheeks. "But I do know one thing—with him gone, our income is zero. Zilch. Nothing. That fact is ground further into my brain every time I pass by that pile of mail out there." She inhaled with difficulty. "What am I going to do, Di? How am I going to provide for Cassie and Sam?"

Di took her trembling hand. "You're not alone. I

want you to know that. There's no reason to panic. We'll go over your money situation together. We'll look at everything. Checking and savings. And I'm sure Stan must have a 401K. Those funds can be used in an emergency."

"But there's no income—"

"Mom."

Releasing her friend's hand, Di turned toward Cassie, who was standing in the kitchen doorway. The teen's hair hung in straight, silky strands just as her mother's had at seventeen. In fact, Cassie was the very image of Fiona at that age. Her large eyes were filled with concern.

"It's okay, honey," Fiona said. "Everything's going to be fine."

Nobody believed that.

Cassie took several steps into the room. "I could give up my cell phone."

Fiona shook her head, smiling reassuringly. "That's not necessary. At least not right now. Your phone is on a prepaid plan, remember? We just bought you and Sam nonrefundable cards worth six hundred minutes. If you're careful, you could keep your phone for a good long time. And maybe by then, things will be... back to normal."

Di heard the doubt in Fiona's voice.

"What about school, then?" Cassie asked. "If we need ways to spend less money, Sam and I could go to public school. There'd be no more tuition. No more uniforms to buy."

"But you love St. Anne's." Fiona was clearly stunned by her daughter's suggestion.

"Of course I do. You know that." Cassie looked down at the floor and then back toward her mother. "But I just heard you say we have no money."

"I didn't say we have no money," Fiona insisted. "I said..." She paused. "Honey, this isn't something you're supposed to worry about. This is my problem."

"Mom, this is my problem, too. And it's Sam's problem. You can't protect us from everything." Cassie's chin lifted stubbornly and Di felt proud of her.

"Dad always said there's nothing wrong with public school," the teen continued. "He graduated from public school, and so did you. It won't kill me or Sam if we have to—"

"Well, let's just hope it doesn't come to that." Fiona reached into the dishwasher and picked up two more glasses.

"It won't come to that," Di told Fiona. "I'll be happy to pay the tuition."

"You will not."

Fiona's sharp tone offended Di. You would have thought she was threatening to rob her blind, not bail her out of a bind. "And why not?"

"I am not taking money from you."

"All right, call it a loan then. Whatever. I have money. If you need money, it would be silly if you didn't—"

"Don't call me silly." She set the glasses on the counter so firmly that they clanged together. "Friends don't borrow from friends. And I'm not taking your money, Di—"

"I didn't call you silly, Fiona."

"Hey, hey."

Di and Fiona stopped bickering and looked at Cassie. "Keep up the 'tude and I'm going to call that hot cop who's been hanging around here."

Di's anger disappeared in an instant and she grinned. "That hot cop, huh?"

Fiona, too, exhibited a quick "'*tude*" adjustment. "I had no idea you'd noticed that Detective DeSalvo was... good-looking."

"She's not the only one who's noticed." Di waggled her eyebrows and Cassie laughed.

"Oh, Di." Fiona opened the cabinet overhead. "He's too young for you. Unless you like those inexperienced types."

"Honey, he won't be inexperienced when I'm through with him."

Fiona just shook her head. Then she noticed the digital clock on the microwave. "I have to pick up Sam. And if I hurry, I can stop by Fox and Associates."

Di cocked her head. "That wasn't on the schedule."

Ignoring her comment, Fiona said, "Cassie, would you order the pizza and then finish emptying the dishwasher?"

"Sure, Mom."

Fiona caught Di's eye and jerked her head toward the living room. They left the kitchen together.

Curiosity got the best of Di. "So why the unexpected trip to Stan's work?"

"I've been living with my head in the sand, Di. And for the past couple of days I've been wallowing in self-pity." Fiona picked up her purse. "I want to thank you for kicking me in the butt in there. You're absolutely right. I need to be practical." She moved toward the front door.

"Tonight, you and I are going to go over my financial situation. But right now I'm going to see James Fox. Stan worked the first half of the month. He's owed some money. It might not be much, but it's some." The hinges of the front door creaked when she pulled it open. "And I'm going to go get it."

The doorknob was cool against Di's fingers. She watched her friend descend the porch steps, secretly thrilled by the notion that Fiona had regained her resolve.

Throughout the years that they had been close, during their teens and into their twenties, Di had noticed and even tried to emulate Fiona's courage and tenacity. But as sometimes happens between adolescent friends, admiration often darkened, manifesting itself in negative ways by becoming a close cousin of envy and resentment. Di was ashamed of the times she'd felt jealous of Fiona even though she knew those feelings must be normal teenage afflictions. However, seeing her friend stalk across the lawn with her chin tipped up and her shoulders square, clearly ready to take on the world, Di just shook her head in wonder.

Softly, she whispered, "Go get 'em, girl."

Chapter Eight

Growing Backbone

What a pain in the butt this idea had turned out to be. Fiona stepped into the elevator located just down the hall from James Fox's office, his receptionist's gaze boring into her back. She jabbed the button that would take her to the second floor. The doors slid shut and she tuned out the soft, canned music floating on the stale air.

Jim had apologized profusely that the air conditioner in the elevator was out of order, as if she cared one whit about such a thing. Her unexpected appearance had flustered him. How did one treat the wife of a missing employee when one had hindered the police proceedings for nearly a week? He'd begun repeating the same excuses about Stan's computer that he'd given her over the phone, but she'd waved him off. She hadn't had time for it.

Over the course of the nearly twenty years Stan had worked here, Fiona had seen a dramatic shift in the working atmosphere at the accounting firm. Early on, Fox and Associates had been extremely family oriented. Jim Fox had thrown holiday parties and summer picnics for the employees, and the staff had been encouraged to bring their spouses and children. But the ever-flattening economy had changed those attitudes. Social gatherings became a thing of the past and employees were expected to double or even triple their workloads. Stan had seemed to understand that the new policies and the mounting responsibility were necessary business maneuvers. As one year rolled into another, however, with no letup, James Fox earned a reputation of being a difficult taskmaster.

Although her unannounced arrival had disconcerted him at first, he'd quickly recovered and had turned on the charm. He'd listened sympathetically when she explained her financial situation, that she needed the income Stan was owed, and that she hoped James would hold her husband's job until he returned home.

Compassion had darkened his smoky gray eyes when she'd talked of Stan's homecoming, and Fiona got the distinct impression he was of the opinion that she was holding on to a fantasy, and he felt sorry for her about that. She would have told him to stuff his pity, but at the mention of Stan's return she'd been jarred by an unexpected flare of anger as thoughts of the pregnant Karen Snow had crashed into her brain. Fiona's stomach had rolled, but she had successfully continued with the conversation at hand.

The subject of money had quickly transformed James into the astute businessman that had secured him his success. She'd been taken aback to learn that he'd already discussed the issue of Stan's continued employment with his financial advisors. "The Money Committee," as James referred to them, had recommended that Stan be immediately removed from the company roster.

Although she'd tried to keep her cool, Fiona had panicked. She hadn't expected any more money than Stan was due, but all she could think about was the loss of medical coverage for Cassie and

Sam—something that hadn't entered her head up to that point. James's promise to continue Stan's salary and benefits through the end of the month had been a small consolation. But the extra money— however small the amount—would buy her some time.

However, when she'd pressed the issue, reminding Jim that her husband was owed for three weeks vacation he hadn't taken, and she'd like to collect those funds as well, he had looked peeved. She hadn't cared a single shred if he was irked by her request. She had her children to think about. She needed every nickel she was due, and she intended to get it.

Luckily, his annoyance abated and he'd instructed her to go to the payroll department on the second floor. However, his final statement had been the kicker that had sent her whole world reeling.

"I'll have someone from benefits call you when the time comes, Fiona," he'd told her gently. "About Stan's life insurance."

Any number of emotive reactions would have been gauged as normal: shock, sadness, fear, panic. But what she'd felt was exasperation beyond belief. Even now, as she descended in this airless musical box, she felt her face flaming with an overwhelming vexation.

Everyone thought Stan was dead. The kids were worried about what was going to happen to them. Di forced Fiona to consider her financial situation. Stan's boss was talking about collecting life insurance. Even Detective DeSalvo was becoming less and less optimistic each time she saw him. The man could barely look her in the eye these days.

Hell, she may as well release her desperate clutch on optimism and don herself in sackcloth and ashes. Everybody else she knew seemed ready to go into bereavement mode. It annoyed her.

It also scared the hell out of her.

Mortgage, utilities, school tuitions and fees, clothing, groceries—

The doors of the elevator slid open and Fiona bolted, more than happy to leave behind the stuffy air and claustrophobic thoughts.

Six women sat at desks that had been situated in clusters of two, each separated by a shoulder high wall. Fiona stalked toward the cubicle closest to her.

"I'm Fiona Rowland. I'm here to collect my husband's check."

"Shirley's on the phone with Mr. Fox now. Have a seat. She'll be right out."

Dodging eye contact, the woman indicated the padded leather and chrome chairs near the door and then turned back to her computer. The atmosphere felt somehow "off." The women concentrated on their monitors too intensely, tapped their keyboards too furiously, avoided looking at her in a manner too pointed to be natural. Fiona had never considered herself a paranoid person, but clearly, James's call to the department had sparked conversation about her among the group.

Too keyed up to sit, Fiona ambled over toward the wall of chairs. A door opened on the far side of the office and she turned. The middle-aged redhead striding toward her could only be described as stunning. The woman paused when she reached the employee who had invited Fiona to take a seat, handed her a slip of paper and issued some instructions in a tone too low to be overheard before directing her attention back to Fiona.

"I'm Shirley Bookerman." Her gorgeous face somber, she reached out her hand in greeting. "We want you to know we've been thinking about you during this difficult time."

The words sounded well-practiced. Fiona murmured her appreciation.

"James just informed me you're to receive a check." She glanced over her shoulder for the briefest moment. "It will only take Patricia a moment to print it out."

This time Fiona nodded to show her gratitude.

"I want you to know," Shirley continued, "that everyone at Fox and Associates thought very highly of your husband. Stan was a wonderful, wonderful man."

Whether it was the stress of her situation or residual tension left over from her conversation with Jim, Fiona couldn't say, but she felt a sudden need to set this woman straight. "Yeah, well the jury's still out on whether Stan deserves all that esteem."

Patricia approached them and handed Fiona an envelope. "Your check," she said, and then immediately retreated to her desk.

The sound of a ragged inhalation drew Fiona's gaze. Shirley Bookerman's vivid green eyes glittered with deep emotion.

"You have no idea how lucky you were to be married to Stanley Rowland." The redhead's tone was quiet but fierce. "What he deserved was to be appreciated by his family."

The blatant accusation so staggered Fiona that all she could do was gape in silence. After staring a second or two longer, the woman muttered a pithy goodbye and then turned and walked away. It was only while Fiona stood there speechless that she became cognizant of the utter quiet that had fallen over the entire room. All activity had ceased, shameless suspense shimmering in the air.

Suspicion is a dark and dangerous thing. Fiona felt as if a rod were being jammed up her spine.

"Ms. Bookerman," she called, loudly enough for all to hear.

The redhead stopped in the doorway of her office, defiance twisting her extraordinary features when she turned to face Fiona.

"Were you sleeping with my husband?"

Shirley's coral lips parted, and Fiona noticed that the lipstick shade didn't coordinate well with the deep crimson that flushed the woman's milky cheeks and neck. There was fury and, yes, even hatred in the glare she leveled on Fiona.

"I'm not even going to dignify that with a response."

"She was angry and evasive. And we all know what *that* kind of reaction means." Fiona paced Detective DeSalvo's small, gray office as she ranted. She'd left Fox and Associates, checked her watch, and then practically flew to the police station.

She whirled on him. "You might not have known about Karen Snow before I sent her to your office this week, but you've been fully aware of Shirley Bookerman from the beginning. You interviewed my husband's co-workers. You knew Stan was a two-timing louse, but instead of making me privy to the facts, you treated me like a felon. I resent that, Detective. You kept making me go over the events of Sunday. Kept grilling me about the state of my marriage." She pointed directly at his chest, her hand hovering over the dented metal desk separating them. "You've thought all along that I'm a suspect... that I've done something to Stan, dumped his body somewhere. But you haven't had the decency to come right out and tell me why."

He stood tall, unmoved by her fury.

"Mrs. Rowland, I'm not required to inform the

public—in this instance that means you—about every detail of my investigation."

"But you've been coming to the house every morning." Her purse suddenly felt heavy, so she plunked it onto a corner of the desk. "You've been telling me..."

Her sentence trailed off and her breath left her in a rush as she realized he hadn't told her much of anything during his daily visits. He'd revealed broad plans, said he was interviewing Stan's friends, or his co-workers, or his students. But she realized now that he barely gave her any of the particulars, just enough to put her at ease. In fact, he'd expertly dodged most of her questions, changing the subject, and turning the query back to her, time and again. She'd been a fool not to have called him on it before now.

She sank into the nearby chair, feeling disillusioned.

"You used me, Detective. You judged me guilty and pumped me for information to prove that theory."

"I was only doing my job."

Hadn't she told herself that more than once?

He shifted his weight, lifting his foot to plant it on the seat of his desk chair. "I did talk with

Shirley Bookerman. And her name came up when I talked to some of the other employees at Fox. There were rumors and speculation. Office gossip. Nothing concrete." He bent at the waist, resting his elbow on his thigh. "So I pushed you because... well—" he shrugged "—who's more likely to organize a necktie lynching for an unfaithful husband than his unsuspecting wife?"

The world tipped and spun crazily. She was a suspect in Stan's disappearance. Just as she'd told Di.

Fiona wasn't an idiot. She knew the most likely suspect in any crime was some injured party seeking revenge. However, she'd assiduously clung to her Pollyanna optimism that Stan was okay, avoiding the whole idea that a crime might have been committed. It was too dark, too scary to ponder. It was a shock, hearing DeSalvo actually string together the words lynching and unfaithful husband and unsuspecting wi—

She stopped cold, blinking. "You called me unsuspecting."

"Ding, ding, ding. The lady gets a prize." He pulled his foot off the chair, and when he plopped down on it, the ancient springs creaked in complaint.

"Do you realize how nonsensical you just sounded?"

He grinned. "Took you long enough to notice."

His tone was breezy, but she was still disconcerted. "So I'm not a suspect?"

"Not any longer." He pushed aside a stack of files. "At the beginning of any investigation I have to be open to any result. A good cop has to be able to imagine anyone as the bad guy, so to speak. It's the nature of the business." He paused. "I'll be honest with you. The fact that you couldn't pinpoint the day and time you'd last seen your husband was... highly irregular. And that placed a huge question mark on your innocence."

Like a vine of poison ivy, guilt crept over her, and Fiona wanted to shift her gaze from his, squirm in her chair from the itchy shame.

"But the more I thought about it," he continued, "the more I talked to you, I realized that the two of you weren't having marital problems per se, but that you seem to have become disconnected."

With an odd detachment, she listened to DeSalvo's impassive portrayal of her marriage. Was that what she and Stan had become? Disconnected?

The detective laced his fingers loosely. "I believe

that's why you didn't notice he was gone. Because you were busy. With your kids. With your house. With all the things you do."

You were busy.

The words reverberated in her head, and that poison vine of self-reproach seemed to spread until it was choking the wind out of her. How could a person be that damn busy?

"Besides all that…"

He avoided her eyes, directing his attention to the pile of manila folders he'd already moved. He shifted them another couple of inches.

"—my gut is telling me you didn't do anything wrong."

Then he looked at her, his intense gaze demanding attention.

"I've dealt with all kinds of criminals," he said softly. "You don't have it in you to jaywalk, Mrs. Rowland, let alone plot to harm someone. So, no, I don't think you harmed your husband. However, I do have to point out that after witnessing your temper just now, and knowing that you've spoken to Ms. Bookerman, were Mr. Rowland to walk in the door right now…"

Humor twitched his lips.

"…I wouldn't leave you alone with him."

Her face burned. She hated that she'd let him see her lose control, but she'd been angry. With Stan. With that gorgeous witch in the payroll department at Fox. And with DeSalvo. Hell, she was angry with the whole damn world! Too bad for the detective that he'd been the one forced to bear the brunt of her wrath.

DeSalvo shook his head. "Man, oh, man, you are absolutely beautiful when your cheeks turn pink like that."

Fiona grew still, dumbfounded by his statement. And just when she began to wonder if he might be flirting with her, she realized that he was as discomfited by his outburst as she.

He hadn't treated her with anything short of stark professionalism since this whole mess began. He was a decent guy, she reasoned. Decent enough to feel bad for her. Decent enough to try to lift her spirits after she'd just discovered that her husband had been an adulterous ass.

Self-consciousness built to an unbearable degree. She stood. "I'm going to be late picking Sam up at school. I have to go."

He shot to his feet. "Of course."

Fiona snatched up her purse and headed for the door. She stopped when her hand settled on the doorknob. "You could call me tomorrow, Detective. Let me know if there's any news." The suggestion was out before she had time to think.

He frowned, obviously confused. "I can do that, sure."

She hurried down the hall and out of the police station, mentally kicking herself all the way. What had she just done? For more than a week she'd lived for DeSalvo's morning visits to her house, desperate for some sliver of information about Stan and the investigation. However, without coming right out and saying it, she'd just implied that he should stop coming to her home and that he should call instead.

What the hell had she been thinking? Had she lost her mind?

She unlocked her car and slid behind the wheel. "Fiona, you're a total nutcase."

Tilting her head, she caught her reflection in the rearview mirror.

Beautiful. He'd called her beautiful.

The feelings swirling inside her were weird. And frightening. She jammed the keys into the ignition and started the engine.

"What are you? A teenager? Grow up, Fiona." She stared at herself in the rearview mirror. Just because a man—even one as young and hot as DeSalvo— offered a woman a compliment didn't necessarily have to imply anything more than what it was. A compliment.

She shoved the car into gear. "Now get your butt to Sam's school."

Chapter Nine

The Volvo

It wasn't until the kids had been dropped off at school on Monday morning that Fiona and Di finally settled in the dining room to sort through the bills. The pile of mail sitting in the middle of the table had looked daunting. Who would have thought, though, that a plain, white, number 9 envelope would hold information valuable enough to put the Delaware State Police on alert? Fiona hadn't imagined that a letter buried in that mound of invoices, receipts, advertisements, post cards, magazines, and department store sale catalogs would turn out to be the biggest break they'd received in the two weeks that Stan had been missing. Or that it would ultimately have a dozen uniformed officers fanned out on both shoulders and the median strip of I-95, searching the overgrown grass and scrub for clues.

Ironically, Fiona had nearly tossed the unremarkable envelope into the trash without giving it a second glance. Because it had been missing a return address, she'd mistaken it for junk mail.

"Open everything," Di had warned, so Fiona had used the letter opener to slice through the top flap.

Her stomach had gone queasy when she'd read that a Wilmington towing company claimed to be holding Stan's Volvo. Her hands began to tremble when she noticed the bold, red Second Notice stamped on the letter. She and Di sorted through the mountain of mail until they found the first notice, which had been postmarked the very Wednesday that Fiona had reported Stan missing. By then she'd been shaking so badly that Di had to dial Detective DeSalvo's number. The utility bills were forgotten as Di drove an insistent Fiona into the city to meet DeSalvo at the towing company. She wanted—no, she *needed*—to see the Volvo with her own eyes.

The instant Fiona had stepped out of the passenger side of her van, the scene took on a dreamlike feel. Several black-and-whites had pulled into the parking lot at different angles, DeSalvo's unmarked car blocking a tow truck that was still running, the driver's door wide open. DeSalvo barked into the face of the truck driver, a man who looked to be in his late fifties. The man wore a greasy blue work shirt with Drew embroidered on the pocket. A bizarre thought ambled through Fiona's mind: it was amazing that grubby Drew could see through the squinty slits of his eyes or communicate with the police, considering the obstinacy that stiffened his whiskered jaw tighter than a steel vise. Meanwhile, several officers had swarmed around Stan's silver Volvo, one dusting the steering wheel for fingerprints while the other two searched the trunk.

DeSalvo continued to grill Drew, pressing him hard with accusations of renegade towing, and making clear the punishment for obstructing an official investigation. Frustration had the detective calling to one of the uniformed officers for a pair of handcuffs before Drew finally caved and offered up the exact location from which he'd towed the car.

DeSalvo approached Fiona. His dark eyes flashed with determination, remnants of gritty energy left over from the intense interrogation he'd just conducted.

"What are you doing here?" he charged. "You didn't need to come. I would have called you."

"I wanted to see... I had to see." *For myself*, she finished silently.

"You shouldn't be here. Go home. I'll call you later."

"But—" she looked over at the officers who worked on the Volvo "—what have they found?"

"I don't know yet. And I won't know if I go over there bothering them. Go home, Mrs. Rowland."

"Was there anything wrong with the car?" she pressed.

"The guy said the car was unlocked. No keys. Do you have a spare with you?"

The keys jangled when Di handed them over, and Fiona fumbled with the ring until she was able to fish off the extra key to Stan's car. She handed it to DeSalvo.

"Go home," he urged.

"I want to know—"

"They have to process the car. It's going to take some time. We've got a truck coming to tow it over to the impound lot." Then he repeated, "Go home."

Fiona was seized with sudden desperation. She couldn't just leave. "Where are you going? What are you going to do?"

"I've got a team assembling now and they'll search the last known location of the car just as soon as I call in the mile marker. I'll meet them there to help."

"I'm going with you."

"Fiona." Di touched her shoulder. "That's not a good idea."

"Listen to your friend." DeSalvo seemed eager to get away.

"I'm going." Fiona wasn't used to the steely resolve that squared her shoulders.

The detective stared at her for a moment. "You'll only be in the way."

"I said I'm going." The volume of her voice garnered glances from several of the police officers present.

DeSalvo didn't look happy, but his tone was patient when he finally explained, "It's been two weeks. We probably won't find anything."

Fiona remained silent, her mouth tightening.

He expelled a resigned sigh. "You'll have to ride with me."

Although she felt as if she'd won a war, she was too keyed up to express her gratitude.

"I can't have an unauthorized vehicle sitting on the shoulder of the interstate." DeSalvo addressed Di. "Can you drive the van back to the Rowlands' house?"

Di nodded and the detective excused himself to talk to the officers near Stan's Volvo. For the first time, Fiona noticed the large black box sitting open by the driver's side door. Forensic equipment, she guessed.

She worried her thumb back and forth across the knuckle of her index finger. "This is bad, Di. This is really bad. I thought he had the car."

Her friend remained silent, but the expression in her blue eyes said she understood Fiona was talking about Stan. Di took her by the shoulders and steered her several yards away from the scene.

"Don't think about that right now. Let's focus on something else. Let's make some plans, okay? You want me to pick up the kids from school this afternoon?"

Fiona's nod was vague. "If I don't get back in

time, yes. Thanks for thinking of it. I have no idea how long I'll be. Or how I'll get home."

"If the detective doesn't offer to bring you, call me. I'll come get you."

"I will. Thanks."

"What else can I do, Fiona? I'll do anything. Just say the word."

"I need someone to wake me from this nightmare."

DeSalvo shouted to her. He was ready to go. Immediately, Fiona hurried toward his car. "Oh, Di," she called after pulling open the passenger door. "There is something... Could you pay the bills? I left the checkbook on the dining room table. It really needs to be done." She frowned. Stan would have a fit to know she'd let Di nose around in the checkbook. But what the hell? Stan wasn't here. "Just sign my name on the checks. If there's a problem, I'll take care of it later."

"Sure thing," Di said. "I can handle it."

I-95 remained jammed with traffic at most times of the day and night. DelDOT used every means available to lessen the congestion, but plainly put, just too many commuters used the highway to access the city of Wilmington and points farther north.

"What did you mean," Fiona asked DeSalvo, "when you accused that man of running a renegade towing company?"

"The city of Wilmington doesn't have the revenue to own tow trucks." DeSalvo flicked on his signal and moved into the fast lane.

His voice was tight. Clearly, he didn't want her here, didn't want to be wasting his time explaining this to her. Using one of her son's favorite sayings, Fiona thought DeSalvo could just suck it up.

"City officials contract private companies to tow abandoned cars. They enter each car's serial number into a computer system. It's done that way so that we—the police—can keep track of what cars are where. The first thing I did after you reported your husband missing was to check the computer. There was no record that the Volvo had been towed."

"So that man back there took Stan's car illegally."

The detective nodded. "He did. And he'll have to face the judge for it. Renegade towing is becoming a problem in cities all around the country. Cars are towed from parking lots and side streets. The thing is, these illegal outfits must contact the owners immediately, before anyone gets suspicious or panics and contacts the police to report their car stolen. They have to keep the police out of it if they don't want to get caught."

The towing company had attempted to contact her right away, but she'd been too distraught to open the damn mail.

"A law-abiding citizen wouldn't know that the company holding their car was acting dishonestly. They don't even know they're being scammed." He made a U-turn, using an opening in the median designated for emergency vehicles only. "They want one thing. Their car. So they pay the exorbitant fee and go about their business. Because the car owner is none the wiser, this particular crime is notorious for going unreported."

He eased over into the far left lane and pulled behind the two white vans parked on the shoulder of the roadway. He shoved the car into Park, cut the engine and leveled his gaze on her. "I want you to stay in the car."

"But—"

"Stay in the car." He pushed open the door and got out.

He really was annoyed with her, but she didn't care. She wanted to know if they found something. She deserved to know. So she listened to DeSalvo's muffled voice as he gave instructions to the party of male and female officers. They broke up into three groups; one stayed on the northbound shoulder very near the vans and DeSalvo's car, one crossed to the wide grass-and-scrub-covered median, and the third dodged the southbound traffic to fan out on the far shoulder. All eyes pointed to the ground, sweeping back and forth. Cars and tractor trailers whipped by her at a velocity that set the car rocking with each pass.

She heard someone shout, and craned her neck to see who it was, where he or she was calling from. A female cop who'd been searching the median waved, and DeSalvo left the group that had been walking the far shoulder of the road. Fiona watched him risk life and limb by ducking between the speeding traffic. The woman was donning latex gloves. She'd obviously found something. Fiona got out of the car and went to stand by the rear bumper.

There was a flurry of activity on the median now. Gloved officers were picking up papers and what looked like manila file folders. DeSalvo called in both groups searching the shoulders to help. Fiona's stomach was doing somersaults. Did the stuff even belong to Stan?

"What is it?" she called, but her question was whipped away on the wind as an earsplitting Harley passed a few feet in front of her.

It seemed she stood on the shoulder of the busy interstate for an eternity before DeSalvo glanced her way. He gave her a thumbs-up, but that didn't ease the tension churning low in her belly.

Finally, the detective left the group, carrying two small parcels. He performed another dash and bob to get to her.

"What is it? What did you find?" The stress etched in his face scared her half to death.

"His briefcase. Keys. And a cell phone. They're still working on the briefcase, but can you identify these as belonging to your husband?"

He held up two clear plastic bags. Fiona recognized the worn leather key strap that Cassie had tooled for her dad as a Father's Day gift years ago. The phone was Stan's, too. A lump formed in her throat as she looked into DeSalvo's face and nodded in answer to his question.

"The briefcase was flung open and papers were scattered all over."

His handsome face was strained. Fiona couldn't stand it any longer. "What is it, DeSalvo? Something's wrong. I can see it in your eyes."

He looked away for a moment. "There's no easy way to say this." He paused as he met her gaze. "It looks as if there's blood on your husband's briefcase." He rushed to add, "It's a small amount." He swallowed. "The officers at the towing place found what looks like blood on the steering wheel and the center console of the car."

DeSalvo's voice seemed to come from a distance, reverberating in some weird echo. The earth spun crazily and she swayed, and the next thing she knew his arms were wrapped around her.

She rested her head against his chest. This was a good place. A safe place. At least for as long as it took her to wrap her mind around what was happening.

Stan's car had been found. And his keys, and his phone, and his briefcase.

And there was blood.

"Maybe it's not his blood," she murmured against his cotton shirt. A button pressed against her cheekbone.

Maybe the car had been stolen before Stan had even gotten into it Monday morning. Maybe that blood belonged to someone else. Maybe some car thief had taken the keys and the briefcase and the phone...

God, what a wild fantasy.

"Maybe." DeSalvo's voice rumbled against her ear. "Hope for the best. But it's best to prepare yourself for the worst. Can you give me your husband's hairbrush? I need some strands of his hair to check his DNA against the blood we found."

Even though it seemed that her mind raced, her thoughts emerged in a sluggish haze as she nodded. The world took on an odd incongruity and it was too much to fathom.

In the secure cocoon of DeSalvo's arms, Fiona allowed herself to remember Karen Snow and her unborn baby and Shirley Bookerman. She had reason—no, she had reasons—not to care where Stanley was or what had happened to him. She deserved not to give a rat's butt if someone had cut out his black heart and flung it out the window of the Volvo. He was a liar and a cheater.

The direct antithesis of DeSalvo.

Fiona exhaled softly and let herself relax against the man who had done his very best to help her since the day they'd met. He'd been up front with her. Well, as up front and honest as a police detective could be. He'd kept her as informed as was possible.

And he smelled damn good.

Fiona racked her brain, trying to remember the last time she'd been hugged. Or comforted.

DeSalvo smoothed his palm down her back, and the heat of him made her want to sigh. A peculiar vibration prickled the pit of her stomach, a feeling that was warm and exciting... and wrong.

Her eyes flew open as alarm bells jangled in her head. She splayed her hand against his chest and shoved herself free of him. Surprise knitted DeSalvo's brow, but he remained silent.

"I want to go home," she told him, and he stepped back stiffly and nodded.

She felt panicky and feared she looked a fool. As frantic as she'd been to accompany DeSalvo out here to the search scene on the freeway, she was now just as frantic to leave. It made no sense whatsoever.

Chapter Ten

Winds of Change

"**I** feel sick. Do we really have to do this?"

"Now, Sam." Fiona took her eyes off the road ahead to glance at her son's reflection in the rearview mirror. "It's normal to be nervous when you're facing something new. It's going to be okay."

She purposefully ignored his question because she didn't want him worrying, but it was clear that drastic changes were necessary... for everyone.

A week ago, when she'd been escorted home by a state policewoman who'd helped recover her husband's keys, cell phone, and bloodstained briefcase, Fiona had been shaken to the core. She'd barely had time to deliver the bad news to Di before realizing that her friend had dire news of her own to disclose.

Fiona was broke.

Even though the check from Fox and Associates had been deposited, once all the bills had been paid, the meager balance in the checkbook was alarming. Di had done a little snooping and had some good news to share. There was a nice chunk of change in the savings account and a nest egg in the 401K, but Di had warned against touching those monies unless it became absolutely necessary, and Fiona had seen the logic in the advice. Realizing that, more than likely, there would be no more income from Stan's employer, she hadn't needed Di to tell her that radical adjustments in their lifestyle were called for.

Fiona's first thought had been a J-O-B. But the very word had instilled terror in her. Having spent the last twenty years as a full-time wife and stay-at-home mom, she fretted over how she could turn her talent of keeping the home fires burning into a marketable job skill.

Di had calmed her, and together they'd started working on a budget. What they'd discovered was that the largest expenditure outside of the mortgage payment was tuition for the private schools her kids attended. Because her financial situation had come to light during the last week of September, Fiona had given herself a few days to decide what to do about her children's education. However, the choice had become painfully obvious.

"Mom's right, Sam." Cassie flipped down the sun visor to check her hair in the mirror. "It's going to be all right. You'll see."

Something about her daughter's devil-may-care attitude bothered Fiona, but she was more concerned with cheering the scowl from Sam's face. "This is a new week. A new month. A new experience. And school hasn't been in session for very long. Just a few weeks. You'll find your place quickly... you'll make friends, son."

She turned onto James Street, and Burlington High came into view. The redbrick building brought back a flood of memories. She and Di had been inseparable when they'd attended high school here. Being "townies," they'd walked to school and had tramped up and down this street what felt like a million times. But because the Rowlands lived miles away from the high school, Cassie and Sam would take the bus, and that would shut down

Fiona's chauffeuring service and free her up to earn some money.

The thought of resumes and job interviews had panic swarming in her stomach.

"I'm the new kid." He thumped the back of the seat with his size ten high top. "And we all know how that goes."

Fiona turned into the visitors' lot and maneuvered into a parking space. She unlatched her seat belt and twisted in the seat. "Do you want me to go in with you?"

He shot her a look that told her he'd rather be gutted alive and carry his own entrails than walk into the school with his mother. Without a word, he shoved open the door, and got out of the car, dragging his backpack behind him.

"Do you know which bus to get on this afternoon?" Fiona called after him, but he just kept trudging away from the car. She sighed.

"It'll be okay, Mom." Cassie touched her arm. "I'll take care of him."

"Okay—" Fiona whirled on her daughter "—what is up with you?"

The teen's eyes widened as if she'd been slapped. "What'd I do?"

"You're carrying this all-is-glory-and-sunshine

act a little too far, and I don't get it. I know you've been trying to be nice to Sam because of, well, because of what's happening with your father. But now you're offering to take care of him? You've got to admit it. That's just plain weird, Cassie." The manila envelope she'd stuffed full of birth certificates, immunization records, and report cards slid onto the floor from the space between the seats where she'd tucked it. "You've been too agreeable about switching schools. Aren't you nervous? Aren't you going to miss Emily?"

Excitement danced in her daughter's hazel eyes. "Emily is writhin' jealous, Mom."

Fiona frowned and Cassie practically sang, "Look around. Just look around."

The teen gathered up her purse and backpack and got out of the car. She slammed the door, laughing. Cassie leaned down to gaze at her mother through the open passenger-side window.

Ever so softly, she whispered, "No more uniforms. And boys, boys, and more boys."

Her laughter rang in Fiona's ears, her little jean-clad fanny swishing as she sauntered toward the school. Fiona groaned, letting her neck and shoulder muscles go limp, her skull thudding against the headrest. She didn't need that idea and all its implications planted in her mind. She really didn't.

Just minutes later, Fiona entered the front doors of the high school, and the aroma that smacked her in the face made her feel like a sixteen-year-old again—a distinct and pungent potpourri of fresh white paper, old textbooks, chalk dust, stale bagged lunches and sour gym uniforms.

The library was located just to her left. She and Di had spent lots of time in there goofing around as teens when they should have been studying. Students milled around inside the library and in the hallways. A boy brushed past from behind, obviously running late.

"Mrs. Rowland?"

She turned and locked eyes with a man in a suit. Her steps slowed when she realized he looked familiar.

"Fiona?" His brown eyes lit with pleasant surprise.

"Neil Sullivan." She hurried to him and gave him a quick hug. "How are you? You look good."

He did. Neil had put on weight, but who hadn't? And his burnished chestnut hair had thinned to the point that she could see his scalp.

"You look great," he told her. "Cassandra and Samuel belong to you?"

Fiona nodded.

"I just met them." He pointed behind him toward the office. "They seem like great kids. They've got their class assignments and are both on their way to their homerooms. I even hooked them up with a buddy for the day."

"I appreciate that." And she really did. "Sam's nervous. I'm worried about him. He complained of feeling sick to his stomach before we came in."

Fiona noticed that the library and hallway were suddenly empty.

Neil nodded. "Freshmen are usually apprehensive their first day. He'll be fine."

"I didn't know you worked at Burlington."

"Taught here for a dozen years or so." He tucked his hands into his pockets. "Then switched to administration. I'm assistant principal."

"That's great."

The blaring bell made Fiona jump. A student came flying out of the library. Neil called out to the girl, "Amanda, you should be in class."

"On my way, Mr. Sullivan." She neither slowed nor looked back, but kept racing down the hall.

Neil chuckled. "Kids."

Fiona glanced at her watch. "I should get to the office. I have an appointment with the counselor. A Mrs. Shrewsbury."

"I came out to head you off at the pass. I'm here in her stead. We had a problem on one of the buses this morning." His height crept up an inch as he explained, "Usually I'm the disciplinarian around here, but this incident involved a special needs student she's been counseling, so she's handling things and I'm taking over her appointment with you, if that's okay." Again, he stuck out his thumb and pointed over his shoulder. "You want a cup of coffee? There's a fresh pot in the teachers' lounge."

"That sounds great." The moment she rounded the corner and saw the door of the lounge, a memory came to her, sharp and clear. She'd visited the teachers' lounge as a Burlington student. On a triple dare from Di. During their sophomore year—or had it been their junior year?—she'd slipped into the room and replaced the sugar in the bowl with salt and the salt in the shaker with sugar. She and Di had laughed about that for days, and they'd actually been disappointed when no mention had ever been made of their little joke by the teachers or crabby Mr. Warren, the school principal at the time.

The lounge was cool and quiet and empty. There was a kitchen set up at one end complete with a Formica-topped table with chrome legs, vinyl covered chairs, a harvest-gold refrigerator, and a drab sofa and chair grouping at the other. Fiona got the clear sense that the decor hadn't changed since she'd been a teen prankster.

"We've missed you at our class reunions." Neil poured coffee into two foam cups and set Fiona's on the table. "We just had our twenty-eighth, you know. This past summer."

"I received the invitation." She stirred some lumpy powdered creamer and a yellow packet of sugar substitute into what looked like very strong brew. Just what her body needed, more artificial chemicals and caffeine. "I'm just—" she shrugged vaguely "—really busy with my kids, and life in general."

The truth of the matter was Fiona hadn't been interested in attending the reunions that had been held over the years. She and Di hadn't been hip enough to be considered part of the Rah-Rahs and Jocks, the trendy, popular crowd. And they hadn't been rebellious enough to fit in with the Grits. And thank God they hadn't been weird enough to be identified with the Geeks, a splintered group that had one faction consisting of the creepily intelligent (these kids tended to participate in discussion and debate or become members of the numismatic club or the philatelic society) and another composed of "artsy" students (band and choir and drama club members; the more bohemian types, even the flag twirlers fit in here because the cheerleaders turned their noses up at associating with them). Fiona and Di had been friendly with kids who'd been stamped with all different labels, but they'd mostly kept to themselves, thereby managing to remain safely on the fringe of judgment. Well, Fiona had, anyway.

"Have you kept in touch with Diane Fleming?" Neil's attention was too focused on the white cup he lifted to his lips.

He wasn't fooling Fiona one bit. "Yes. In fact, Di's visiting with me now."

He stirred a little too briskly and hot coffee sloshed over the rim, scalding his fingers and making him wince. He recovered quickly, though. "That's great. How long will she be in town?" Snapping up a napkin, he dabbed at his hand and then at the mess on the table.

"Don't know for sure." Fiona's taste for coffee—and this conversation—dried right up. She left the cup sitting on the table and fiddled with the corner of the envelope she carried. "Di's come to help me... you know... through my trouble."

"Your trouble?"

Apparently, the counselor hadn't explained Fiona's situation. She told him about Stanley.

"You're that Rowland? I had no idea. Does Susan know? Mrs. Shrewsbury."

Fiona nodded. "The counselor promised to talk to my kids if the need arises. Cassie and Sam are going through a lot right now, Neil." Her stomach felt knotted and she was glad she hadn't sipped any of that coffee. "It's important that this school transition go smoothly."

"I've seen kids bounce back from a lot of things that their parents thought they wouldn't," he said. "Kids are resilient, Fiona. Trust me. I've worked with teens for a long time. You should probably step back a bit. Cut the apron strings, so to speak. Don't be so protective. I'm sure your kids are hardier than you think."

A tiny frown bit into her brow and her lips parted. She couldn't believe it. She'd never heard anything more insensitive in her life. Everything that made her children feel safe had been ripped from their lives—their father, their schools, a steady income, even their damn health insurance, damn it. How could this asinine Geek stand there and act so blasé about what her children were facing? She wanted to rip his hard, cold heart right out of his chest.

Needless to say, the meeting went downhill from there.

"The man was a royal ass." Fiona stirred sugar into the mashed strawberries simmering on the stovetop.

"What do you want?" Di asked with a casual shrug. "He's a man."

Di wanted her to laugh, but she was too upset. The kids were due home soon and she'd been worried sick about them all day. And then there was that pesky problem of income that kept gnawing at her.

"Oh, come on." Di picked up the bottle of almond extract that was sitting on the counter. "I'll agree that he might have been a tad thoughtless. But is it possible that you're being a little too sensitive? He might have been sincere in his efforts to assure you."

"By telling me to cut the apron strings?" Fiona pulled the pot off the burner. "Give me that." She snatched the extract from Di, unscrewed the cap, and tipped some into the strawberries, eyeballing a teaspoon.

"Why don't I remember Neil Sullivan?" Di twirled the aluminum measuring cup around in a circle.

"You should. He was a band geek and he had a mad crush on you."

"He did?"

Fiona nodded. "He took me out once. To see the The Texas Chainsaw Massacre."

Di chuckled. "Not such a wise choice in a date movie."

"But all he did was ask questions about you. After the third or fourth gruesome killing, I excused myself to go to the restroom and stayed there until the movie was almost over. He'd thought I'd gone home, and was fuming."

"I remember that, and I remember him! The skinny redheaded kid who played the tuba."

"That's the one." Fiona dropped cubes of cream cheese into the hot strawberry mixture. "He's grown into his nose, and his hair has darkened considerably." She thought about what Neil had said to her. "But he's still a colossal geek."

Di laughed just as the kitchen timer buzzed.

Fiona pulled the pie pan from the oven and set it on the granite countertop to cool.

"That smells good. Sweet. Not anything like a regular pie crust."

Fiona smiled. "It's not. I use shortbread cookie dough for the crust of my strawberry cream pie. It's Sam's favorite. I thought it might lift his spirits. He was so down when I dropped him off this morning."

Di dipped a spoon into the pot, blew across the strawberries and then tasted. "Mmm. It's luscious. You really should write a cookbook."

"It'll be even better once I put it all together and it has a chance to cool." She busied herself slicing a second bag of thawed strawberries into chunks for texture, letting them fall into the pot.

"Sam's favorite, huh? He's going to be surprised."

"I hope so." She hated thinking that her son was miserable about changing schools, but it couldn't be helped.

"Cassie did say she'd watch out for him," Di said, as if reading her mind.

Fiona didn't even want to think about her daughter or what new friends she might be making.

"That crust is huge." Di had ambled over to the stove.

"It's a restaurant-size pie pan." Fiona had relaxed enough to chuckle lightly. Cooking did that to her. "When I bake, I don't mess around."

"Restaurant-size," Di murmured.

Once the strawberry cream mixture was ready, Fiona picked up the pot and filled the crust. "For really special occasions I pre-bake a lattice top. It's really easy. I bought this gadget that just presses out the lattice circle. I bake it, pop it on, and, presto, I have a gorgeous pie."

"You sure do." Di's tone was whispery soft as though her thoughts were elsewhere. Then she said, "That sour cream cake you made the other day was delicious, too."

Fiona licked a drip of strawberry filling from her finger. "Wait'll you taste my four-layer coconut cake and my chocolate fudge raspberry torte."

Di groaned. "I've gained five pounds just listening to you." She leaned in to sniff the pie. "Fiona, have you ever thought of selling your desserts?"

"I have sold them. At all the school fundraisers and—"

"No, no. I mean really sell them. For profit. As in starting your own business."

Fiona laughed. "I couldn't do that."

"Why not?"

"I wouldn't know where to start."

"I'd help you."

Her humor faded. Di was serious.

"You could call it Fiona's Fantastic Desserts. Or Fiona's Famous Sweets."

"But my sweets aren't famous—" she arched her brows "—and neither am I."

Di grinned. "Not yet, maybe."

The two of them had talked, ad nauseam, for the past week about what kind of job she might qualify for. Neither of them had come up with any employment options that might offer the kind of income she and the kids were used to.

The idea of earning a living doing something she loved made her stomach quiver strangely. She almost gasped when she realized what caused it. Hope. Something she hadn't felt in weeks.

The kitchen door swung open and Cassie waltzed in, her face beaming. Fiona couldn't help but smile.

"Looks like you had a good day," she said to her daughter.

"Absotively!" She laughed, and Fiona and Di couldn't help but join her. "I had the most wonderiffic day. Johnny Williams goes to Burlington. We sat together at lunch. Emily. Is. Going. To. Die."

Then the teen did the most extraordinary thing. She leaned toward her mother and kissed her on the cheek. Fiona was absotively stunned.

Before Fiona could react, Cassie was across the room. "I've got homework, then I have to call Emily. I'm sure she's dying to hear from me. And a couple of girls from school took my number—"

"Whoa," Fiona said. "Slow down a second. Don't go filling up your whole evening. I'm cooking dinner."

"Mom, no. It's only Monday."

She shot her daughter a narrow-eyed, warning glance. "I want to sit down together. I want to hear about your day."

Although Cassie offered her the infamous eye-roll, Fiona knew her daughter would acquiesce.

"Where's your brother?" she asked.

The teen wrinkled her nose. "He's coming."

Fiona's hopes fell. "He had a bad day?"

Sam clomped in through the back door, and after one quick look at his face, Fiona knew her son hadn't just had a bad day. He'd had an awful, horrible, ghastly, no good day.

Dinner would have been a quiet affair had Cassie not yakked like there was no tomorrow. She told them about every class, every teacher, and nearly every new student she'd met, especially those of the male persuasion. Di was obviously enjoying Cassie's nonstop banter.

Sam's fork clattered onto his empty dessert plate. "Would you shut the hell up?"

Fiona gasped. "Sam!" Her children had been so good to each other lately. There'd been no bickering, no nastiness. This turnaround hit her out of the blue. "Don't talk to your sister like that. And don't use that kind of language."

"Yeah, Sam," Cassie said, glaring. "Do you have to be such a bahoozle?"

Fiona glanced at her daughter, then, feeling at a loss, shot her gaze toward Di for some deciphering help. But Di only leaned back in her chair and offered a tiny shrug that conveyed she, too, had no idea if Cassie had used bad language or not.

Before Fiona could reprimand her daughter against name calling, Sam shoved his chair back a good foot from the table.

"You've been there one day and you're already talking like those freaks."

"They're not freaks, freak!"

"Stop!" Fiona's shout stunned her children into silence. She looked at her son. "What's the matter with you?" Sam's angry, narrowed blue eyes were so much like his father's.

"That school sucks. The kids are wads. And the teachers are stupid." His shoulders rounded in a sulk. "I tried to tell Mrs. Angelo that I'd already had Algebra II last year. That I'd passed the class. But she wouldn't listen."

"Honey, that can be fixed," Fiona told him gently. "I'll call the school tomorrow morning. I just took them your report cards, and they'll receive transcripts from your school soon. It might take them a couple of days to get your schedule straightened out, but they will. You have to be patient."

"I saw the track coach." High emotion made his words sound strangled. "Asked if I could try out for cross-country. But he said the team had already been chosen." He muttered, "Coach Gray is a butt wipe."

Fiona nearly choked on her sharp inhalation, but the tears of frustration and disappointment filling her son's gaze forced her to hold back her reprimand.

Sam tossed his napkin next to his plate. "The captain of the team—"

"Brian Lowe," Cassie supplied. "He's a senior."

"—he called me a loser under his breath, and the jerk laughed at me when I was walking away."

Fiona thought her heart was going to break.

"I'm sorry, Sam," Di said.

"Look at it this way—you can always try out for the team next year." Sincere sympathy softened Cassie's voice.

"But I was on a team already. I'd already proved myself. It's not fair—" he thumped his fist on the table and made the dishes jump "—that I don't even get a chance to try. What do you know about it, anyway? Everything is so easy for you."

"It isn't easy for me," Cassie said, her affront evident. "I just make the best of things, that's all. I had bad stuff happen to me today, too, Sam. I choose not to dwell on it."

Hearing that his sister had troubles too seemed to help Sam relax.

"What are you talking about, Cassie?" Di set her water glass down on the table. "What happened?"

When it looked as though her daughter was

going to clam up, Fiona prodded, "Oh, come on. Vent."

Sam snickered suddenly. "Yeah, Cassie. Vent."

"Make fun of me and you'll be doing the dishes." Fiona grinned at her son in the hopes of lifting his mood.

"It was nothing, really." Cassie waved both her hands in small arcs. "Some kid named David Snow cornered me at lunch. He called Dad dirty names. Said that his sister was one of Dad's students and that Dad was fooling around with her and got her pregnant."

Fiona couldn't breathe. She looked over at Di, who'd grown too still.

"He's a stoner, obviously," Cassie continued, but clearly, recounting the incident unsettled her. "It couldn't possibly be true. Dad wasn't like that. He wouldn't have done something like that to us. He just wouldn't have." Her prattle slowed and she finally noticed the unnatural static that had fallen over the room, and the conclusion contained in the silence seemed to shake her confidence in her father. "He wouldn't have. Right, Mom? Well, aren't I right?" Sudden doubt and fear made her go pale. "It isn't true, is it?"

Fiona wasn't ready for this. A massive hot flash

whooshed over her entire body, threatening to burn her alive. Without thinking, she snapped, "Damn it, Cassie, why would you bring something like this up in front of your brother? He's too young to have to deal with this kind of thing."

Chaos broke out and everyone started talking at once.

Sam: "I'm not a baby, Mom!"

Di: "That's not what your mother meant, Sam. I'm sure."

Cassie: "But you told me to vent!"

Di: "She's not angry with you, Cassie."

Fiona: "Stop yelling at me. Both of you."

Sam: "My dad was a good guy!"

It wasn't until the wee hours of the morning, while Fiona sat alone and wide awake in her room that the realization dawned on her: both of her children had spoken about their father in a past tense that was gut-wrenchingly emphatic.

Chapter Eleven

Echoes from the Past

The setting sun glowed blazing red on the horizon. Di zipped in and out of the last remnants of rush hour traffic on Kirkwood Highway, people fighting to get home from work and those brave enough to venture out early for some Friday night entertainment. Her stomach did a little trilling somersault when she scooted in front of an SUV, the driver honking at her an instant after she stomped on the gas pedal and sped away.

Her baby was an absolute dream to drive, maneuvering curves with ease and flying along straightaways. The 500 horsepower engine purring beneath Di excited her more than sweaty sex.

She'd bought the Viper SRT 10 as a gift to herself the very day she'd received the largest bonus ever earned at Roche Advertising. That had been four years ago, the same year she'd won her third Employee of the Year award, the same year she'd made East Coast division vice president, the same year Cliff Bowers had become her fuck buddy.

Oh, how the mighty do fall.

The yellow light didn't deter her from buzzing onto Lancaster Pike.

Fiona was going to be exhausted this evening. She'd received favorable reactions from nearly all the area chefs she'd phoned about her desserts, and she'd made appointments with several for the coming weekend. So Fiona had planned to spend the day in the kitchen, baking. The hesitation that had met her offer of an extra set of hands had let Di know her friend wanted to do the job herself. Di hadn't been offended in the least. In fact, she understood perfectly. There had been a few projects at Roche she'd handled on her own. There were times when a person wanted—*needed*—to accept the full risk of possible failure or complete success.

Di had taken the opportunity to drive into Philadelphia. Even though she'd been away for weeks, she'd found her house in great shape. Even the leftover milk and yogurt had been removed from the refrigerator. Go Merry Maids! The violent messages from Jonni Jean Bowers clogging her voice mail had curled Di's hair. After listening to the first three, she'd hit the delete button. She was no longer an employee of Roche Advertising, no longer a threat to Jonni Jean, so Di tried to put the woman out of her mind. She'd sorted through the mail, paid her bills, and stopped in at the post office to fill out a "hold" request form. She'd had lunch with Sandy and was sad to hear that her former assistant hadn't yet found a job. However, Di's late afternoon appointment with her financial advisor had resulted in some positive news. Now that the money from her severance package had been added to her prior holdings, she could anticipate some nice dividend checks. She wouldn't have to worry about income for a while. Maybe never if she guarded her pennies. Of course, that would surely mean a future that included no more Vipers or Manolo Blahnik stilettos, and she couldn't imagine the horror of such an existence. But it was good to know that she could spend some time with Fiona without worrying about money. Di had a sneaking suspicion that the worst was yet to come for her friend.

The flashing lights reflecting in her rearview mirror made her whisper a vulgar epithet. Traffic stops were a common occurrence for a platinum-blonde in a candy-apple-red sports car. Di had pretty much perfected the get-out-of-jail-free smile that normally resulted in, at best, an invitation to dinner or, at worst, a lecture on the hazards of speeding. The fact that she'd never been issued a moving violation filled her with a prideful satisfaction that more law abiding citizens might find appalling. Downshifting, she pulled to the shoulder of the roadway, determined to keep her perfect record.

The waning daylight made it impossible to see the officer's features in her side mirror as he approached, but he was tall... and built. Just as his crotch entered the periphery of her vision, she pushed the button that opened her window.

"Evening, Officer." She looked into his face, and her bright smile nearly faltered. Nearly. Her instant recognition of the man stirred a resentment that had been long dormant. Not that Eli Osborn had ever done anything to deserve the bitterness that prickled inside her. It was just that her teen years had been filled with bad experiences—some of them her fault, most of them not—but seeing anyone from the past aroused an odd anxiety in her.

He had changed little since high school. If anything, the years had honed Eli's features and his Adonis-like body. A Jock to the nth degree back in school, he'd been an above-average student who had played on both the basketball and football teams. Guys with that much going for them never thought to give Di a second glance. Well, that wasn't entirely true. She'd received lots of looks, but only because she was stacked and the boys were horny little shits who imagined she was one of "those kind of girls." Unfortunately, she feared she'd fit that category a time or two, but thankfully, Eli had been too respectable to come sniffing around. "May I see your license and registration?"

"Of course." Di dug into her purse to retrieve her license, and then leaned over to access the glove box where she kept the registration card, lengthening her torso so her top would ride up and flash a bit of midriff skin. Ah, yes, she had the technique down pat.

She handed over the information, and as he scanned the cards, he said, "I followed you for several miles. Do you know how fast you were driving, Miss—" hesitance wavered in his tone "—*Fleming?*" He bent an inch for a closer look. "Diane Fleming? Di from Burlington High?"

Di flashed her pearly whites. "That's me. I wondered if you'd remember me, Eli." She cut the engine, pushed open the door and exited the car, making sure she tensed her calf muscles to their best advantage.

He looked momentarily stunned, blinking as he backed up a step. "You look great."

Delight bubbled in her chuckle. "So do you. I didn't know you were in law enforcement." She tapped the badge on his chest with a lacquered fingernail. "You're a county boy, huh?"

He nodded. "I worked for the town of Newark and then the city of Wilmington. I've been with the county for over five years. Just put my resume in with the state police." He glanced down the length of the Viper. "Looks like life's been pretty good to you."

"I can't complain." Her baby made all the men drool.

"You living in town?"

She crossed her arms, propping her hip against the car door. "No. Just here for a visit. Helping a friend in need. Fiona Simpson. She was in our graduating class. She married Stanley Rowland."

"Rowland. That rings a bell." His brows arched. "Isn't he the guy who—"

"That's him."

Eli whistled. "Tough thing to go through. We got a quick briefing on the case. He's been missing what? A month?"

"Almost."

He shook his head. "Doesn't give me very good vibes."

She knew exactly where he was coming from. He adeptly changed the subject and they talked about more mundane things for a few moments. Then he asked, "You married?"

"Never found Mr. Right. You?"

"Divorced." He shifted his weight from one foot to the other. "Got a thirteen-year-old son. Zack. Cheryl lets me have him almost every weekend." He smiled. "He's a good kid."

"You sound like a devoted dad."

Eli studied her face for a second and then looked at the ground. Panic swept through Di. Things were about to get too personal. She could feel it.

She liked men who were safe. Guys who were a bit quirky. Or who weren't the sharpest pencils in the case. Or who, like Cliff Bowers, didn't need impressing because they were going home to their wives after drinks and a quick wrestle in the sack.

Guys who were easy to get, easy to keep, and easy to get rid of, that was her preference.

Why the hell did good, solid, decent guys instill that little niggling fear in her? There was no doubt that Eli was a good guy. He had a steady job. He had aspirations and ambitions for his career. And he spent his weekends with his kid.

He lifted his gaze to hers, and before he could speak, she pointed to her license and registration in his hand. "You going to do anything official with those, Mr. Police Officer?"

Eli chuckled, and Di went still as a warm, funny feeling jostled her insides.

He offered her the cards and she took them. "I guess not. But you need to slow down, woman."

True concern softened his green eyes. Yep, he was a good guy all right. Di reached for the door handle.

"It's been fun chatting with you, Eli, but I need to get going." She opened the door and slid behind the wheel. "Fiona's waiting dinner on me."

The lie rolled off her lips with ease. It was a skill Aunt Viv had taught her quite early. One at which she'd become proficient as a teen. She'd all but abandoned the practice as an adult, though. Keeping track of lies was like herding ants. But this one was harmless enough.

"Listen, Di." Eli leaned toward the window, resting his forearms on the door.

Crap! She'd hoped to avoid an actual turndown.

"Would you like to go out for a beer sometime?"

Pushing in the clutch with her left foot, she twisted the key. "Sorry, Eli." She revved the engine and he straightened and took a backward step. "I've never been a beer drinker."

Yeah, and you're going to fibbers' hell. She high-tailed it fast enough to kick up pebbles and road dust, Aunt Viv's croaking cackle ringing in her head.

The smells filling Fiona's kitchen made Di salivate: warm berries, vanilla, tangy lemon, coconut, chocolate, and toasty walnuts.

"Hi, honey, I'm home!" she called. "Have I died and gone to sugarplum heaven?"

Fiona stepped out of the pantry, hefting a five pound bag of flour in one hand. "Hey, Di. How was your day?" she asked. The sack thudded onto the counter and Fiona pulled open the top before dumping it into the ceramic canister. She immediately scooped some into a measuring cup.

Exhilaration glazed her friend's blue-green eyes, and Di suspected that if she were to reply that she'd had a wonderful time milking goats in Peru, Fiona probably wouldn't even notice.

"I baked the pies and cakes early." Fiona measured flour into a mixing bowl. "The tortes are in the oven. I've searched through my files and found the recipe I concocted years ago for a four-layer orange cake. I'd forgotten all about it. Took it to some gathering or other—" she dumped the flour into a mixing bowl "—I can't remember where, but I do remember that everyone raved about it. I think I can get five of them made in time."

"Five?" Di slipped off her heels. "You do intend to get some sleep tonight?"

"I have five appointments this weekend, so I'm making five of everything," Fiona rattled. "I have no idea what each chef will be interested in and I wouldn't want to take a half-eaten dessert into a restaurant, you know? It just wouldn't look very professional."

That made perfect sense. Di slid onto the stool near the counter.

"And, yes," Fiona said, measuring more flour into the bowl, "I plan to get plenty of rest. I want to be bright-eyed and bushy-tailed tomorrow." She snapped the lid onto the canister and tossed the empty flour bag into the garbage can.

"You're excited," Di observed.

Her gaze danced as she nodded. "And scared to death."

"They're going to love you... and your desserts."

Fiona smiled and went right back to measuring salt, baking powder, and other dry ingredients into the bowl.

"Where are the kids?" Di kicked off her shoes and hooked her bare toes on the rung of the stool.

"Sam's upstairs. Emily called, asking Cassie to go to the mall. They just left a few minutes ago. I practically had to force Cassie to go." She stirred the flour mixture slowly with a whisk. "The world keeps turning. We have to keep living, right?"

Di knew she wasn't expecting an answer.

"The damn phone has them both unnerved." Fiona set the whisk on the counter.

"Another call?"

Someone had been calling the house since last

weekend and hanging up a few long, drawn-out seconds after the phone had been answered. The calls weren't being made every day, but there was enough regularity to make it evident that these were not wrong numbers. Strange how the ringing of the telephone could impart a creepy feeling.

A frown marred her friend's brow as she nodded. Fiona went to the refrigerator for eggs. "Cassie said she thought it might be someone from school. One of the new boys she's met who might be interested in her, but who's too afraid to actually talk." Fiona cracked an egg and let it plop into the bowl of the stand mixer. "She tried to laugh it off, but I could see she's worried." She cracked another egg. "Sam seems to think it's that boy from the cross-country team. Brian Lowe. Sam says the kid's been taunting him." The shells from a third egg landed in the sink. She rested her hands on the counter for a second. "He looked scared, Di. And angry. I'm thinking I should go to the school."

"I doubt they'll do a thing unless you have proof." Di had disregarded the calls at first, assuring everyone that she thought they were harmless. But after hearing Jonni Jean's promises to "hunt you down like a dog" on her answering machine this morning, Di now had to wonder if the woman intended to make good on her threats.

"Oh, speaking of the school—" Fiona went to the fridge and tugged a slip of paper from beneath a magnet "—you had a visitor this afternoon."

"Oh?" Thoughts of Jonni Jean made Di's heart hammer. She took the paper from Fiona and saw a name and phone number scrawled on it. "Neil Sullivan? From the high school?"

"The vice principal."

"Why would he come to see me?"

Fiona grinned as she turned the mixer on. "He wants to take you to dinner."

"What?"

"I was a little annoyed when he showed up unannounced, but then he told me he'd come to see you—" she went to the microwave and pulled out a glass measuring cup containing melted butter "—and that he'd hoped to take you out to dinner tonight. He was so disappointed when you weren't here." Di glanced down at the local number again, and then crumbled the paper between her palms.

"Hey! What are you doing?"

"You said he was still a Geek. I can't date a Geek. It would ruin my reputation."

Fiona laughed. "I shouldn't have said that. You

might have been right when you said I was being too sensitive. He was nice when he was here tonight. Funny. And he asked how the kids were doing. Said he'd been keeping an eye on them."

The skinny, wiry-haired tuba player floated through Di's mind. Easy to get, easy to keep, easy to get rid of. Neil seemed to fit all the criteria. She smoothed the wrinkles from the slip of paper. "Maybe I will give him a call."

By midnight all the cakes had been baked and Fiona had spread the finishing touch of a rich cream cheese frosting on each. The movie Sam and Di had watched had long been over. Cassie had long since returned from an evening of shopping. And both kids had gone to bed.

Di and Fiona had donned sweaters against the dropping fall temperatures and were enjoying cocktails out on the back porch. Di had purchased vodka and had made them cranberry cosmopolitans.

"I just wish he had a friend," Fiona murmured. "Someone to lean on. To talk to. To turn to."

"Sam's going to be just fine." Di toyed with the button of her sweater.

Fiona looked over at her. "I want for him what we had as kids, you know?"

"What we had was special. It wasn't just a friendship. It was a sisterhood. Something like that doesn't happen very often, I'm thinking."

Her friend nodded in agreement.

Memories swam through Di's mind as she drained the last of her drink, her thoughts tumbling back to when their friendship first began. "I'll never forget your facial expression, Fiona. Not in a thousand years. You'd given your report to the class on homeless children in Africa, and Mrs. Edwards started asking you questions. You looked petrified having to talk off the cuff."

"I thought I was going to pee myself."

"And that's not even the expression I'm talking about."

Fiona looked at her curiously over the rim of her glass.

"It was when Mrs. Edwards asked that last question. The one about why you chose homeless children as your topic."

School had been difficult for Di. It was hard to pay attention when your empty stomach wouldn't stop grumbling. But Mrs. Edward's sixth grade class had been extra difficult. The teacher seemed to have some sort of extrasensory perception that allowed her to see right through the little lies Di conjured in order to get by, and the woman called her on every one.

"You went very quiet," Di continued, her voice as soft as the velvety night, "but your eyes shone with a sadness so profound that every child in that room halted, almost breathless, waiting for you to answer. I was just as enraptured as the rest of them."

"The witch caught me off guard." Fiona pulled the facings of her sweater together.

"Do you remember your answer?"

Fiona's groan was answer enough.

"'*Sometimes I feel homeless*,' you said. '*Sometimes I feel abandoned*.'"

"And when Mrs. Edwards reminded me that I had a house and a father, the whole class started snickering and laughing at me."

"Not me," Di told her.

Fiona smiled up at her. "Not you." She set her glass down. "You moseyed up to me at recess. I panicked, Di. Did I ever tell you that? The girl who beat up boys was staring down at me."

"Hey, if you beat up the boys, the mean girls left you alone." Di chuckled. "Those poor boys had been taught not to hit girls. And they were too embarrassed to tell." She stretched out her legs, her bare feet gleaming white against the dark wood decking as she released a sigh. "I made it up to most of them in high school, though."

"You looked me right in the eye and said you knew how I felt."

"And I did. I don't know why we didn't hook up sooner. I mean, I had always known that, like me, you didn't have a mom around. But you were different from me." This kind of talk made Di nervous. "You know. Your dad had money."

Fiona looked surprised. "We weren't rich or anything. We were middle class, Di."

"You had some money, whereas Aunt Viv and I had none." Di took a deep breath. "We were the kind of family that relied on the local churches to supply our holiday dinners."

"Trailer trash" is what many of the kids had called her. Well, they'd call her that once before she did her damnedest to rip their ears off their heads. Even if she could get them to stop saying it, they still thought it, and they let her know with their looks and their determination not to have anything to do with her.

But she'd found Fiona. During recess in the sixth grade. And her whole life had grown brighter. Not that she'd have described it that way back when it was happening. No, it had taken many, many years of life experience for her to realize the extraordinary gift that was her relationship with Fiona, and it scared the crap out of her to know how close she'd come to screwing it up.

"You know, we should go to the next class reunion. We could drive up there in my Viper. I'd wear the most expensive outfit I own. I could show them all. Diane Fleming made something of herself." She was on a roll. "They expected so much out of you, and so little out of me—" her laugh came out harsh and short "—and look what happened."

That hadn't come out quite right, and when she saw Fiona's spine straighten, she grew alarmed. "Wait, Fiona, I didn't mean—"

"It's okay," Fiona assured her. "It's true. I've always been sorry I didn't finish college. Earn my degree. I had—"

"No! Stop that." Offending Fiona had never been her intention. "That's not what I meant at all." She sat up straight. "You should be proud of what you've accomplished. You've been a great wife. You have a wonderful home. And two great kids. Cassie and Sam are your crowning glory."

"They are, aren't they? I'm so proud of them I

could bust." Fiona shook her head. "I'm not so sure I was a great wife, though."

"What are you talking about?" Di scoffed. She reached for her glass, realizing that it was empty. "Of course you were. You loved Stan."

"Di, I have so many doubts about my marriage. I feel guilty one minute and furious the next. After what I've discovered, if Stan's not dead, I'm going to kill him myself." She was quiet for a moment. Her tone went whisper soft. "If I was a good wife, why would he stray?"

"That wasn't your fault."

It was as if Fiona hadn't even heard her.

"Would it have hurt me to make his lunch without grumbling about it? Or put his clean clothes in the dresser drawers rather than setting them on the bed?" She looked up at Di, emotion glistening in her eyes. "Small things like that are important between a husband and wife. I might have kept him from, you know, turning to some other woman."

"Or women." Di grimaced when she saw she'd shocked Fiona. "I'm sorry. But I can't sit here and let you take the blame for his bad choices. I know you. You're a good person. You've always been very giving." When Fiona looked unconvinced, Di tried again. "You were faithful to him, weren't you? You don't even need to answer that. I already know the answer. He's the only one responsible for his infidelities."

Fiona remained skeptical. "Whoever's at fault... I'd do it all again, Di. Does that make me crazy? I'd marry Stan all over again... I'd go through all this scariness... I'd even face the fact that my husband was disloyal just so I could have Cassie and Sam."

Di gazed at her friend for a long moment. "That doesn't make you crazy."

Chapter Twelve

Butterflies and... Kisses?

Earning money did something for a person's self-esteem. The checks Fiona had collected from the restaurant owners who ordered her desserts had her walking a little taller, feeling more sanguine. Of course, with a job baking for only four small local restaurants, she couldn't provide her children with the lifestyle to which they were accustomed. But Fiona had a plan.

Although her weekend of meeting with chefs had been nerve-racking, it had also been enlightening. One of the first lessons she'd learned was that she wasn't charging enough for her products. Elizabeth Underwood, the fifty-something, been-around-the-block-a-time-or-two chef and owner of Underwood's Table, had bluntly told Fiona that her desserts were easily worth twice what she was asking (and she'd been right). Of course, the helpful advice hadn't been offered until after Fiona had agreed to provide her two pies a day, six days a week, for a full month. After the initial trial period, however, Liz would be open to renegotiation and maybe adding other unique confections to her order. After thirty days, she'd know if her customers liked the pies. Her strong suspicion that they would had made Fiona ecstatic.

Another thing Fiona had learned was that chefs are highly territorial. Liz insisted that Fiona sell her strawberry pies exclusively to Underwood's Table. Fiona still couldn't believe she'd had the prudence and the chutzpah to dive headfirst into an impromptu bargaining session. The women had finally come to the agreement that Fiona wouldn't provide strawberry-and-cream pies to any other eating establishments within the Wilmington city limits. That's when Fiona started formulating her plan, mentally listing the eateries she intended to solicit in neighboring towns and boroughs. Widening her selling area would add to her traveling costs, but if she charged more for her desserts, she could expand her selling area and still make more profit than she'd first expected.

Her learning curve, she was fast discovering, was sheer-cliff steep.

On this crisp October Monday morning, Fiona was driving home with the intent of putting her feet up for a couple hours before getting back to work. The toot of a car horn had her glancing into her rearview mirror in a double take—the first time, seeing DeSalvo's familiar smile, the second, tentatively returning his friendly wave.

Two weeks ago, when the Volvo had surfaced and the police had found Stan's bloodstained briefcase, Fiona had sought and found solace in DeSalvo's arms. Although her need for consolation had lasted mere seconds, she'd been mortified by how she'd acted. However, the weakness that had embarrassed her had brought out a powerful protective instinct in the detective. His behavior toward her had changed in other ways, as well. He treated her with more gentleness, an intimacy that was as comforting as it was disconcerting.

She pulled into a gas station parking lot.

"Morning," she called after they'd both gotten

out of their cars. "I haven't heard from you in a couple of days."

He slammed his door shut and rounded the car. "Been working on a case."

Fiona frowned. "That little girl?" She'd heard on the news about the six-year-old who'd gone missing, her battered body found a mile from her home just hours after her mother called the police.

DeSalvo nodded. "The mother's boyfriend confessed this morning."

A deep empathy tightened Fiona's throat. "What that poor woman must be going through."

"It's been rough. Everyone at the station is sick about how that child died. I'm taking the afternoon off. Just need to get away." Strain pulled his features taut as his dark eyes met hers. "I was on my way back to the station to give you a call. Then I saw you and thought I'd flag you down."

"You have news?"

"Only that we're releasing your car. We've gotten everything off the Volvo that we can. There's no reason for us to hold it any longer. You can pick it up anytime." He pulled a business card from his wallet. "This is the address and phone number of the holding yard. If you'd rather, I can have someone drop it off at the station house."

"No, no. Don't go to that trouble." She took the card from him, unsettled by the odd undercurrent rippling between them. "You're not closing the case, are you?"

"No." He slid his hand into his pocket and his loose change jingled. "But I have to tell you, I've exhausted all leads. There's no one else to talk to. It's been over a month."

He didn't have to remind her. What they'd thought were going to be the two biggest breaks in the case—the discovery of the Volvo and the return of Buck Snow just a day later—had been nothing but disappointments. Stan's car had only provided more questions. And the detective finally had to admit, after thoroughly interrogating Snow, that the only thing the man was guilty of was being a sad drunk looking for someone to take responsibility for his daughter's pregnancy. The past two weeks had been bone dry of clues. In fact, DeSalvo's daily contact had dwindled to a phone call every two or three days. Fiona feared it wouldn't be long before the police gave up the search for Stanley altogether.

The detective didn't like disappointing her; that was clear in the apology shadowing his dark eyes.

Fiona's tone was soft. "I need answers."

After a moment, he replied, "And I promise I'll continue to try to find them for you."

She offered him a smile of appreciation.

"So, how are you doing? How have you been?"

"I'm doing fine," she told him.

"No. I mean, really. How are you doing?"

Sincerity had him so solemn she chuckled. "I'm really doing fine. Better than fine, actually." She thought of the checks she'd collected this morning. "I'm earning some money. I've started my own business. Fiona's Fabulous Confections."

"That's great."

"It is. It really is." She told him about Di's idea of selling her desserts, about filing forms for an honest-to-goodness business license, and about her terrifying but informative weekend meeting with the chefs. Then she proudly listed off the restaurants that made up her current list of clientele.

"But I will add to my customer base," she rushed to assure him. "I'll have to if this little venture's going to succeed. And I'm determined that it will. I haven't been this excited about anything for a very long time."

Something in his brown eyes made her pause. "What? What is it?"

"Nothing." He glanced away, but only for a moment. "I'm happy for you. And I'm sure you're going to achieve great things."

"Thanks." The giddiness in her stomach was a nice feeling. She was glad he was encouraging. She didn't need any naysayers at this point. Right now, her business and her feelings surrounding it were too new, too susceptible to disappointment.

"Hey, listen—" he swiped his open palm down the upper thigh of his trousers "—I'm on my way to the park for a quick hike and a picnic lunch. How about joining me?"

"Oh, thanks but—"

"If you've been working half as hard as I think you have, then you deserve a few hours' downtime. Come on. It'll be fun."

How long had it been since she'd had some fun? Oh, the time she'd spent in the kitchen had been stimulating in a frenetic kind of way, but she couldn't remember the last time she'd enjoyed any "downtime," as DeSalvo had called it.

"The leaves are beginning to turn. Some of the maple trees are already crimson. Brandywine Creek is beautiful this time of year. The park has hiking trails. You'll enjoy yourself."

"Okay, okay." She laughed. "You've convinced me. I'll go."

They sorted out the particulars and she ended up following him to the police station so he could switch cars. She left hers in the lot and he drove them to a nearby deli for sandwiches and bottled water. It didn't take long before they were tramping along a packed-dirt trail.

"I love autumn. It's my favorite season." He shifted the strap of the backpack that contained their lunch.

"Oh, come on, now." Fiona brushed a pine bough out of her way as she passed and then held on to it until he went by. "There's something nice about all the seasons."

"True." After a moment, he said, "I like that about you. You try to see the best in everything."

The compliment made her feel good, but for the life of her she couldn't fathom how and when she'd given him that notion.

A few mothers had their preschool-age children on the swings and slides, but practically no one used the hiking trails at noon on a Monday. Fiona and the detective trekked a couple of miles, and when they came to a bench at the edge of a meadow, DeSalvo suggested they sit.

"Are you married?" she blurted out the question before thinking it through. She should be shocked at herself for delving into his private life, but she couldn't deny that she was curious.

"No." He unzipped the backpack.

"Got a steady girlfriend?" She accepted the sandwich he handed her, their gazes holding a second or two longer than they should have. This hadn't been the wisest or safest of subjects for her to broach.

He shook his head. "Nope." He set her bottle of water on the bench close to her hip.

Fiona grinned. "I get it. You're having too much fun enjoying your freedom. You've probably got girls crawling out of the proverbial woodwork."

"Actually, I don't date much."

"You're kidding me." She didn't bother trying to mask her surprise.

"I wouldn't do that." He set his own sandwich and water on the bench between them.

Something else was there between them, too. A provoking heat that felt off-limits. A nuance of hunger that had nothing to do with sustenance or thirst.

Pulling the wrapper off her sandwich, Fiona inhaled the scents of rye bread and mustard, ham and Swiss, and found them grounding. "You should ask Di for a date. She'd go, I'm sure. She's commented on your hot factor. She's young at heart. As well as ready, willing, and very available."

Fiona took a bite and chewed, identifying what she was feeling as pure sexual desire, and realizing that bringing Di into the conversation was an attempt to cool the embers that seemed to smolder around them.

He gave more attention to zipping up the backpack and placing it on the ground than the chore required. "I don't particularly find your friend's availability all that appealing. She seems too wild for my tastes."

Fiona wiped her fingers on a paper napkin. "Men usually stumble over themselves for the opportunity to test Di's wildness."

He shrugged. "What can I say? I like my women a little more tame."

The hint of disapproval in his comment made Fiona leap to her friend's defense. "Di had a rough childhood. She didn't know either of her parents. Her mother left her in her aunt's care when she was a baby. To hear Di tell it, the woman walked away and forgot she gave birth to a daughter."

The trailer Di had grown up in had been run-down, and the woman who had raised her had been perpetually down on her luck. "Di's Aunt Viv married and divorced so many times I lost track of her last name. That woman was always on the hunt for someone to take care of her, but her drinking ruined things, time and again. She lived off the state most of the time, and she wasn't what you would call good parent material. There was no discipline to speak of. No routine. No rules. It was more like Viv and Di coexisted.

"Di didn't complain, and neither did I." Fiona grinned. "I spent a lot of time at Di's, and being kids, we took advantage of all that freedom. But when I think back—" she gave a soft whistle "—I can't believe some of the things we got away with. Let's just say it wasn't the best environment for children." She took another bite of her sandwich and chewed, becoming contemplative. "I think Di saw her aunt as, I don't know, helpless. Viv's inability to take care of either of them did something to Di. Instilled in her a drive to succeed. To become something. To make something of herself. Independence can foster a rowdy boldness, you know?" She chuckled. "Nah, that can't be it. She was bold and rowdy even when we were kids."

Her gaze swung around, and she found DeSalvo

staring at her. He hadn't taken a single bite of his lunch, and heat stippled her cheeks when she realized how she'd gone on about Di.

"Sorry," she murmured. "I didn't mean to go off on a tangent."

"No problem." He picked up his water bottle. "The two of you seem—" he twisted off the lid "—so different. Almost opposites, actually." He took a long, deep drink.

"You could say that." Fiona wiped her mouth with the napkin. "But we did have one thing in common. Both of us grew up without a mother. Mine died giving birth to me."

And her father never forgave her for that.

"It was almost as if Di and I had some kind of cosmic connection. We were twelve when we became friends. She's the sister of my heart."

Conversation petered out, and all that talk of Di had dissolved the tension. Fiona was relieved.

They ate in silence for a while, and after he'd finished off his sandwich, he picked up his water. "I was married once."

"Oh?" Fiona balled up her own paper wrapping. "I bet I can guess what happened. She couldn't live with the danger of your job. I can imagine it would be horrible sitting at home waiting to see if your spouse will walk through the door, safe and sound, at the end of the day. I can see how that would cause a lot of marriages to fail for people in your line of work."

"That is the cause a lot of the time. But that's not what happened between Laurie and me." DeSalvo looked her straight in the eye. "I couldn't give her children."

Fiona tilted her head. "You didn't want kids?"

"Not wouldn't. Couldn't."

Her mouth formed an "oh" of understanding. "I'm sorry to hear that."

"No need to apologize. I've come to terms with it. My condition, I mean." A gleam lit his brown eyes and he lifted his hand. "Doesn't affect my performance. Let's get that straight right up front."

His in-your-face attitude regarding his sexual prowess made her grin. There wasn't a man on earth who wouldn't want that fact straight and fully understood.

"But it makes it impossible for me to father kids." He lifted a shoulder. "And Laurie wanted kids." He took a drink. "The docs called it torsion. Testicular torsion. The blood supply cord becomes twisted and..." He glanced at her pained expression. "I can see you're not interested in the details."

She shook her head quickly. "Not really."

His smile was easy and he hooked his ankle over his knee. "There's not a damn thing I can do about it. It's just one of those things you have to live with."

Fiona suspected he was hiding some real regret behind his take-it-all-in-stride facade.

He asked her more about her budding business, and she was eager to tell him all about it. He asked about Cassie and Sam, and she was eager to tell him about them, too. It was nice to have someone to connect to, someone who seemed truly interested.

Finally, they stuffed their sandwich wrappers, napkins, and empty plastic bottles into the backpack, and when DeSalvo stood, he reached out to help her from the bench. She slid her palm into his as if it was a completely natural thing to do. Their gazes caught for the merest second, and then he released her hand. The intense longing entangled itself around them once again.

Back on the trail, Fiona indulged the jarring excitement churning in her. The purely sexual energy was thrilling. It was also wrong. She knew it, but suddenly she didn't care.

It had been years—no, decades—since she'd had lunch with someone of the opposite sex (who wasn't her husband, anyway). She'd forgotten how good it felt to talk to a man. To tell him about her plans. To share her dreams. It felt intimate. It felt *wonderful*.

Two yellow butterflies flitted across the path and Fiona stopped to watch. DeSalvo was so close behind her she could feel his breath against her hair.

"Butterflies always make me think of my father." She watched the insects cavort in the dappled shade of a pin oak. "Right before he died he motioned for me to look out his window. Several butterflies were darting and dancing just like that. We watched them for several minutes. Then he called me by my mother's name." She turned to face DeSalvo, but she was lost in the past. "He took my hand and lifted it to his mouth. I was sure he was going to kiss my fingers, but then the fog seemed to clear from his gaze and he recognized me." She swallowed around a ball of raw emotion. "He frowned and then let go of me. He turned his face back to the window... and died."

Hot tears welled in her eyes. "He blamed me, you see. For the death of my mother." Her tone went whispery as she added, "Blamed me until the day he died."

DeSalvo's hands were gentle as he turned her around; then he reached up and cupped her face. "You didn't deserve that. You didn't deserve a minute of it. Let alone a lifetime." His tenderness astounded her, rocked her to her bones.

"You don't deserve any of this."

Instinct told her he wasn't talking about her father anymore. His fingertips were soft against her cheek.

"You're a good person. A wonderful, caring mother. You're worthy of much better from... from—"

A frown creased his brow, and she guessed he was fighting to find the right words to communicate his thought.

"—life."

His gaze bore into her and she felt her body quicken. He made her feel pretty. Desirable. He leaned toward her, his hand sliding to the curve of her neck.

Their kiss was reckless and powerful and brief. Fiona broke contact with a gasp.

"I can't do this, DeSalvo!"

"Call me Chad."

She shook her head. "I can't do that. And I can't do this." Turning on her heel, she walked swiftly away from him.

"Don't run away, Fiona. Talk to me."

Consumed with skittery, frantic energy, she stalked back to him. "You make me feel... things. Dangerous things." The look on his face irritated her. "Don't smile. That wasn't a compliment."

But the curls at the corners of his mouth didn't wane. If anything, they widened.

"I shouldn't have to remind you that I'm a married woman. And my husband is missing. I've got children to think about. I can't... I can't go around—" Her brain shut down, trying to describe the activity they'd just been involved in. Was she such a damn prude that she couldn't say the word kissing?

She stopped ranting and forced herself to take a deep breath. But her heart continued to hammer in her chest. With as much matter-of-factness as she could muster, she said, "Besides, you are *way* too young for me."

That knocked the humor right off his face.

"Wait a minute. You tried to get me to hook up

with your friend. If I'm not mistaken, she's your age."

"That's different. Di can handle affairs with younger men. I'm sure she's very proficient at loving 'em and leaving 'em. I'm not like that. And I have a strong feeling you're not, either. And that's what makes this so damn scary." She didn't like the intensity she read in his eyes. "I'll admit that this, this—" she waved her index finger back and forth between them, once again at a loss to express herself.

"Attraction," he stated.

Forbidden attraction, she wanted to clarify, but she didn't dare.

"Whatever!" She refused to verbalize what she was feeling... what she'd surrendered to. "I admit that it's the most exciting thing I've felt in... in... a really long time." Her inability to articulate was frustrating the hell out of her. "But there's just too much going on in my life right now. Too many reasons that I cannot do this." Feeling like a complete fool, she found herself repeating, "You are much too young for me!"

She'd never moved so fast down a dirt path in her life. All she could think of was escaping the panic, escaping these illicit feelings, escaping *him*.

"It's all right if you want to blow me off, Fiona," he shouted from behind her. "Just make sure you're doing it for a reason that makes sense."

Chapter Thirteen

The Race

"**I**t's him. I know it's him."

Angry frustration flamed Sam's face and glazed his watery gaze, and it distressed Di to see Fiona's son so upset. He was already nursing a bruised elbow and a scraped knee from a tumble he'd taken, compliments of Senior Snot, on the bus ride home from school.

If black looks were laser beams, the Rowland telephone would have melted into a gelatinous blob of plastic. The teen tossed the cordless phone onto the couch.

"Why won't he just leave me alone?" Sam

lamented. "I go out of my way to avoid him. At school and on the bus. Why can't he do the same?"

Di felt ill at ease. She knew Sam needed comforting, but she wasn't quite sure how to go about it. He was nearly six feet tall, all arms and legs. Hugging all that gangliness would be awkward, she suspected. Cuddling was probably the last thing he wanted from her right now, anyway. What he needed was his mother, but Fiona had been asked to attend a fundraising meeting at St. Anne's, Cassie's old school. Apparently the committee was finding their efforts floundering since their star chairperson had left the ranks.

"I'm proud of the way you handled the call. Put that back on your elbow." Di pointed to the ice bag he held in his hand. "I could see you were shaken when no one responded to you, but you stayed calm. That's good. Never Let the Bastards See You Sweat is my motto."

Fiona had warned her about her language, but she wasn't here, and if ever a situation called for strong language, this one did. Di could plainly see that Sam felt helpless, and he was angry and physically injured. This Brian Lowe—Senior Snot, as Di had dubbed him—was a real jerk for causing

Sam to get hurt on the bus. And the fact that he went about it so sneakily irked Di to no end.

"It might not be him." Her attempt to calm him fell flat.

"Oh, it's him. I know it."

"You know where this kid lives?" she asked Sam.

"Yeah, he gets off the bus before me." His eyes narrowed. "Why?"

"I think we should pay him a visit."

"Oh, no. Thanks, but—" he let the ice bag drop away from the lump on his elbow "—that wouldn't be a good idea."

The more Di thought about it, the more perfect the idea sounded to her. "Sure it is." She grabbed up her purse and her keys. "That kid needs to know you're not alone. That you have friends and supporters. Old Snot-boy doesn't understand that some people get pissed when those they love get bullied."

"Please, Di."

When she realized Sam wasn't following her toward the front door, she snapped her fingers twice in quick succession. "Come on, Sam!"

"But Mom wouldn't—"

"We're going!" She held open the screen door, waiting for him to pass. "Your mother has enough problems on her mind right now. You and I can handle this. And if that kid gives me any lip, I may tear him a couple of new nostrils." She hadn't taken this kind of crap from her classmates when she was Sam's age. He needed to learn not to take it, either.

The rolling hills of Hockessin were a patchwork of farmland, mushroom houses, and neighborhoods of sizable, prestigious homes. But older homes dotted the landscape as well. These houses had been built before the region had acquired the label of "the" place to live and up-and-coming professionals from Wilmington began flooding the area, forcing the property values—and the taxes—higher and higher.

"There." Sam pointed. "That's his house." Fear tinged his voice when he added, "That's him right there."

A lanky teen pushed a lawnmower across the front yard of a small Cape Cod style home; the only things keeping it from being described as quaint were the need for a fresh coat of paint and a good day's weeding of the overgrown landscaping.

Brian Lowe stopped, ogling Di's Viper as she slowed, and then, recognizing Sam in the passenger seat as they pulled into the drive, he glowered.

The lawnmower's engine died a quick death. "What do you want?" he asked. Senior Snot wiped the sweat from his brow with the sleeve of his gray T-shirt, his hostile gaze never leaving Sam.

Di slammed her door and walked around the car. "We're here for you, chump."

The animosity left Snot-boy's face, and for a second, Di thought he was going to let out a bark of laughter. Okay, so she hadn't chosen the most malicious of monikers, but Fiona just might find out about this escapade and she'd be furious to hear Di had called the boy a nasty little shit like she wanted to.

"I'm onto you." *Oh, come on, Di, you've got to do better than that.* "You're a class A bully, and you're not going to get away with it. Where are your parents? They need to know what kind of person their son is."

"My mom works. We don't have it easy like private school prissy boy."

Di wanted to slap his face. The fact that he was willing to express his antagonism toward Sam right to her face took her off guard. This kid wasn't a nice person, and the situation could easily turn precarious. But then, she should have realized the extent of his meanness when she'd seen Sam's lumps and bumps. She was too angry to ponder all the possible consequences. "Sam's elbow is bruised and his knee is banged up because of you."

"I never touched him."

She took a step closer, her finger pointing directly at his sweaty weasel face. Anger made her tone lower. "You sneaky bastard—" *oops!* "—you might think no one knows about your not-so-innocent foot sliding out into the aisle of the bus, but I know. And if it happens again, you little fuck, you'll contend with me." This kid needed to know she could stoop to his level if that became necessary.

Derision pervaded Senior Snot's chortle as he glanced at Sam. "Your mommy doing your fighting for you these days?"

"She's not my mom." Sam looked at her, desperately trying to keep from out-and-out pleading. "Di, I can fight my own battles."

Well, crap! Not only had she not intimidated Brian Lowe in the least, she had succeeded in completely embarrassing Sam.

She snapped, "I know you're fully capable of fighting your own battles!" Sam seemed startled by her tone. Then she pointed at Snot-boy again. "In fact, Sam here could whip your ass any day of the week."

Brian's jaw dropped a fraction, his dry lips sticking at the corners. Di sensed Sam go utterly still beside her.

"I'm not talking about a fistfight, you moron." She sneered at Brian. "I mean in a footrace."

Both boys seemed taken aback.

"How far is Burlington High from here, Sam? Five miles? Six?"

"Something like that," he muttered.

"How about it? A showdown. If Sam kicks your ass, as I have every confidence he will, then you back off and give him some space."

There was no chemical known to man more powerful than male testosterone. Oh, shit. What had she done? The teens eyed one another. The gauntlet had been thrown. She'd left them no chance to back out. The only way for them to hang on to their pride would be to accept the dare.

They yielded to the challenge at the same moment. Snot-boy and Sam both struggled out of their T-shirts. Sam let his shirt drop to the ground while Brian tossed his behind him. Di watched the gray jersey fabric arc through the air and settle on the handle of the lawnmower. The boys crossed the narrow road and hoofed across the rolling field.

She groaned, instantly regretting not having thought this through. She'd gone from one bad suggestion to the next. Those boys were bound to trespass onto private property, cut though farmland and use winding, narrow roads in their quest for the shortest distance to the high school. What she'd thought to be a brilliant plan she quickly saw as a stupid idea that could easily get one of those boys hurt. If Fiona found out about this, Di was dead meat.

Burlington High held not a single pleasant memory for her. Just thinking about those years made Di want to cringe. Shoving people into boxes and slapping labels on them was cruel, and adolescents could be merciless. Way back in middle school she'd been branded as *trailer tramp* and *double-wide diva* (the idiots had no idea she'd have considered herself lucky to live in a double-wide). The hated nicknames had followed her all the way into community college. She hadn't shaken them until after she'd graduated, packed up, and left town.

It aggrieved her having to admit that her stupidity and naiveté had suckered her into caring about the opinions of her peers. Today, she'd have boldly looked them in the eye and told them to go fuck themselves. Especially Geneva Wattson.

As the daughter of the mayor of Hockessin, Geneva had thought a flowery fragrance wafted from her excrement. She also thought it was her life's objective to cruelly criticize and condemn those she saw as beneath her. Di had been shoved into this category, like it or not.

During one mortifying incident, Geneva had paused next to Di's desk and announced to the entire class that someone needed to let a "certain trashy girl" know that Right Guard was deodorant for *males*, and that it would be better for a "certain trashy girl" to stink than to go around smelling like a man.

When the welfare money ran out before the month was over, which happened often in Aunt Viv's house, personal hygiene products were the first things dropped off the shopping list. Di often lived without simple amenities that others took for granted, things like shampoo, deodorant, or toothpaste. The aerosol can of Right Guard had been left behind by one of Viv's men friends, and without thinking about it, Di had decided to put it to good use. Once.

Geneva's words had embarrassed her, but the laughter that rang out in the classroom had been crushing.

It had taken several days of wooing before she'd succeeded in squaring the score with Geneva. Sleeping with the twit's boyfriend felt like sweet victory, but the triumph was extremely short-lived. Jerry Prichard had been happy enough to betray Geneva for a quick piece; however, after Di's fifteen minute conquest had ended, the creep had suggested it wouldn't be a good idea for them to be seen together outside the back seat of his Ford Pinto. Eventually, Geneva and Jerry had patched things up. Di, however, remained the despised, poor white trailer trash.

Di shut off her car and got out, scanning the horizon for Sam and Senior Snot. She'd parked near the student driving range located at the far north end of the school, sure that the boys would approach from that direction. But whether they'd arrive on James Street or cut across the sports field was anyone's guess. Nervous energy had her pacing. What if Sam couldn't run fast enough to beat that jerk? Would her grandiose scheme only land him into deeper trouble, with more heartache and torment than he'd already been enduring? God, she was a pinhead.

The faint strains of laughter carried by the breeze caught Di's attention. She glanced toward the school and saw a small group of teens emerging from the double doors of the gymnasium at the far side of the building.

Two of the four boys jostled in friendly horseplay. A coppery-haired girl squealed when the boys bumped into her. Cassie's long, straight, golden-brown hair glistened in the late afternoon sun, and Di gasped.

Holy crap! She'd gotten so involved with Sam and helping him to face his fear of that bully that she'd forgotten she was supposed to pick up Fiona's daughter. Cassie had decided to join the yearbook committee, and because Fiona was busy at her meeting, Di was to pick up the teen at five o'clock.

Di didn't know how Fiona handled all her responsibilities with the kids. Simply remembering who had to be where when was mind-boggling. But Fiona handled it extremely well, reminding Di of a professional circus juggler who kept a dozen balls in the air at all times. How in the world did single moms work a full-time job and raise their children? That was what Fiona was these days—a single mother. And since starting her business, she was busier than ever.

It wasn't as if Di didn't know the meaning of responsibility. One didn't reach her position—or rather her former position—in any business without being dependable and accountable. But there was a huge difference between Di's job in marketing and Fiona's job as a mom. Where Di once created ad campaigns meant to promote and sell this or that product to the public, Fiona had the awesome and often daunting task of influencing the lives of children, shaping them, nurturing them, teaching them.

And Fiona was damned good at it.

Cassie was oblivious to everything except the kids joking and chatting around her. Di lifted her hand, ready to call out, but the greeting died in her throat when Cassie casually accepted a cigarette from the redhead and several of the kids lit up.

Now, what the hell was she supposed to do with *this* information? Go to Fiona and tell her what she'd seen? Di was certainly no rat fink. Should she approach Cassie and lay down the law against smoking? Cassie would love that. Should Di turn a blind eye and pretend the incident hadn't happened?

The questions were still rolling around in her mind when she noticed Sam and Senior Snot loping across the sports field. Panting, sweating and red-faced, the boys were locked in a dead heat. Di's heart pounded and she pressed her fist to her mouth to keep from cheering Sam on.

They were headed straight for her and she quickly realized they'd pegged the spot where she was standing as the finish line.

Come on, Sam, she silently chanted. *Run faster! Faster!*

Fifty yards from the finish, Sam was still holding his own, but Di clearly saw his confidence and his stamina fading. Senior Snot's pace remained strong. At twenty-five yards, Snot-boy pulled away.

"Move your ass, Sam!" Di could no more have stopped the shout from ejecting from her throat than she could have kept the moon from rising.

Brian Lowe picked up speed, sprinting the final few yards, and the race was over. A trooper to the end, though, Sam continued to run until he, too, had crossed the imaginary finish line.

Snot-boy walked in circles, gulping in air, his

hands resting on his narrow hips. Sam hunched over, his palms cupping his knees, as he did his best to catch his breath. Di felt horrible, and she was sure Sam would be angry with her. She'd only made his problem worse. She wanted to apologize, but didn't dare speak while the bully was within hearing distance.

"Walk it off, man. Or you'll get cramps." Brian approached Sam and got him moving. "Hey, man, that was great."

Apparently, Sam only had enough energy to nod and shuffle a few steps.

"I mean it," the older teen continued. "You stayed with me the whole way. We have plenty of runners on the team who don't have that kind of endurance."

The unexpected compliment had Sam straightening. His chest heaved as he mumbled his thanks.

"I'm going to talk to Coach. See if he'll let you come to practice. We could use you on the team."

A mixture of surprise, doubt, and amazement rounded Sam's blue eyes.

Di pointed a warning finger at Senior Snot. "No more prank calls."

He stared at her for a few moments while he

continued to suck in huge amounts of oxygen. Then he glanced as Sam and asked, "Who is this woman?"

"I mean it! Don't call Sam's house again." The kid might have won the damn race, but Di refused to back down.

Brian Lowe ignored her. "I haven't called your house." He heaved one more inhalation, his chest expanding, as he combed his sweaty hair straight back off his forehead with his fingers. He lifted his chin at Sam. "I'll see you around school." Then he started walking back across the sports field.

Di saw that the group of kids by the gym had broken up, and her shout must have caught Cassie's attention because the teen was making her way over to them. If she wanted to apologize to Sam without an audience, Di knew she was going to have to do it now.

"I'm sorry, Sam. I never should have—"

"Did you hear that?" Excitement sparked the question. "He's going to talk to the coach about gettin' me on the team. He said I was better than some of his teammates."

Di hesitated. "You're not angry with me?"

Sam shrugged. "I never thought about racing

him. But it was a good idea, I guess. How else could I really show him what I can do?"

Di flattened her mouth. "Still, I should never have—"

"Really, Di. It's all right." Then Sam grinned. "You know he thinks you're nuts, don't you?"

"Sometimes the perception of being crazy can work in a person's favor."

Sam looked across the field at Brian. "Should we offer him a ride?"

"Hell, no." Di crossed her arms. "Let him walk. Serves him right. He shouldn't have been such a shit to you."

He laughed, and then he shook his head, his smile nearly touching his ears. "I might get a chance to make the team." The lead balloon of guilt that had taken up residence in her chest suddenly filled with helium and took flight. She smiled at Sam, unable to articulate how relieved she was and how happy it made her to see him happy.

Still too far away for a verbal greeting, Cassie waved at her. Di lifted her hand, wondering what she was going to do about having seen Fiona's daughter smoking.

Sam had reached into her car for his T-shirt, and

tugged it over his head. "Um, listen, Di." He looked suddenly shy. "Thanks. Okay? I mean, really." His intense gaze pleaded for her understanding. "Thanks. Mom would never have done anything like this for me. Never in a million years."

She let out a loud laugh. "Oh, wow. Now ain't that the truth? Your mother would never have stood on someone's front lawn and acted like a complete and utter idiot. She's an intelligent and civilized human being, Sam." Di arched her brows. "That's something I'm still working on."

Chapter Fourteen

All Dressed Up

"**I** guess what I'm trying to say is that I'm surprised you agreed to go out with him again." Fiona stood next to Di before the mirror in the bedroom of the apartment above the garage. One of the earrings Di had asked to borrow lay in Fiona's palm while Di inserted its mate into the pierced lobe of her ear. "I mean, I know I warned you against ruling him out immediately. But you said Neil kisses like a bass out of water. You said he was strange—"

"Strange in a cute kind of way." Di plucked the

earring from Fiona's hand. "And it might be fun to teach him to kiss."

Fiona let her hand fall to her side, grinning. "He's our age. You know what they say about old dogs. The same holds true for old fish, I'm sure." She was surprised to realize that her friend's moue expressed insult.

"Di, I'm sorry." She put her hand on Di's shoulder. "I was joking. Do you have feelings for Neil? Can you see yourself with him long-term?"

Some unreadable emotion shadowed Di's blue eyes. "Who said anything about long-term? I'm going out to dinner with the guy." Frustration knitted her brows and she let out a groan before she sank onto the edge of the bed. Fiona followed suit, settling beside her on the mattress. "I look at you, and sometimes I get the feeling that you have sole proprietorship of the American dream," Di confessed.

The defensiveness that welled up in Fiona was a knee-jerk reaction that was easy enough to quell. The misery expressed in Di's tone let her know the comment hadn't been meant as a personal dig so much as it was a lament of life.

"Just look at the warm and fuzzy Fionaville you've created for yourself. I can't help but wonder if I've had it all wrong." Di's lips glistened in the lamplight. "I've worked my ass off earning money to buy things. Then I come here and see you with Cassie and Sam, and I feel like I've been doing nothing but spinning my wheels all these years."

"Don't do that. My life is nowhere near enviable."

"Oh, but it is," Di insisted. "You have a good life, and up until a month or so ago, you had a foundation, a stability that I could never imagine."

"Need I remind you that Fuzzy Fionaville is also inhabited by the likes of Karen Snow and Shirley Bookerman?"

"No, no... let's not go there. Not now. I only meant to focus on the good. There's so much good, you know? You said it yourself. You'd do it all again for Cassie and Sam."

Fiona nodded. That was true enough.

"At the rate I'm going, I'll never have kids." Di fiddled with her thick gold bracelet, her tone whispery. "My eggs are probably all dried up by now."

"Don't talk like that."

"Could you see yourself having a baby, or chasing around after a toddler, at our age? Right. I didn't think so." Di laughed, her white-blond hair bobbing as she stood abruptly and went back to the mirror. "I need to get ready. Neil will be here soon." She picked up her hairbrush, her gaze meeting Fiona's in the mirror. "You know, I never was able to understand it. Your attraction to Stan, I mean. I know I nicknamed him Studly back then, but that was because I was having some good, mean fun." She grinned.

"You think I didn't know that?"

Di ran the brush through her hair, her smile fading. "I never said it, but I always thought Staid Stanley would have been a more befitting name. He was so... dry... so humorless... so damned analytical."

Fiona shrugged. "I can't deny it."

"What did you see in him?" She set the brush down, turned, and rested her bottom on the edge of the dresser. "What was it about him that attracted you?"

Sighing, Fiona gazed down at the bedspread and smoothed her fingers over the cool fabric. "Stan was smart. I really liked that. But he was also gentle. And kind. And he was truly concerned about... me. About my emotional well-being. I guess what I loved most about him was that he loved me." She feared the simple comment sounded stupid. Fiona looked at her friend. "You know how my father was. Yes, he kept a roof over my head and food in the cupboards. But he didn't really... care." Emotion swam around in her chest, threatening to rise up and choke her.

"Besides that," she said, feeling the desperate need to forget about her past, about her father, "there was a time when Stan could be pretty wild." She nodded. "He had quite the imagination."

Di set the hairbrush aside, seeming to shimmer with sudden curiosity.

"When we were newlyweds—" the memory made Fiona flush "—he used to dress it up."

"*It?*" Di lunged toward the bed, tugged up the hem of her dress and scooted next to Fiona. "As in his beef bayonet? His trouser trout? His bologna pony?"

Fiona laughed. "What are you? Thirteen?"

"Hey, I'm not the one who played dress up." Di lifted her hands, palms up, and waved her fingers furiously. "Start spilling, baby."

An odd shyness rushed at Fiona. She tucked one foot beneath her and shifted to face Di. "On our first Christmas, I was introduced to Rudolph the One-eyed Reindeer. Stan had used a brown pipe cleaner for antlers, and a red Sharpie for the nose, not realizing it was a permanent marker." She snickered. "He toted around that red dot for weeks."

Di gaped at her, clearly delighted.

"And I celebrated one very memorable Halloween with Casper the Sexually Addicted Ghost. I was sore the next day, but very satisfied, if you know what I mean."

Di laughed so hard her eyes watered. "Oh, shoot. I gotta stop or I'll smear my mascara."

The women moved into the bathroom so Di could touch up her makeup.

Fiona leaned her shoulder against the doorjamb. "For the life of me, I can't figure out how or when Stan and I lost our way. I do know that I'd begun feeling a bit resentful. For the last few years I've been pestered with nagging questions. Is being a wife and mother all I'll ever have to define me? What the heck am I going to do when the kids leave for college? What could I have accomplished if I'd earned my degree instead of marrying and having babies so young?"

Di capped her mascara and spun around. "You, missy, are getting way too Eeyore on me. Keep this up and I'll have to cancel my plans. It's Saturday night and I want to party, but if you're gloomy I can't possibly go out and leave you."

"Are you really sure you want to go?" Fiona continued to have trouble picturing Di and Neil together, and she felt guilty for urging Di to call him to begin with.

"Didn't you understand a word I said?" Di flipped off the bathroom light and shooed Fiona out of the doorway. "I want in on it. The kind of American dream you have. I'm looking for a man who can offer me some stability. Neil has all the qualifications. He's dry, humorless, and damned analytical." She waltzed through the bedroom, picking up her sweater from where she'd tossed it on the chair.

"That's all fine and good." Fiona followed Di into the living room area of the small apartment. "But don't go out with the man because you think he fits some kind of criteria. Find someone you're attracted to. Someone who excites you."

"I'm attracted to Neil. He's... he's—" Realizing Fiona saw right through her lie, Di heaved a short, tight sigh and tossed her sweater over the arm of the couch near her purse. "I'm going out with him and that's that." She slid her feet into turquoise stilettos that had been dyed to match her dress.

"Hey, speaking of exciting men, why don't you call your cute detective and the four of us can go to dinner."

The proposition so shocked Fiona that her mouth fell open.

"Oh, come on." Di smoothed her hands over the fabric covering her hips. "Don't try to deny there's something there."

"Something where?" Fiona felt flustered.

"Between you and DeSalvo, silly. You think I haven't noticed that you've started calling him Chad? Or that he showed up for coffee out of the blue yesterday morning? And how awkward the conversation was between you two? And that he couldn't take his eyes off you? And how you tried hard not to look at him?"

Fiona couldn't think of a single thing to say, and even if she could muster up some words, she doubted she could form them.

Di beamed. "You are so busted." She went to the kitchenette, grabbed a glass from the cabinet and filled it with water. "You look dazed and confused. Is that because I noticed something was going on or because you believe there's something wrong with your thinking he's good-looking?"

Ever since their walk in the park—and their

kiss—she'd done an excellent job of ignoring the feelings Chad stirred in her, or she thought she had, anyway. Even when he'd showed up unannounced at the house yesterday morning bearing a box of chocolate-dipped crullers, she felt she'd acted properly. Responsibly. Yet Di had seen something in her behavior, and that mortified Fiona.

Without taking a sip of the water she'd poured, Di set the glass on the counter and came to Fiona. "You're not feeling guilty, are you? You're not thinking it's wrong that you find him attractive?"

Fiona's mouth had never been this dry.

"Cut it out right now. Honey, you need to stop being so hard on yourself. You're human. A woman has needs. I know. I've been there."

Annoyance cut Fiona to the quick. "I'm married, Di." In case she hadn't been heard, she repeated, "I'm married!"

The gentleness of Di's touch as she slid her fingers around Fiona's upper arms cooled the heat raging in her.

"I think it's wonderful and admirable that you want to honor your marriage," Di said softly. "Was Stanley as wonderful? As admirable?"

Fiona's shoulders rounded. She and Di both knew the answer. Di's eyes lit with mischief.

"If I were you, I wouldn't even think twice about DeSalvo." She waggled her eyebrows. "I'd snatch up that delicious man and have my way with him."

Fiona heaved a sigh. "Well, that's where you and I are different."

Di clicked her tongue and shook her head, and as if suddenly remembering her thirst, she returned to the corner kitchenette.

"I can't act impulsively—no matter how enticing the impulse." Fiona swiped imaginary lint from the back of the upholstered armchair. "I care what people think of me."

She hadn't meant to be cruel, but the words were cutting. Di took her time drinking from the glass. Finally, she looked at Fiona.

"I used to care what people thought of me. But it hurt too much. Then I grew up." She hesitated. "We've always known we were different, you and I. It never seemed to matter."

"It doesn't matter. It didn't then, and it doesn't now. I didn't mean to hurt your feelings, Di."

Di smiled, setting down the glass again. "You know my skin is thicker than that." Then she asked, "He is enticing, though, isn't he?"

Fiona chuckled softly. Di would never change. "He is." Not wanting to come off as holier than thou, she decided to be honest about the matter. Her smile widened. "He's a good kisser, too."

Di inhaled a gasp. "He kissed you? When? Where? No wonder you two were so awkward together yesterday. Why didn't you tell me?"

A groan grated deep in Fiona's throat. "Because I didn't want to think about it. How could something feel so right and so wrong at the same time?" Agony knotted her stomach. "I've got the kids to consider."

Di crossed the small room again. "I know you do. And I know you'd do anything to keep them from being hurt." She led Fiona to the sofa. "Sit down with me for a second." Once they were settled, she said, "It makes me so sad to think that you feel bad, or guilty, or wrong, just for feeling something that's completely natural between a man and a woman. I'm not saying that you have to act on what you feel today or even next week or next month. But, Fiona..." Di paused, as if measuring her words "...you have to get back to living sometime." She hesitated, and when she spoke again, her voice held an amazing tenderness. "All the evidence tells us that something bad happened."

Instinctively, Fiona knew Di was talking about Stan.

"I know there's no proof. Not a shred. But if there were... if you had... confirmation that he was... not coming back—"

Clearly she was having difficulty with this complex and thorny topic.

"—how long would you wait... before you—"

"Longer than five weeks, I can tell you that much," Fiona declared.

"Okay, okay." Di backed off. "I understand. I'm just saying that... you don't have to put on some kind of grieving act. You might be a widow, but you're also a woman who's been... wronged. Stan was a—" She stopped suddenly, frowning with frustration. "Why the hell aren't there any derogatory names for a man who screws around on his wife? I mean, had the situation been reversed, people would be calling you a hussy, a tramp, a whore, a slut." She gazed off into the distance, concentrating. "There's horn dog, of course. But I think most men wouldn't find that insulting in the least. In fact, they'd wear it like a badge of honor. Why is it that—"

"Stop!" Fiona chuckled, shaking her head. "It just amazes me that, no matter how serious the conversation gets, you never fail to make me laugh."

Di's eyes grew warm with affection. "That's because I love you." She slid close enough that their shoulders touched. "You know what amazes me? That we were friends at all. There was such a disparity in... everything about us. You lived in a big brick house in a nice neighborhood. I lived with Aunt Viv in Sunset Trailer Park. You were quick-witted and scholarly. I was a mediocre student at best. You chose hearth and home, while I focused on a career. You became a one-man woman. And me? Hey, I've got so many notches on my bedpost that my bed is rickety." Then her humor withered. "We really are different. We've always known it. But with you and me... it never mattered." Emotion swirled around them.

Fiona reached over and took her friend's hand. "It never really mattered."

Chapter Fifteen

Forced Confessions

Fiona hurried out of the extra bedroom that had been converted into an office years ago, her excitement so palpable she barely felt her feet touch the floor. She raced down the stairs.

"Di! You won't believe it. Liz Underwood has doubled her order. And she didn't even wait a month! She agreed to pay full price." Fiona shouted at the top of her lungs as she passed the living room doorway. Where the heck was Di? Giddiness bubbled up and she let it surge from her in a chuckle as she moved through the house. She thought of the new clients she'd taken on this week. "How on earth am I going to get all this baking—"

She bounded into the kitchen and found Di and Cassie.

"—done?" She couldn't help finishing her thought; however, her enthusiasm died in a snap. She'd obviously interrupted a private conversation. She hadn't heard a word of it, but the looks on their faces said it all. Whatever the topic, they hadn't meant for her to know.

Surprised to see her daughter home from school, Fiona glanced at the clock. She'd been on the phone with the restaurant owner longer than she'd thought.

"Where's Sam?" She inched farther into the room.

"He's on his way." No one could pull off true petulance better than her daughter. "He stopped to talk to some kids at the bus stop."

"What's going on?" she asked, looking from Cassie to Di.

"Nothing." They answered nearly in unison, although their tones were night-and-day different. Cassie clearly felt her mother should keep her nose out of what was none of her business, while Di's attempt at casual indifference irritated Fiona.

Something hit her. Hard. Fiona pressed her hand to her stomach, realizing what it was. She felt passed over, left out, and she didn't like it at all.

"What's going on?" she repeated, putting one hand on the back of a kitchen chair and nailing her daughter with the unyielding "mother look" she'd perfected over the course of the past seventeen years.

"Cassie and I were just talking, Fiona. It was nothing."

Studying her daughter, Fiona remarked, "It sure seems like something judging from the way you two clammed up when I came into the room." She pressed the issue. "In fact, I think I'd be safe in guessing it was something significant."

"Nope," Cassie said. "It was nothing."

Fiona continued her steady stare. Had this been any other time in her daughter's life—in all their lives—she might have backed off. But Cassie was dealing with too many changes at the moment. If she was having a hard time handling the issue of her father, or if some problem existed at her new school, Fiona thought she was only being a prudent mother in wanting to know. Just as she expected, her daughter caved.

"Di caught me smoking last week when she

came to the school. She was reaming me out about it."

Drugs? Holy hell. The child had only been in public school for a few weeks. Fiona would never have faced this with the hawk-eyed Sisters watching over Cassie.

"How could you?" Disappointment overwhelmed her. "You know the dangers of pot. You know—"

"*Mom!* It was a cigarette! God, I hate you people!" She picked up her backpack and headed out of the kitchen.

"Get back here, Cassie," Fiona called, but the teen pretended deafness.

"Just because it was tobacco," Di shouted loudly at the empty doorway, "doesn't make it okay. Lung cancer kills, you know."

Cassie stomped up the steps.

Alone in the kitchen with Di, Fiona felt her pulse race. Di looked unfazed.

"She hates us people." Di's mouth quirked. "Do you care? Because I don't care."

"You should have told me."

"Oh, come on, Fiona." Di laced her fingers and rested her elbows on the table. "Calm down. It was a cigarette. Every kid tries smoking. You did. I did.

She's in a new school. Trying to fit in. If it had been pot, I'd have told you. If she'd been having sex in the locker room, I'd have told you. If she'd been drunk out of her gourd, I'd have told you. But this—" she unlaced her fingers long enough to wave her hand for effect "—was nothing. She knows she shouldn't. She says she doesn't like it. That it tastes nasty. Makes her hair stink. And her clothes. She's working it out for herself." Di tilted her head. "So let her work it out."

"Like we worked things out for ourselves?"

"We didn't do too bad."

Ready to launch into a diatribe on responsible parenting, Fiona actually started when her son burst into the kitchen from the back door.

"Di! Di!" Sam's face was flushed, his breathing labored. "You won't believe it. I'm on the team! Coach took me out of gym class today and let me run." He dropped his backpack onto the table. "He told me to show 'im everything I had, and I did. I showed 'im."

"Good for you," Di said. "Congratulations. That's great, Sam."

"I'm only an alternate, which sucks." He wiped the sweat from his forehead and then dried his damp palm on the belly of his T-shirt. "But Coach gave me a uniform and everything."

Fiona watched the exchange, thinking there was something odd about her son's tunnel vision where Di was concerned. It seemed just a little strange that he hadn't addressed Fiona even once while presenting his exciting news. He hadn't even looked her way or offered a greeting.

"When's your first meet?" Di asked. "Your mom and I are going to want to be there."

The instant Di mentioned his mother, Sam glanced at her. "Hey, Mom." His demeanor turned awkward. "I, uh... I'm on the cross-country team. Coach let me try out today."

What did he think? That she had miraculously appeared out of thin air? "I heard. I'm surprised he let you try out after he'd been so adamantly against it at first. You must have really impressed him. Congratulations."

Her son's discomfort was unmistakable. Looking at Fiona seemed difficult for Sam. And Di's smile was much too innocent for Fiona's liking.

"Okay. What have you two been up to? Let's have it."

Her son's uneasiness appeared outright painful.

And Di? Well, as usual, Di looked cool, confident, and totally composed. No doubt about it. They were hiding something.

"You know what?" Fiona threw up her hands, palms out in surrender. "Never mind. I don't want to know."

"Anyone up for a movie?" Fiona shouted up the stairs toward her kids' bedrooms later that night. "There's hot buttered popcorn."

"I guess." The sounds of video game guns and bombs went silent and Sam clomped across his floor. "Be right down."

Cassie came to the top of the stairs. "What's the movie?"

"Can't remember," Fiona told her honestly. "It's a psychological thriller."

"I need ten minutes to finish this chapter. Will you wait?"

Sam gave his sister an ornery nudge when he passed, and she called him a dweeb before flouncing back into her bedroom and slamming the door. Fiona made her way back toward the living room, shaking her head when Sam created more noise than a pack of wild animals thumping down the steps.

"I'm going to grab a soda," he called.

"Decaffeinated." She didn't need a wired teen on her hands.

Her children had pretty much returned to normal. Yet all of their lives had changed drastically. Yes, Sam and Cassie participated in an extra-curricular activity or two, but those meetings and practices took place directly after school, so most of their evenings were now spent at home. Six weeks ago, Fiona had abandoned all of her commitments in order to focus on her children and the crisis they were facing. As the weeks passed and their lives had settled somewhat, she could have returned to some of her clubs and meetings, but she hadn't for several reasons. First and foremost, she'd forgotten what it was like to spend a quiet night at home. Keeping up with all those friends and acquaintances and commitments had forced her to dance to some swift-paced music, and the syncopation, she now realized, had been endless. Now that she'd turned off the tunes, her life had become so much more gratifying. She truly enjoyed spending more leisure hours with her kids. She only wished her husband was with her, benefiting from this new, liberated environment. All those nights of racing to and from clubs and study groups and team sports might have contributed to their well-roundedness, but it had stunted their well-*groundedness*. It also kept them exhausted.

Fiona's Fabulous Confections excited her more than anything she'd experienced in a very long time. She spent some long but gratifying hours in the kitchen. Then there was the shopping for supplies and the delivering of the desserts, but the work only energized her. The income thrilled her. Her clientele list was expanding by a restaurant or two each week. A slow, easy start, maybe, but this success was just what she needed to help ward off the doubt and fear and confusion that crept under her skin whenever she thought about Stanley and how they would survive without him.

She might never know what had happened to her husband. She had to face that realization. She also had to make some decisions—such as what to do with his car, which continued to sit, unused, in the garage. She'd offered it to Cassie, who had qualified for her license last year. But the idea of driving the Volvo had only made the teen tear up. Fiona was also going to have to decide about the house. Yes, her business was picking up, but she wasn't earning nearly enough money to keep up with the mortgage payment. She was going to have to downsize, and she was going to have to do it soon.

But she wasn't going to have to do it tonight. Banishing the dire thoughts, Fiona entered the living room and plopped down on the couch next to Di, who'd already begun munching on popcorn.

"Ten minutes to showtime," Fiona told her friend.

"Oh, good." Di stood, brushing a few hulls from her lap. "Just enough time for me to take a potty break."

Fiona propped her feet up on the coffee table and picked up the DVD box to read the name of the movie she'd rented from the self-service Redbox. Middle age was hell. It seemed short-term memory was one of the first things to go.

"I'm going to get a glass of wine," Di said from the doorway. "Want one?"

"I'd love that."

The doorbell sounded.

"Stay put," Di ordered. "I'll get it."

Curiosity had Fiona twisting to peek out the front window. She didn't recognize the large, black

SUV sitting in the driveway. Events became chaotic so quickly that later, once the dust settled, Fiona had trouble sorting through the facts for the police.

She remembered frowning at the sound of Sam's heavy footsteps scuffing the hardwood of the hallway leading from the kitchen, and thinking she wished he would pick up his feet when he walked. The sounds of raised voices at the front door had urged her to her feet.

When Sam called out to her, the alarm in his tone set her into motion.

Fiona arrived at the living room doorway just in time to hear Di firmly state to whoever was at the door, "I'm not coming out there." Then a hand reached into the house—the sight of the long, brick red manicured nails would be forever burned into Fiona's mind—clutching Di firmly by the front of her blouse. Her head jerked backward and she disappeared from sight. The scuffling noises made Fiona's heart jump right up into her throat.

"Mom?" Sam's voice was frantic now and filled with fear.

"Stay there," she ordered her son, and then she went to the door.

Di was rolling over onto her side from where

she'd landed in a heap at the base of the porch steps, sticky blood oozing from various scrapes on her knees and one shin.

"Hey!" Fiona shouted. "Stop!"

The woman on the stairs turned. She was tall and broad-shouldered, and she hefted a baseball bat like a pro player. Her fiery hair was cut short. She lifted the bat and pointed the top of it at Fiona.

"This is between me and Di," she said. "You don't want to get involved."

"Who the hell are you?" Fiona asked, feeling a keen need to keep the woman talking.

What struck Fiona as strange was that the woman didn't seem angry. But the determination and absolute resolve reflected in her flat, dark eyes chilled Fiona's blood.

"Di knows who I am. And she knows why I'm here." The redhead turned back toward Di and descended several steps.

Di scrambled to her feet. "Jonni Jean, you don't want to do this."

"Oh, yes, I think I do." Jonni Jean stepped off the bottom stair, swinging the bat with amazing force. Di jumped back just in time to avoid being hit, pea stones skittering into the grass.

Fiona looked at her son, who stood motionless

in the hallway, a can of soda in his hand. "Call the police." When he didn't immediately obey, she yelled, "Dial 911, Sam!" He reached for his back pocket for his cell phone.

"You thought I wouldn't find you, didn't you? Well, I refused to stop looking. Because someone needs to teach you a lesson, Di."

The redhead swung again, and Fiona flinched at the hairbreadth of space between her friend's shoulder and the bat. Clearly, the woman wasn't meaning to frighten Di. She intended to injure... or worse.

Fiona looked around the foyer for a weapon. A flimsy little lamp. A few framed pictures. Nothing that could compete with Jonni Jean's solid chunk of wood.

"And I think that someone's going to be me. You need to learn that your actions can hurt people." Jonni Jean had backed Di up until they were in the middle of the yard.

Di dodged another swift arc of the baseball bat. "I never meant to hurt you, Jonni Jean. And I'm sorry. It's over, you know. And it's been over for a long time."

"Your apology doesn't mean shit. I want to see you in pain. I want to see you hurtin' so bad you can't stand it. Then maybe you'll realize how I felt when I found out what you did."

"Mom, the guy wants to know what's going on." Sam came up behind Fiona, his phone pressed to his ear.

Cassie skipped down the last few steps. "What's going on? What's all the shouting about?" She peered over her mother's shoulder from the foyer. "Who's that out there?" Her voice became shrill. "What the heck is she doing?"

"Hush a minute." Fiona's mind swam. She took the phone from her son. "I have the police on the line," she yelled at the women in the yard.

The redhead glanced toward her, an icy calmness in her expression. "Thanks for the warning. I'll be quick."

Before Fiona could inhale to scream, Jonni Jean raised the bat with both hands and swung it... hard. Di lifted her arm to ward off the blow. The sound of wood splintering bone made Fiona sick to her stomach.

Jonni Jean stared down at Di, who lay crumpled in a heap on the grass, mewing like a kitten and cradling her forearm, which was now bent at an unnatural angle.

Fiona couldn't remember if she'd spoken a single

word to the dispatcher on the other end of the phone.

"Okay," the broad-shouldered redhead declared, "I'm satisfied." Then she stepped over Di, tossed the bat into her SUV, got in, and drove away.

As Fiona raced to Di's side, she heard sirens sounding in the distance.

"She's going to be groggy soon because I gave her a pill for the pain," the E.R. nurse told Fiona. "It was a nice, clean break. It should heal well."

Fiona chewed her bottom lip.

Nearly three hours had passed since Di's arm had lost its battle with Jonni Jean's Louisville Slugger. Two police officers had arrived just minutes after the crazy redhead left. They'd assessed the situation, called for an ambulance and then alerted Dispatch regarding the identification and description of the perpetrator and the black vehicle she'd used to flee the scene.

Refusing to leave her children at home while Jonni Jean was still on the loose, Fiona had loaded Sam and Cassie into the van and followed the ambulance to Christiana Hospital. With the excitement over, the kids now sat in the waiting room looking bored.

"Can I go in with her now?" Fiona asked the nurse.

The woman nodded. "Exam room three. Follow me."

Fiona caught her kids' attention. "Stay put. I'll be right back."

The security guard behind the Plexiglas partition buzzed them into the inner regions of the E.R. The oppressive scent of disinfectant hung heavy in the air. One wobbling wheel on the phlebotomist's cart creaked as a young man pushed it into a nearby exam room. An elderly patient held the back of her thin cotton gown closed as she inched her way down the hall, leaning on the arm of a male aide. Several nurses reviewed charts at the center station. Someone's heart monitor beeped loudly. An orderly emptied wastebaskets.

What would Stan have thought about all of this? Not much. He'd rarely had anything nice to say about Di, and this debacle would only add fuel to his discontent. The question and answer soughed through Fiona's head, unnerving her. Had this really been the first time today that she'd thought of her husband?

"Here you go. I'll be back in a sec with her release forms. Once she signs them and I go over instructions, you can take her home."

Fiona thanked her, and the woman walked toward the nurses' station.

The wooden door of the exam room was surprisingly heavy, and once Fiona closed it behind her, the quiet was so keen she felt as if she'd stepped into another world.

Her face pasty, Di reclined on the bed with several pillows supporting her back. She looked tired. Her arm rested on a tray table, a cast covering it from just below the elbow to the middle of her hand.

"They come in designer colors now." Di reached up with her other hand to swipe her bangs off her forehead. "But I wasn't feeling very fashionable, so they gave me basic white. Goes with everything, you know."

"Don't." Fiona shook her head. "There's not one thing about this that's funny. I need some answers, Di."

Di's eyelids slid shut momentarily and she

sighed quietly. "I know you do. Once the police arrived, everything got pretty hectic."

"An officer questioned me. What could I tell him? I didn't know that woman. I didn't know what that was about. He didn't believe me and kept pressing me for answers... answers I didn't have." The terror that had taken her too long to squelch resurfaced like crude oil bubbling up in water. "Who was that, Di? Why would anyone do such a thing? She could have killed you. My kids watched her..."

The rest of her sentence trailed off. It was unfair of Fiona to hold Di responsible for someone else's actions, especially when she was the unfortunate recipient of those actions.

"I know, Fiona. And I'm so sorry. Truly, I am." Di shifted on the bed. "When I opened the door and saw Jonni Jean standing there, I thought I could reason with her. I didn't want to believe she would actually show up at your house."

"Who is she? How do you know her? And what did she mean about you needing to be taught a lesson?"

Di dipped her chin nearly to her chest, her jaw muscle tensing. She lifted her gaze to Fiona's. "She works at Roche Advertising. Her husband does, too. I sort of... well, I kind of... slept with him for a while."

Fiona just stood there, speechless. Di rushed to explain.

"It was not an affair," she stressed. "There was nothing remotely intimate between us, Fiona. Jonni Jean had nothing to be worried about. Cliff meant nothing more to me than a big 'O' every now and then. Every woman needs to have her world rocked every once in a while, doesn't she?"

Neither woman smiled.

"I never dreamed this would happen, Fiona. You have to believe me."

Unable to think of anything to say, Fiona remained silent.

Di winced as she wiggled the fingers of her broken arm. "I guess I deserved this. I'm a real slut, aren't I? An adulterous slut."

"Nobody deserves this. You can't be held entirely accountable for what happened. That man was the one who was married. He's the one who broke his commitment to his wife, not you."

"I helped him along," she murmured. "That's for sure. Funny thing is, it had been over for weeks by the time Jonni Jean got wind of it."

Remembering the pain she continued to feel

whenever she thought about her own husband's infidelities, Fiona scowled. "I don't care how long it had been over, if you ask me this Cliff person is the one who deserves the broken arm."

"Oh, he had his run-in with Jonni Jean's baseball bat."

Fiona went still.

"Cliff showed up at my house with all the windows busted out of his Grand Cherokee and a big, blue goose egg on his forehead. He warned me Jonni Jean was angry. Told me to get out of town."

"You *knew* his wife was dangerous? You knew she might come looking for you? Yet you came to my house?" Irritation flashed through Fiona. "Di, that woman is deranged. She could've killed you. She could've hurt my kids."

"I never imagined she'd find me in Hockessin. I didn't talk about my past to anyone at work. I've been here a month and a half. I thought surely things had died down in Philly."

"*Things?* With an s?"

Di's mouth drew into a thin line and she glanced away yet again, alerting Fiona that more drama was forthcoming.

Then something heavy—shame, Fiona

suspected—rounded her friend's slender shoulders.

"I didn't leave Roche on the best of terms. In fact, Hal Roche booted me out on my ass."

Her eyelids closed for an instant and Fiona suspected the pain medication Di had been given was taking hold.

Di's tone grew weaker. "I've had so much time to think since I came home. Too much time, doing too much thinking. I would love to blame someone. *Anyone*. And I have. I've cussed Aunt Viv again and again for showing me how easy it is to manipulate and use people to get what I want. I've blamed my worthless mother for walking away, for not caring about me. But you know something, Fiona? There comes a time when everyone has to take responsibility for their own actions, for their own choices, for their own life."

She went quiet, and for a moment Fiona thought she had drifted off to sleep. But her head lolled forward and she opened her eyes.

"I stepped on a lot of people's faces on my climb up the corporate ladder. Oh, I was good at my job. I helped to build that company into what it is. I deserved every single perk I earned, Fiona. But I didn't have to go about it as ruthlessly and maliciously as I did. I cut people out and screwed them over and—" she took a deep breath "—I'm not so sure anymore that all that was necessary."

She frowned. "What amazed me most was that, in the end, my impressive sales record and the long list of clientele I'd brought on board and all my company awards hadn't mattered once my enemies decided to shut me out. And they were my enemies because that's what I made them."

Exhaustion seemed to get the better of her and she rested her head back against the pillow. "Jonni Jean might have been right. I probably did need to be taught a few lessons." There was a knock on the door and the nurse came in with papers and an envelope containing pain medications. She spent several moments going over the doctor's orders with Di.

"There's a wheelchair parked at the nurses' station for you," the woman finally said. "Anytime you're ready, you're free to go."

Just as she was leaving, a police officer arrived—a man who looked vaguely familiar to Fiona. Osborne was the name on his badge. Di had told Fiona about being pulled over by their classmate.

"Eli." Di's greeting sounded drowsy but pleased. "Come in. Fiona, you remember Eli from school?"

Fiona and Eli exchanged greetings.

"I heard about your accident over the radio. I came straight here once my shift was over. How you doing?"

"I'm good," Di told him. "Just tired."

"They got her." He stepped closer to the bed. "The Philadelphia police picked up the Bowers woman at her home. She's in custody and they'll bring her back here tomorrow to face charges."

Di lifted her broken arm off the tray table and gingerly set it on her lap. "What if I don't want to press charges?"

The question clearly startled Eli. "I don't think you have a choice in the matter, Di. The woman hurt you."

"I hope they put her away for a good, long time," Fiona said. "She could have killed you, Di."

The door handle clicked and Neil barged into the exam room, lugging a large bouquet of daisies and sprigs of exotic grass. "I was watching the ten o'clock news and couldn't believe my ears when I heard what happened to you."

Fiona was forced to back away when Neil bustled closer. He thrust the flowers at Di and bent to kiss her. Di twisted her head so his lips landed on her jaw.

"The ten o'clock news?" Di groaned, evidently unhappy to have her name broadcast all over the tristate area.

"Yeah." Neil beamed, completely oblivious to Di's melancholy. "The Philadelphia stations are picking it up, I think, because you live there. My girl is famous."

Di lifted her head from the pillow, and it looked to Fiona that her friend was trying to decide if she'd heard Neil's last statement correctly.

"Fiona," Neil said in greeting. His head cocked when he glanced at the officer. "Don't I know..." He grinned. "Hey. Eli. How've you been? Long time no see."

The men shook hands overtop of Di. Then Neil picked up the bouquet, which she'd set on the tray table, and handed it back to her. "Do you have any idea how many stops I had to make to find flowers this time of night?" That's when Di sneezed, and pain strained her pallid face. "But I don't mind." He smoothed possessive fingers over Di's hair. "Nothing's too good for my girl."

Clearly irritated, Di shooed him away awkwardly with her good hand. Fiona lifted her fingers and pressed them against her lips to conceal her grin. If he wasn't careful, Neil was about to feel the wrath of Di, Fiona sensed it.

However, she was surprised when Di closed her eyes and took a long, deep breath. When Di next looked at Fiona, her blue gaze held a definitive calmness, as if she'd willed away her aggravation.

"Fiona," Di said, "could you and Eli go get that wheelchair the nurse told us about?"

"Sure." Fiona automatically moved to the door. Eli did the same.

Fiona closed the door of the exam room behind them.

"So, uh," Eli began, "how long have they been a couple?"

"They're not, as far as I know." Fiona paused to let a nurse pass in front of her. "They've only dated a couple of times."

Eli only nodded.

They'd barely had time to retrieve the wheelchair and head back to Di's room before Neil exited. Dismay knit the man's brow, but he wasn't bruised or bleeding and all his limbs were intact. Fiona took that as a good sign.

"Di was asking for you," Neil said to Fiona. He nodded a quick goodbye to Eli. "It was good seeing you."

Neil walked away with his head held high. He didn't look at all like a man who'd been blasted. Fiona took that as a good sign, too.

"I'll wait out here," Eli told her. Fiona nodded and slipped into the room.

Di struggled to get down off the high bed.

"Hold on. Wait." Fiona rushed forward. "Sit still until I get all your stuff together."

"What was all that 'my girl' crap? Has Neil completely lost his mind?"

Evidently, Di's annoyance had returned, and it had her feeling moody. Fiona only shrugged at the questions.

"Damn, Fiona." Di tucked her grass-stained skirt between her knees. "You'd think we were engaged or something. I only went to dinner with the man. Talk about presumptuous."

"What can I say?" Fiona folded Di's sweater and tucked it into the plastic bag that the nurse had left them. "Some men become smitten faster than others."

This elicited a weary chuckle from Di. "You'd have been proud of me, Fiona. Although I was really firm about ending it, I was actually nice. I let him down very easy."

"I suspected as much." Fiona bent and slipped

Di's shoes onto her feet. "He wasn't clutching his private area when he walked out of here."

Di laughed again. "I even went so far as to tell him it wasn't him. It was me."

Telling a white lie to protect Neil's feelings. Wow, maybe Di really had learned a few lessons from all of this. Fiona tucked the paperwork and the envelope of medications into the plastic bag.

Sliding off the bed, Di swayed unsteadily on her feet. Fiona wrapped an arm around her friend's waist. "Whoa. Careful. Eli's right outside with the wheelchair." They started toward the door. "What about the flowers?"

"Leave them," she snapped. "I'm allergic to weeds."

Fiona didn't bother to curb her smile. Lessons were one thing, but she was happy to know Di didn't intend to completely stifle her feisty spirit.

A nippy breeze blew through the window she'd opened, but Di didn't have it in her to get up and close it. As fuzzy-headed as she felt, she should be sleeping. A dull ache throbbed in the middle of her forearm, the spot where the baseball bat had fractured her bone. However, the pain wasn't what kept her awake. She wished these thoughts would quit chasing through her head.

Her face-off with Jonni Jean had brought so many things into crisp clarity. Every swing of that bat had been an awakening. The very instant the wood had smashed against her arm, the agony had opened her eyes to the truth—she hadn't been a very nice person up to this point in her life.

Relief had flooded through her when she'd seen Jonni Jean's taillights departing. But as she had lain there on the ground, she'd thought about the people she'd used and abused, and it sickened her to know that she had never given them a second thought. To her, it had all been a game. A game she'd intended to win. As the police sirens got closer, she'd been aware of the pain in her arm, felt the coolness of the grass beneath her, the vibrations of Fiona's footsteps pounding across the ground toward her. Di had closed her eyes, finally comprehending the error of her thinking. People's lives where not something to play with.

The realization had prompted her to be completely honest with Fiona in the hospital. Well, almost completely honest. She hoped to God she never had to come totally clean. Leaden guilt gathered in her stomach.

There had been a hole in her heart for the past twenty odd years... ever since she'd left Hockessin, and Fiona, behind in order to go after the career she'd craved. But that hole had filled, had healed over beautifully during the six weeks she'd spent with Fiona.

Di had missed her best friend terribly, and she couldn't imagine not having Fiona in her life. She loved her. Would do anything for her.

Tears of remorse filled her eyes, fracturing the soft moonlight spilling into the bedroom. Di had never been a religious woman, but she prayed that Fiona would never discover her dirtiest secret of all.

Chapter Sixteen

Saturday Night Fever

"**D**o I have to wear these stupid gloves?" Sam snapped the latex encircling his wrist.

Fiona slipped on a fresh pair from the box. "You do. Who knows where those fingers have been?"

"You look cute in that hairnet, Sam."

"Shut up, Cassie." Then he muttered, "My butt is cuter than you."

Cassie pulled an ugly face and darted across the cavernous kitchen with a squeal when Sam lunged at her.

"Cut it out, you two. We came here to work, so let's get to it." Fiona went to the center island, where she'd placed a row of various-size baking pans and pie tins. "Sam, start buttering and flouring the cake pans like I showed you. Cassie, unload that box for Di."

"What's the matter, Di," Sam called down toward the other end of the room. "Your arm broke?"

Di stuck her tongue out at him and Fiona gave her son a playful smack on the arm. Right after the scary incident with Jonni Jean Bowers, everyone had tiptoed around Di. But the tension had loosened considerably during the five days that had passed, and now the kids were teasing her mercilessly. It just proved to Fiona that her children could endure a great deal more than she ever thought they could, and that hers was a family of survivors. It made her proud.

She couldn't believe that Cassie and Sam had agreed to give up their Saturday afternoon to help her. The owner of a catering company had called Fiona, asking if she could provide desserts for a Sunday brunch anniversary party. Apparently, the bakery shop owner they had contracted to do the job had suffered a death in the family and had been forced to fly out of town immediately. The money they had offered had made Fiona's mind reel. She knew her own small kitchen didn't have the equipment she'd need to complete the job. But she wanted that money. And even more, she wanted the challenge of providing dessert for those five hundred guests!

After making a few calls, she'd barely contained herself when the president of the local VFW Ladies Auxiliary had agreed to let her use the newly renovated kitchen in their lodge. After Fiona had explained her circumstances—that she was a single mother and a new business owner—the woman offered the use of the kitchen this once at no cost. Firecracker excitement had burst inside Fiona, but then she'd wondered how on earth she could do all the work herself. That's when her kids, and one-handed Di, had come to her rescue.

Fiona dumped butter and sugar into the mixer and set the beaters spinning.

It had been Cassie's offer that has shocked her the most. Since having been forced to reveal she'd gotten caught smoking, her daughter had been moody and on edge, as if she were anticipating and dreading an attack complete with a motherly lecture and some sort of punishment to go with it. Normally, that's exactly what Fiona would have doled out, but Di had assured her that Cassie would work this problem out. The girl was seventeen. Fiona couldn't trail around after her every minute, nor could she control her every move.

"You want all of these oranges zested?"

Fiona looked across the kitchen at Di. Cassie had washed the fruit and Di was doing her best to dry it.

"Yes. But only the orange part of the skin. The white pith is bitter. And I need the juice, too."

"Gotcha." Di reached into a bag, pulled out the grater Fiona had packed from home and handed it to Cassie.

Fiona cracked eggs into a bowl and then poured them into the lemony-colored creamed butter and sugar.

"Pans are ready," Sam announced.

"Think you can chop up the walnuts in the food processor? Just chopped, not pulverized."

Excitement gleamed in his eyes at the prospect of getting his hands on a piece of electrical equipment.

The four of them spent all afternoon and a good part of the evening measuring and whipping and cracking and stirring at a feverish pace. At the end of the day, Di supervised Sam by the sink where he washed bowls and pans and beaters and spatulas. It was Sam's least favorite job, but he was performing it with little complaint. Fiona would have to find some way to repay her kids.

"We did pretty good, huh?" Cassie sidled up to Fiona, who was wiping down the stainless steel countertop.

"We did better than good," Fiona told her daughter. Her hand stilled. "I can't tell you how much I appreciate your help."

Cassie nodded, looked away, then rolled the dish towel she carried in one hand around the fingers of the other. "I'm not a bad person."

The breath left Fiona in a soft rush and she straightened.

"I just wanted you to know that, Mom. I don't want you to think I'm some kind of scuz."

The appeal clouding her daughter's hazel eyes melted Fiona's heart.

"I would never think that."

"I told the girls I wasn't doing it anymore. You know, smoking. They made me sick to my stomach. Gave me a headache." The kitchen heat had her cheeks all rosy. "The cigarettes, not the girls. It was stupid. The whole thing. Emily said so. But..." She shrugged.

You needed to figure that out for yourself, Fiona wanted to say, but didn't dare. Her daughter was growing up before her very eyes, maturing, learning from her own mistakes. Pride washed over Fiona.

"I knew you'd do the right thing." It was only a tiny lie. The hours she'd spent worrying about her daughter buying and smoking cigarettes, and the trouble she could get into—not to mention the health risks—confirmed, at least in her own mind, that she hadn't really been certain. What mother could be?

"I just—" more fidgeting with the towel "—didn't want you to be mad at me."

"I'm not angry." And to prove it, she teased, "In fact, I'm relieved to hear you're not a scuz."

Cassie smiled then for the first time, and she inched forward. Her daughter's arms slipped around her, and Fiona basked in this loving moment of peace and harmony. It was wonderful. However, she wasn't stupid enough to think that another teenaged catastrophe wasn't lurking in the shadows... probably closer than anyone realized.

Fiona sat in the kitchen thumbing through a

magazine as she waited for the pizza bites to heat up in the oven. Di and Sam were watching the end of some silly sitcom on TV and she'd offered to make them a snack. Cassie had gone out to a movie with Emily and was due back before eleven.

The triumphant feeling Fiona had experienced at the VFW kitchen earlier that day continued to lift her spirits. She wondered if it was too early in the game to decide she really could make a go at this. The fact that eight out of ten small businesses failed mattered little to her at the moment. Fiona's Fabulous Confections would be a success. The giddy sensation in her gut told her so even though the voice of logic in her head warned her to keep her hope in check.

However, all she had left to do was fill and frost the cakes and deliver all the desserts by midmorning. Then she'd have that fat check in hand, secure in the knowledge that she'd completed the massive task she'd taken on. And she'd done it all on top of her regular baking. Damn, accomplishment felt good!

The phone rang, and her heart skittered a beat. Then anger knifed through her. If this wasn't a legitimate call she was going to be pissed. She wished whoever was calling the house and hanging up would just stop. It was irritating and frightening. Chad had suggested she change her phone number, but Fiona had had Cassie list it on the business cards she'd made on her computer, as well as all the advertising brochures they'd printed, so it just wasn't feasible to get a new number now.

She picked up the phone on the second ring. "Hello?"

"Fiona? George Harrigan here."

Surprise squared her shoulders. Hearing from her husband's friend and co-worker had been the last thing she'd expected on a Saturday night. "George. How are you?"

"Fine. Fine. I'm fine, Fiona."

A disconcerting anxiety crackled over the line. The buzzer sounded and she automatically moved to the oven and switched off the timer.

"How are you?" he asked. "How are the kids?"

"We're well. Really, we are. The kids have changed schools. They're going to Burlington High now, and they're thriving, George. They are." She paused, then instantly felt the need to fill the silence. "And I've started a business. I'm selling desserts. Pies, cakes, tortes. I had to do something to earn some income."

After a moment, he said, "I remember that

delicious strawberry pie I had at your house years ago. That's great, Fiona. I'm... happy for you."

The pitch of his voice clashed with the words he spoke. Her frown deepened. "George, what is it? What's wrong?"

"Fiona..."

The sound of dead air made her stomach clench. "George?"

"I, um... I, uh..." He heaved a sigh. "I saw Stan."

Fiona couldn't breathe. "What? Where? When?"

"This evening. Just a few minutes ago, in fact. Connie said I should call the police, but—"

"Was he okay? Did you talk to him?"

"No, I didn't talk to him."

"Why not? You're sure it was him?"

"I'm sure. He's grown a beard, lost a little weight, but it was Stanley, all right."

Her heart pounded furiously and blood whooshed through her ears, making her light-headed.

"Connie and I have a condo at the beach. We were down there this weekend. Ocean City is great this time of year. The tourists have gone home, but the weather's still nice."

"Maryland? Or New Jersey?"

"Maryland." He paused and gave a little cough to clear his throat. "We were on the boardwalk, and that's when I saw him. He seemed in a rush when he passed right by us. I told Connie I thought it was Stan—"

"You thought?"

"I'm sure it was him, Fiona. We followed him for several blocks. To a place called the Crooked Crab. It's a pub. A bar, really. A little hole-in-the-wall place. He's working there, I think."

"You went in? But you didn't talk to him? I don't understand. You saw him working?" She needed air. The questions were coming too fast.

"No. But he was wearing a T-shirt. You know, the kind with the business name and logo on it. A low-budget uniform, of sorts. And when he opened the door of the bar, I heard the people inside cheer his name, and I was a half block away."

Stan was alive and well and working in a bar in Ocean City, Maryland.

"Like I said, Connie thought I should call the police. But I started thinking about all you must have been through during these weeks, the anguish you and the kids suffered, and... well, it made me... angry. I felt you should be the first to know. So the minute I got back to the condo, I looked up your home number on the internet."

When she didn't respond, he added, "Fiona, on the ride back to my condo I thought of something. A conversation Stan and I had. Months ago. It was back in the spring, I think. I'd forgotten all about it. The office was in an uproar at the time."

CPA offices all across America were in an uproar during the hectic tax season.

"Stan and I were fantasizing about getting away from all the work and the irate people we deal with. He asked me where I would go... how I would do it. I told him I'd slip away to Ocean City in the off season. It would be a quiet place to hide. I never in a million years thought he'd do it. I feel awful thinking I planted the idea into his head."

Fiona didn't know what to say, but common courtesy urged her to somehow assuage his guilt. "Don't feel bad, George. Stan's an adult. He's responsible for his own choices."

"But he just left. You. And the kids. His job. His responsibilities." George's inhalation was tight. "Maybe Connie was right. Maybe I should have called the police and reported the bastard. Fiona, I'm sorry. I'm sorry this has happened, and I'm sorry I'm the one who had to bring you this news."

Silence stretched for several seconds. "I, um, I sure hope I did the right thing in calling you."

"Oh, yes, George. You did the right thing."

Her hands were trembling when she hung up.

"Show's over." Di breezed into the kitchen. "What happened to the snacks?" After one look at Fiona, she tensed with concern. "What is it? What's happened? Your face is ghost white. Who was that on the phone? Did something happen to Cassie?"

"Where's Sam?"

"Up in his room. Said he was going to answer email. Wha—"

"I've got to call Chad. And Cassie. She needs to come home to be with Sam."

"What is it, Fiona?"

"Stan's alive. We're going to Ocean City."

The words had barely left her mouth when the shrill of the smoke alarm made them both jump. The pizza bites were burnt to a blackened crisp.

The two-and-a-half-hour drive to Ocean City flew by. Fiona spent her time either ranting against her selfish-assed husband (when a person became this distraught, it became impossible not to cuss) or silently fuming. Chad had firmly insisted on driving them to the seaside town. He sat behind the wheel, unresponsive to her sporadic tirades. However, conducting herself like a true friend should, Di had sympathized or agreed with—and sometimes added to—every disparaging remark Fiona had spoken. Fiona's anger and indignation were white-hot by the time they'd passed the final ten miles of endless strip malls, restaurants, vacation homes, high-rise condominiums, fast-food joints, and mini golf courses that made up Ocean City.

Chad parked on a side street close to the address George had given them. Fiona unhooked her seat belt and opened the car door while the engine was still running, ready to find her husband and give him an earful. Feeling Chad's firm hand on her forearm made her roll back into the seat, irritated that he'd thwarted her forward momentum.

"I want you to take a deep breath, Fiona, and get yourself under control."

"I am under control." She forced the words through gritted teeth.

His hand remained latched to hers and his dark gaze sharpened. "I am not the enemy."

The firmly spoken words gave her pause and the

angry haze in her brain cleared a bit. "I know that, Chad. I do. And I may have given you a hard time about coming with us, but I really am glad you're here. I can use the support." Resentment boiled to the surface and she grumbled, "You can keep me from killing the worthless son of a bitch."

Tension thickened the air.

"That's not funny, Fiona."

Evidently trying to lighten the mood, Di chuckled. She scooted to the edge of the back seat. "Oh, now, lighten up, Chad. You know she's kidding."

But the strain remained.

"Fiona, my job has taught me that you can't barge into a situation with preconceived notions. You have to prepare yourself."

"Prepare myself?" She heard the resistance in her tone. "I think I'm quite prepared, thank you very much."

"What if he's not working in this bar? What if he won that T-shirt George Harrigan told you about in some contest or raffle? What if he found the damn thing? What if he's not even there? What if he recognized George and he's already left town? What if you walk in there and find that he's suffered some medical problem—a stroke or something—and he doesn't even recognize you?" Chad glanced out the windshield. "I listened to your tirade for a hundred miles, hoping you'd spew out all that anger and it wouldn't have such a strong hold on you once we arrived. But that hasn't happened. I have to warn you about facing your husband when you're not in your right mind."

Leave it to levelheaded Chad to bring her back to earth. He'd been an anchor through this whole disaster.

The overhead streetlamp threw shadows across the angles of his face. The seductive allure that crept between them, humming across her nerve endings, shouldn't have been there. Not now. Not when she was about to come face-to-face with Stan. But the complicated feelings seemed to have no concept of right or wrong, and, as always, they scared her just as much as they enthralled her.

Di placed her hand on the back of the front seat, and Fiona sat up straighter. Now was no time to get caught up in fantasy. Hard, cruel reality had to be dealt with.

"I'm okay," she told him, and Chad offered no resistance when she eased her arm from his grasp and got out of the car. All three car doors slammed shut. The auto-lock caused the car horn to toot.

"I thought George said the tourist season was over," Fiona commented, surprised by the sea of people cruising the boardwalk.

"They're probably weekenders." Di stood beside her.

Fiona nodded. "Like George and Connie, I guess. Come on. Let's find the Crooked Crab."

An autumn chill edged the salty breeze, and the muted sound of the surf was a constant backdrop to the squeals and laughter and conversations of the crowd. The three of them waded into the human current. It didn't take long to find the bar.

The glossy black door was propped open and music spilled out into the night. Fiona started for the entrance, but Chad's warm fingers encircled her wrist. Their gazes met.

"Remember," he gently warned, "no matter what we find in there, I want you to stay calm."

She took a moment just to breathe, and then she nodded.

The Crooked Crab was little more than a dive. A triangular stage was snuggled in one corner, where a live, four-member band played a rock-a-billy tune. Several couples danced on a small square of scuffed hardwood. A half-dozen tables surrounded the dance floor and more tables flanked one wall of the deep, narrow room. A bar ran the length of the back half of the opposite wall. People laughed and talked and drank and sang, living it up on Saturday night.

Fiona stood just inside the door, scanning the patrons and wait staff, while the music assaulted her ears. Disappointment swept through her.

"I don't see him," she shouted at Chad.

He pointed two sharp jabs toward the back of the bar and she wove her way through the throng. The walls were decorated with wire traps, fishing nets, a clam rake, old buoys, and antique fishing rods. Drunkenness had one man sitting at the bar bleary-eyed and swaying on the stool. Fiona's gaze bounced from one face to another, and that's when she saw him.

She stopped dead, her heart thudding a louder beat than the drummer in the band. Chad was so close she could feel the solid mass of him just behind her right shoulder.

"Okay, take it easy." Evidently, he'd seen Stan, too.

Emotion clogged her throat, so she simply nodded.

"Let me—"

She started forward, and the rest of Chad's

words were swallowed up by the music and the loud banter of the crowd. Her eyes locked on Stanley. His whole face lifted in merry laughter as he shared the punch line of a joke with a man sitting at the very end of the bar.

A young woman edged in front of Fiona and was elbowed out of the way. A chair scraped the floor when the woman grabbed it for balance. "Hey!" she complained, but Fiona ignored her.

Prepare yourself. Stay calm. Chad's words echoed through her mind.

She wanted to remain composed, truly she did. Somewhere in the very depths of her brain she was aware of Chad calling her name, but it was easy to disregard. Every step that took her closer to her husband brought to mind another misery she and her children had suffered since he'd been gone.

The dread that had filled her that first morning when she'd turned to see that his side of the bed hadn't been slept in.

The utter betrayal she'd felt when Karen Snow had arrived on her doorstep pregnant and claiming that Stan was the father.

The fear that had knotted in her stomach when they'd found his car, and his bloodstained briefcase—a fear that had never left her for a single moment.

The humiliated chastising she'd received from Shirley Bookerman.

The worry that had plagued her over their finances.

The trepidation she'd experienced when she'd enrolled the kids in public school.

The anxiety Sam had suffered when he'd first started at Burlington. The bullying he'd endured.

The peer pressure that had compelled Cassie to make some poor decisions—decisions she later regretted.

An all-consuming fury engulfed Fiona, beating back logic, crushing common sense, compressing her composure.

Everything around her seemed to shift into a lower gear. Stanley happened to glance her way. His blue eyes registered blatant surprise, his whiskered jaw tensed, his lips parted and formed her name.

The music amplified in her ears, jarring and garish. The fury raging through her was feverish, agonizing in its vehemence. Normally, Fiona didn't have a violent bone in her body. But something happened to her in that moment. She was overtaken by some sort of insanity. A stark, raving madness.

She flung an empty bar stool out of the way. Almost of its own accord, her hand balled and her arm swung in a wide arc. She made contact, cold-cocking Stanley square in the nose. He fell backward, sending a shelf of glassware and liquor bottles crashing to the floor.

A single act of aggression had never felt so good.

Chapter Seventeen

Crying Foul

A barrel-chested man charged out of a back room, seeming to size up the situation in an instant: Stan on his butt behind the bar and Fiona gingerly stretching her fingers, shaking off the pain of the punch. The man didn't seem the least bit fazed that a woman had been involved in the ruckus. Apparently, he'd seen too much to be surprised by anything.

He pointed his short, stubby index finger at Fiona and bellowed, "I'm callin' the cops, lady."

Chad flashed his badge, and sausage finger looked delighted.

"Arrest that woman," he demanded. "I own this place and I want her the hell outta here. But I want her name and address because she's gonna pay for these damages."

Stan slowly pulled himself to his feet and blinked, but he wasn't yet fully cognizant of what was going on. He touched his nose and sucked in his breath. He mumbled, "I think it's broken."

The kid behind the bar had to be twenty-one if he was serving liquor, but he didn't look a day over sixteen. He gave a toothy grin. "That woman knocked you on your ass, Stan."

All conversation at the back end of the bar had gone quiet, and everyone openly gawked, waiting to see what would happen next.

Stan shook off the fog and then touched his upper lip, staring at the blood on his fingertips. "Damn, Fiona. You broke my nose."

"You're lucky I didn't break your neck." She leaned forward and he took a backward step, glass crunching under his feet.

"Everyone needs to calm down." Chad put his hand firmly on Fiona's shoulder. "I mean it."

"I want you to arrest her," the owner of the bar said to Chad. "She can't just come in here and manhandle my people." His gaze jerked to Stan. "Wha'd you do, anyway?"

"I didn't do anything."

The man sitting at the bar who had been laughing with Stanley a moment before parroted, "He didn't do anything, Bud. I was sitting right here. That bitch just came up and popped him. Sucker punched him right in the face for no reason."

"Didn't do anything, my ass." Fiona shrugged out from under Chad's hand. "So you're a liar on top of being a deserter and a cheater, huh, Stan?"

Her husband's skin went pale and his guilty blue eyes slid from Fiona's. The kid behind the bar slipped a towel to Stan, who put a great deal of attention into cleaning up his fingers and face.

Chad approached the bar owner and introduced himself. "Could we use your back room for a few minutes?"

"Nobody goes in my office but me," Bud blustered. "I don't even know what the hell's going on, or who this woman is. The broad comes in here and socks my friend and then starts throwing accusations—"

"I'll be happy to tell you what's going on." Fiona pointed at Stan. "Your friend over there just happens to be my husband. Two months ago he decided to walk away from it all—me, the kids, his job, everything. I've had the Delaware State Police looking for him for weeks."

Bud shook his head. "No way. I can't believe—"

"Bud, wait." Stan shuffled out from behind the bar. "Let us use your office, okay? I do need to talk to them."

The owner of the bar glared at Stan, then heaved a sigh before heading toward the front of his establishment. Avoiding Fiona's stare, Stan looked at Chad and indicated the back office with a tiny tilt of his head before disappearing through the door. Chad, Fiona, and Di followed him.

The office was cramped, but adequate for their needs. Stan winced. "Hell, Fiona, I can't believe you broke my nose."

Determined to feel no sympathy, she leaned back against the filing cabinet and crossed her arms over her chest. "Quit whining. All I see is a little blood. You don't know that it's broken."

"So, Mr. Rowland—" Chad stepped forward "—am I correct in assuming that you left your home of your own accord? You weren't coerced or kidnapped? You didn't suffer any medical abnormality?"

"I left, yeah," Stan admitted.

"How could you do that?" Fiona threw her hands into the air. "You left the kids. Your job. Your *life*. You just walked out like it meant nothing."

"What I walked out on was our marriage."

She felt as if he'd slapped her. "You rotten son of a bitch."

"Maybe. Maybe so. But tell me something, Fiona. How long was I gone before you noticed?"

Guilt walloped her harder than a heavyweight's punch, but she refused to break eye contact with her husband. Anger made it hard to draw in a breath. "Your children's lives have been turned upside down."

"I'm sorry that I hurt Cassie and Sam. I've missed them terribly. I've called the house just to hear their voices."

Fiona muttered an obscenity and rushed at him, but Chad blocked her attack. "Those phone calls had the kids scared to death," she yelled, struggling to get at Stan.

"Stop," Chad ordered Fiona. "Just stop." Although she relaxed, his grip on her remained firm.

Chad stared at Stan, and Fiona could feel the

detective reining in the antagonism he felt toward her husband. He was good in a crisis, and she thanked her lucky stars he was on her side in this.

"I can't help but think there had to have been a better way to handle this, Mr. Rowland." His voice softened when he addressed Fiona. "I don't know that there's anything more we can do here. You know he's okay. He hasn't broken any laws. We should go before the Ocean City police get involved in this."

"But he abandoned his children," Di said, her hand on her hip.

"He left them in the care of their mother." Chad kept an eagle eye on Fiona as he loosened his grip on her. "That's not a crime."

"I refuse to allow you to push the blame on me." Fiona glared at Stan. "You ran away because your life was a mess. How could you sleep with a girl barely older than your own daughter?"

A deep V gouged Stan's brow.

"Oh, come on," Fiona ranted. "I know all about it. Karen Snow came to our house. Told me she was pregnant with your baby."

"I don't know what you're talking about. Karen is—"

"Damn it, Stanley. Be a man! Stop lying and take

responsibility for your actions. You've been sleeping around, having affairs. I know what you've done."

Stan's astonished gaze shifted to Di. "I can't believe you told her about that. You are such a bitch."

Fiona wasn't aware that earthquakes rocked Maryland's eastern seashore, but one was shaking her world to pieces at the moment.

Her husband's top lip was smudged with dried blood. "What happened between me and her meant nothing. It was years ago, Fiona. Before we were even married. You have to believe me. And when it happened she was the one who came on to me."

For an instant, Fiona thought her knees were going to buckle. *Stan and Di?* Fiona's mind reeled. "I was talking about Shirley Bookerman. I talked to her. Saw for myself what she feels for you."

Stan's complexion went downright cadaverous and it took him several seconds before he asserted, "I have not been unfaithful to you, Fiona." His gaze darted to Di. "What I mean is... I mean... not with anyone from my work." He rushed to add, "Or with any of my students."

Nausea churned Fiona's stomach. He was a lying

swine. He'd admitted deceit. She refused to believe a word he had to say.

"I have to get out of here. Right now." She brushed past Chad, took a single step and came nose to nose with the person who had claimed to be her best friend. She glared, unmoved by the tears sparkling in Di's big, blue eyes. "Hey, what do you know?" Her tone was nasty. Downright mean. And she didn't care. "You've been right all along. You really are a slut." Shoving open the office door, she stormed out.

"You idiot!" she overheard Di exclaim to Stanley.

Fiona snaked through the crowd, oblivious to the music and conversation.

"Hey, lady! What about those damages?" Bud called out to her when she reached the front door.

She only gave him a cursory glance and flipped him the bird. "Bite me, Bud." She stumbled out into the salty night air.

It had felt so good to belt Stan in the face. The lying cheat. She hoped she *had* broken his stupid nose. She rubbed her bruised knuckles as every detail of the upsetting exchange replayed in her mind. The memory of him shaking himself out of a daze she had induced was priceless.

But the knowledge of Di's betrayal banished even that small satisfaction.

The drive home was made in a stony silence the likes of which the world had never known. Only once had Di attempted to talk, and Fiona sharply warned that if another word was spoken Di would walk the hundred miles back to Hockessin. Di shut up.

Chad dropped them off at home just after one a.m., and the first thing Fiona had done was check on her children. Cassie and Sam were safe and asleep in their beds.

She hadn't told them where she'd been headed or why. She hadn't wanted them worrying. But now they'd need to be informed that their rat fink of a father was alive and well, and that he had decided to leave them high and dry while he partied it up down at the beach.

Of course, she couldn't use that particularly biased explanation. Hurting her kids was not an option, even if their father was a no-good son of a bitch.

Cassie and Sam had still been sleeping when she'd left the house this morning for the VFW. The sight of Di's fancy red sports car had made Fiona grind her teeth as she'd pulled out of the driveway.

Luckily, she'd had her work to keep her mind occupied. She'd spent the early morning hours putting the finishing touches on the desserts. Then she'd carefully loaded the cakes, pies and tortes into the van and transported them. Ultimately, it had taken two trips, but she'd delivered everything on time.

The extra check she'd walked away with no longer lifted her spirits to soaring heights; however, it did give her a small sense of relief. She needed some sense of security in this train wreck of a life she was living.

She pulled into the driveway around noon to find Sam cutting the grass. And she hadn't reminded him. Wonders never ceased. Cassie had written a note and left it on the kitchen counter, announcing she'd gone to the store with Di.

Fiona filled the kettle with water and was setting it on the stove to heat just as the phone rang. Well, one good thing had come out of all this, she thought, reaching for the telephone. This wouldn't be one of those silent calls. And she had little fear that the person on the other end of the line would be Stan, not after she'd shown him how angry she was last night. Warmth permeated her body when Chad asked her how she was doing.

"Things could be better." She leaned her hip against the kitchen counter. "But I've decided I'm going to live." He chuckled, and the sonorous vibration made her go all tight and needy inside.

"I never doubted it, Fiona. You're a strong woman." After a short pause, he asked, "How did Cassie and Sam take the news?"

"I haven't told them yet." She sighed. "It's sure not something I'm looking forward to. I don't know what to say or how to say it."

"You'll figure it out. No one knows your kids like you do. You're a great mom, Fiona."

She smiled. "I guess the case is closed?"

"Yes. It is. Or it will be once I file the final report tomorrow morning." He hesitated. "Fiona, I know you've been hurt by all of this. But I really do believe that this outcome—as angry and shocked and upset as it's made you— was better than it could have been."

Just thinking about sitting Cassie and Sam down and explaining a more ominous conclusion made her shiver. No mother wanted her children exposed to death.

"I agree. I do."

The sounds of footsteps and crinkling grocery bags made her swing her gaze to the kitchen door. She pushed herself away from the counter.

"Cassie just walked in," she told Chad. "I should go."

"Listen, um...before you hang up—"

Tentativeness was atypical for Chad.

"—I just want you to know that I'm here for you. If you, you know, need to talk or anything."

Her voice went silky with gratitude. "Thanks." She didn't trust herself to say anything more. She ended the call.

"Hey, Mom." Her daughter plopped the grocery bag onto the island countertop.

Di followed on Cassie's heels, and Fiona's whole body tensed at the sight of her. Di's eyes jumped from the bags, to the floor, to the window, taking in everything but Fiona.

"I ran out of—" Cassie's voice dropped to a whisper "—tampons." She pulled a box of cereal from the bag. "Di offered to take me to the store. We were out of milk and Cheerios this morning, so I picked some up while we were there."

"Thanks, hon." Fiona automatically took the milk out of the bag and headed toward the fridge. "Would you run out and get Sam for me?"

Cassie closed the pantry door. "He'll be in soon. He's nearly finished cutting the grass."

That was the trouble with kids who started taking on more responsibility. They tended to stop doing as they were told.

Fiona paused with her hand on the refrigerator handle. "Cassie, go get your brother. I need to talk to you both." Cassie's bouncy attitude vanished. She stared at her mother. "I'll be right back."

A thick awkwardness descended once Fiona and Di were alone. Di moved farther into the room and set another grocery bag onto the counter.

"Fiona, I—"

"You didn't say anything to Cassie about Stan, I take it."

Di mouth flattened and she shook her head. "I'm smart enough to figure out that that's your job."

"Damn right it is." She put the milk away and shut the door. "I need some time alone with my kids."

For a second it seemed that Di intended to argue, but then she turned to leave. At the threshold, she paused. "I thought about packing my bags and heading home. But I decided against that. I'm not leaving for good until we talk." Di closed the door behind her.

Fiona shoved the female Judas from her mind. She had bigger fish to fry right now.

The teakettle began to whistle when her kids filed into the kitchen. She poured boiling water into a mug. "Anyone want a cup of tea?"

"No, thanks." Sam went to the sink to wash his hands. "But I would like a Coke."

"Sure, son. I'll get it."

Sam turned off the faucet. "Whoa. Mom." He pulled off a paper towel and wiped his hands dry. "Soda in the morning? You gave in way too easy on that one. What's up?"

"I told you, Sam," Cassie said. "Something's wrong." She looked at her mother. "They found Dad, didn't they? He's dead. They found his body." Tears welled in her eyes.

"No. No. That's not it at all." Fiona handed her son the cold can of soda from the refrigerator. "Sit down. Both of you."

The three of them settled around the kitchen table. Fiona wondered where to start, what to say.

"The news is good actually," she began. "We did find your dad, and he's alive. And well."

"He's okay?" Skepticism strained Sam's young face.

She reached out and touched his arm. "He's okay."

"He's okay," Sam repeated.

The news was sinking in. Fiona nodded.

Cassie slapped her palms down on the table. "Then where the hell has he been?"

"I'm not sure." She wanted to be honest without revealing her own personal feelings. "All I know is that he was in Ocean City last night. That's—"

"That's where you went last night with Chad and Di?" Sam asked.

Before she could answer, Cassie huffed, "He's at the beach? He walked out on us and went to the beach?"

"Now, hold on." Fiona tried hard to keep calm. "You should know that your father is very sorry for upsetting you. He was very clear last night that it was me he needed to get away from, not you two."

Cassie rose from the chair so quickly that the wooden legs grated against the floor. "How fucking rude!"

Shock made Fiona's jaw go slack. "Cassandra Diane!"

"I hate him!" She raced away, down the hall and up the stairs, screaming that she hated his guts and never wanted to see him again. Her bedroom door slammed hard enough to rattle the ceiling beams.

Sam hadn't touched his soda. Trouble brewed in his blue eyes. "Is he coming home, Mom?"

Fiona lifted her hands. "I don't know, honey. I honestly don't know."

Later that afternoon, Fiona slid two cakes into the oven. Sunday was a slow day, as several of the restaurants she baked for were closed on Mondays. She set the timer and looked out the window to see Di awkwardly wielding the bamboo rake in her one good hand in an attempt to gather up grass clippings and the leaves that had begun to fall from the trees.

Fiona went out the door and crossed the lawn.

Di wore her guilt like a horsehair shirt. "Hey." Clearly, Fiona's appearance surprised her.

"You don't have to do that." Fiona clipped the words. "In fact, you probably shouldn't be doing it with that arm." She turned to go back into the house.

"Fiona, please. Talk to me. I'm going nuts."

Fiona whirled on her. "You want me to feel sorry for you? To take pity on you? To care about you?"

She shook her head. "Aw, isn't it a shame? Poor Di's going nuts. Poor Di wants to talk. Poor Di wants to lie her way out of another mess." Oh, crap. She was acting like a seven-year-old, but she couldn't help it.

She held her hands out, fingers splayed wide. "You've done a lot of low-down things in your life, but not in my deepest, darkest, wildest nightmare could I have ever imagined that you would betray me like this."

Di planted the rake on its tines, her face scrunched and pale. "I'm sorry. I'm sorry I hurt you."

"No, you're not. You're sorry you got caught."

"It happened a long time ago, Fiona."

"And that's supposed to make it better? Make it hurt less? If anything, it makes it worse. You kept this from me for over twenty years, Di." Her eyes went narrow and her tone scathing. "Oh, how you must have gloated."

"I did no such thing." Di's hand slid several inches down the rake handle. "I'd slept with my best friend's fiancé. I was ashamed. Mortified. Why do you think I packed my bags and left town? I couldn't face you."

Overwhelming emotions roiled in Fiona. Her

voice was whispery when she asked, "Why? Why would you do it?"

Di's eyes rolled closed and she heaved a sigh. "I don't know. I don't know! Oh, shit," she said on a heaved sigh. "Of course I know."

It took a moment before she could look Fiona in the eye. "I was jealous. Of all you had. Of all you'd accomplished. You had some college under your belt. Not some piddling business school certificate, but real credits from a real university. You'd met a guy you loved. A guy who adored you. You were planning to have kids and a house with the white picket fence. Damn it, you were on your way to having it all." Di shifted her cast. "Can't you understand that I was lime-green with envy? I just wanted a small taste of—"

"So you slept with Stan?" It baffled the hell out of Fiona, and infuriated her. "I don't believe you were jealous. I believe you wanted to ruin things for me."

"That is not true."

"You've never been able to stand it if the spotlight wasn't blaring right on you. I had found a little bit of happiness, and you had to try to wreck it. You might as well admit it."

Di pressed her lips together, condemnation

weighing heavy on her. She swallowed. "I'm not that person any longer."

Fiona's brows arched and her gaze shifted pointedly to Di's broken arm.

Big, watery tears turned Di's eyes a crystalline blue. "Shit," she breathed. "I don't want to be that person anymore. I don't like that person."

"Yeah, well, right now I don't like that person very much, either." Fiona turned and stalked back toward the house.

Chapter Eighteen

Men

Fiona had lost her mind. That had to be true. Why else would she be standing outside the door of Chad's apartment at nearly eleven o'clock at night?

She'd been feeling out of sorts and restless at home. The kids had been subdued since she'd told them about their father this afternoon. Cassie and Sam had barely touched their dinner, and they'd both holed up in their rooms for the duration of the evening.

Anger was like an acid, and it was eating Fiona alive. She could think of little else except what

Stan had done. To all of them. He'd claimed he'd walked away from Fiona, but she hadn't been the only one affected by his actions. The lives of her children had been completely upended during the last two months. Resentment burned inside her, bonfire hot.

She'd paced the house, frantic to clear her husband from her thoughts so she could get some rest. However, if Stan wasn't plaguing her, then backstabbing Di was.

Many times in the past, Di had shown her underhanded ways. During their senior year of high school, Di had stolen Fiona's homework so she could copy it. When she'd gotten caught red-handed by the teacher, Di refused to fess up to thieving, but had instead let Mrs. Buck believe that Fiona was in on the scheme. And, unable to bring herself to out Di, Fiona had kept her mouth shut and had served a week's worth of detention for her trouble.

Incident after incident had rolled through Fiona's mind, until she felt as if the walls were closing in on her. If she hadn't left the house, she'd have crawled out of her skin.

Sam had already fallen asleep, but Cassie was still up. Fiona told her daughter she was going for a short drive and wouldn't be gone long. Although it was unusual for Fiona to leave the house this late at night, Cassie hadn't commented.

With her shoulders square, Fiona rapped on Chad's door.

It took a few long, stomach-sinking moments before she heard the thunk of the dead bolt, and then he pulled open the door.

Just seeing him was like inhaling a deep breath of fresh air.

Concern darkened his brown eyes. "You okay?"

She shook her head, noticing how the muted light turned his hair golden. He was shirtless and his jeans rode low on his hips. His feet were bare. During their day hiking in the park, she'd already noticed he was muscular, but his broad chest with its short, springy blond hair made her fingertips itch to touch him. She shifted the strap of her purse just to have something to do with her hands.

"Come in," he said, stepping back so she could enter.

He closed the door behind her and followed her into his living room.

"I was having a beer. You want one?"

She nodded, and the instant he disappeared from sight, she headed down the hall in search of his bedroom as if it were a common, everyday occurrence.

The room was neat, just as she'd imagined it would be. The air held his scent. She placed her purse on the dresser, then went over and sat on the wide mattress.

Nearly a full minute passed before he appeared in the doorway.

"Fiona?" He carried a dark green beer bottle in each hand.

"When we were at the park, and things got... and I told you that I couldn't... and I stopped it..."

He set the bottles next to her purse and approached the bed. He grinned. "You stopped it, all right. You ran away from me."

The simmering silence seemed to have an audible resonance. He was waiting for her to smile, but she couldn't. Her emotions were too overwhelming. She reached out and took hold of his fingers. It was the scariest—most freeing—thing she'd ever done. "I was afraid of what I was feeling for you. I felt all chained up by... circumstances." She swallowed. "But I'm not running now."

He sat next to her, and she murmured, "I'm sorry I made you open those." Her glance darted toward the dresser and then back at him. "It's not beer I want."

The statement obviously pleased him.

"I guess breaking a man's nose can be liberating for a woman."

She grimaced. "Do you really think I broke it?"

The delight glimmering in his eyes was answer enough. He ran the back of his fingers along her jaw.

She closed her eyes. "I've been miserable. Hurt, confused, enraged." He cupped her face and she pressed her cheek to his palm. "You make me feel... good. I need to feel good, Chad."

He skimmed his lips against her neck and a groan rumbled deep in her throat. His kisses were feather-light and luscious. She kissed him back, nibbling, tasting. It had been too long since she'd wanted a man this badly. She whispered his name.

"Shh." No hint of reproof tinged his voice. It was more a melodic response that was followed by another kiss, this one deep and exploring.

Fire flickered in her belly. He ran his hands down her arms, his fingertips tickling the insides of her wrists, and then he fumbled with the hem of her sweater until he'd succeeded in pushing the knitted cotton up far enough that he could touch bare skin. The heat of flesh on flesh made her burn hotter.

With a sigh of pleasure, she touched him, smoothing her hands over hard, bunched muscles. When her fingers settled on the fly of his jeans, she was surprised by how easy it was to unfasten. She sat back when he stood to kick his way out of his trousers. Caught up in anticipation, she tugged her sweater over her head and flung it to the floor. Then he was beside her again, hugging her to him, pulling her down onto the mattress, their hearts beating, their breath, and lips, and tongues intermingling.

The desire pulsing through her brought a delicious giddiness rippling through her body. She smiled. Kissed him deeply. Then, shoving her hair out of her eyes, she whispered, "You can try to kiss me senseless, but I'm still worried about the age difference between us."

He chuckled. "Are you kidding me? You should count yourself lucky that you've snagged a young, sex-loving stallion like myself."

He rolled so that he was on top of her. She curled her arms around his neck, teasing him with an alluring look. He smoothed her hair back, tickling her ear with a light touch. His kiss was hot and sweet. Desire smoldered in his dark eyes, tensed his face. "Tell me you're doing this for the right reason."

The request rattled her. "What do you mean?"

"When you ran away from me in the park you used our ages as an excuse, but there were other reasons. Other problems. Lots of them."

What he said was true.

"The problems haven't been solved," he whispered. "But you're here. In my bed."

His tender caress of her breast was distracting.

"I just need to know that you're here because you want to be. Because you want to be with me."

She reached up and ran her finger over his full bottom lip. "Of course that's what I want. Why else would I be here?"

He stared for a moment. "Revenge," he gently suggested. "Against your husband."

"I wouldn't do that." Her voice was soft and sincere. "I wouldn't."

He smiled and kissed her bare shoulder, ready to believe her.

"I'm not going to lie. Angry doesn't even begin to describe how I feel about what he's done. I don't think I can ever forgive him. He's hurt the kids. And me."

Chad eased down next to her on his side. He bent his elbow and cradled his head in one hand, the other nestled on her stomach, his middle finger tracing her belly button.

"He's been unfaithful at least once." She raised one arm, relaxing it on the bed above her head. "With Di."

Bitterness surged, but she did her best to tamp it down.

"In all our years of being married," she continued, "I've never known Stan to lie to me. And that's what has me so confused. That he said he didn't mess around with Karen Snow." She shifted, her hip nudging Chad's flat belly. "He insinuated that he hadn't messed around with anyone but Di." She frowned. "If that's so... if he wasn't worried about facing problems with other women... then why would he just pick up and leave like that?"

She was oblivious to the shifting of weight on the mattress. "Was I such a lousy wife that he had to run off?"

Every fiber in her being screamed against making such an admission, but then she remembered voicing regrets to Di weeks ago. Remembered wishing she'd been a more attentive spouse. Taking the blame for an unhappy marriage hadn't been difficult when she'd thought Stan might be dead. Now, though, it wasn't so easy.

Could her husband have left her because she hadn't been a good wife?

She moistened her lips nervously. Shame barraged her when she realized she'd asked herself that question while lying half-naked in another man's bed.

The sound of a metal zipper made her sit up. She hadn't even realized Chad had gotten up. "What are you doing?"

"Getting dressed." He sighed.

She suffered a second assault of guilt when she saw the disappointment on his face. Coming here had been a huge mistake.

"Chad, I—"

"Don't, Fiona. Don't say anything." He hooked his thumb in his pocket. "You need to go home now. You also need to talk to your husband."

Teens could be intuitive creatures. When Cassie and Sam arrived home from school Monday afternoon, they took one look at their mother and knew something was awry.

"Your dad called," Fiona admitted. "He's coming to pick up some things."

Ire jutted her daughter's chin. "Well, I'm not going to be here when he comes. Take me to Emily's."

"I'm not taking you anywhere."

"Then Emily's mom will come and get me."

"There's no time." Fiona folded the tea towel in her hands. "Besides, I think both of you should be here. You have to face him sometime. You might as well make it sooner rather than later."

"Mom! I don't want to see him. I don't care if he falls off the face of the earth. I hope he—"

"Cassie, spare me the drama, okay? Just this once? He's coming, and you're going to be here, and that's that."

Highly insulted, her daughter clamped her mouth shut. Fiona looked at her son. "You okay?"

He shrugged, and she had to force herself not to reach out and ruffle his hair. Leave it to easygoing Sam to take all this in stride.

The doorbell rang, and Cassie said, "I'll be in my room."

Fiona nailed her with a look scary enough to stop her in her tracks. "You'll stay right here. In fact, why don't you make a pitcher of tea?"

As she headed down the hall, she heard her daughter grumble, "He can die of thirst for all I care."

Something told Fiona this was not going to be a pleasant visit.

Her anxiety over how her children were going to handle seeing their dad had preoccupied her to the point that she hadn't had a chance to give her own feelings any thought. The anger purling in her hadn't abated a bit. She felt bitter and resentful toward Stan—incensed by what he'd done to their family—and at this point, she had no idea how to even begin to get over those feelings.

She might feel angry, roaring angry, but she refused to lose control in front of her kids. And that's what this moment was about. Helping Cassie and Sam through the difficulties of their father's reentry into their lives. Fiona pulled open the door.

The white nasal splint was the first thing she saw. Then she noticed the bruises at the inside corners of both his eyes. Although he was clean-shaven and dressed in the business suit he must have been wearing the day he walked off, his appearance still managed to shock her. He looked like a man who'd been mugged. And he had been—by her. But it hadn't been his wallet she'd wanted. What she'd intended to rob him of was his dignity.

She had no desire to celebrate her victory, but she still couldn't bring herself to feel remorseful, either.

"You could have just come in," she told him.

"I thought it would be better to ring the bell." He stepped into the foyer. "For everyone."

"The kids are in the kitchen. Go on back."

"Is that Di's flashy car out there in the driveway?"

She didn't want to talk to him about Di, so she ignored his question.

He slowed down. "Listen, Fiona, I had to use the credit card. I needed money to get home."

She only nodded. Looking at him, she felt her anger rising. She turned and walked to the kitchen. "Kids," she said as cheerfully as possible, "look who's here."

Stan scuffed into the room, appearing wary. "Hey, guys. How's it going?"

Cassie stood next to the refrigerator, her tightly crossed arms shutting him out, her gaze directed at the floor. There was no indication that she was even aware of her father's presence.

Sam's fists were buried deep in the pockets of his

baggy jeans. He nodded at his dad awkwardly, his expression a conglomeration of troubled emotion.

The silence felt clumsy and uncomfortable.

"How are things at school?" Stan tried again.

Sam's Adam's apple bobbed when he swallowed, and he looked pleadingly at her.

Fiona rested her hand on the corner of the cabinet. "The kids are going to Burlington High now. It was a little rocky at first," she said, "but they're both doing well."

"I'm, ah, I'm surprised the kids changed schools." Defensiveness reared its ugly head. She didn't want to respond. What she wanted to do was to call him vile names and toss a few steak knives in his direction. Instead, she gritted her teeth.

"Stan, we had no income. I had to do something to cut the budget." The words came out sounding pleasant enough, but inside she seethed.

"There was money in sav—"

"I don't think we should do this now, do you?"

"You're right," he said. "We can talk about it later. What's important is that the kids are okay."

"No thanks to you," Cassie spat out. She hadn't moved, hadn't looked at her father, but continued to stare a hole in the floor.

Silence stretched out like a thick, cumbersome rubber band.

Sam asked his dad, "So what happened to you?"

"Oh, this?" Stan reached up and gingerly touched the end of his nose. "I had, um, a little accident. I'll be fine."

"Isn't that just too bad?" Cassie aimed a hateful glare directly on her father.

"Cassie," Fiona warned.

"It's okay, Fiona." Stan turned his attention to his daughter. "I understand that you're angry. And it's okay. You have every right to be upset with me."

He took a hesitant step toward her, then he stopped. "Look," he said, gazing from his daughter to his son, "I know you're both unhappy with me. I know you probably need some time to get used to... everything that's happened. But I want you to remember one thing. I love you both. Very much. It may not look like it from where you're standing, but it's the truth."

He pulled a slip of paper from his pocket and set it on the table. "Here's the address where I'm staying. I'm going to see about getting a new cell phone. Until I do, you can use the number there under the address. Call me if you need me. Any time of the day or night. I know this is a lot for you to deal with. But nothing good can happen unless we start talking to each other, right?"

Fiona got the distinct impression her husband was including her in that "we."

"I know it's going to take some time. I can be patient." Stan then looked at Fiona. "I'm going upstairs to pack some things."

She continued to chew her top lip while she nodded.

Alone with her children, Fiona nervously tried to assess how they were handling this thorny situation.

Cassie stalked to the table and picked up the paper her father had placed there. "Well, we might as well throw away this piece of trash."

"You will do no such thing."

"He's a jerk, Mom," she huffed.

"You will not talk about your father like that, young lady." Sheesh, how long had it been since she'd called her daughter that? "I understand that you don't like what he's done, but he's still your father."

"He left us." Sam shifted his weight from one foot to the other.

"He didn't leave you, Sam. I already explained that. He left me."

"He left us, too." Antagonism contorted Cassie's face.

Now it was Fiona's turn to cross her arms over her chest. "Okay, you two. Here are the facts. Your dad was gone. And now he's back. He was your dad the two months he was gone from your lives, and he's your dad now that he's home. That hasn't changed. It isn't going to change. So get over yourselves and try to find some way to forgive him. All I can tell you is, you're going to have to work to find some middle ground."

Cassie was clearly exasperated. "How can you take his side? After all he's done."

"I'm not taking his side. I'm not taking anyone's side. I'm trying to deal with this the best way I can. And the only thing I know to do is deal with the facts."

"Okay, so the fact is he's our dad," Cassie said. "But he's your husband."

Her daughter's statement held a huge measure of accusation.

"Listen to me, both of you, because what I'm about to say is very important." She tried to keep the sharpness from her tone, but knew she failed miserably. Usually her motherly lectures were delivered with an abundance of nurturing love and caring, but this little sermon would be interpreted as nothing but blunt. However, she couldn't help that. Her kids needed to face reality. "Every day, married couples all over this country decide they can no longer live together. There are thousands of reasons why couples separate. Now, I'm not a clairvoyant. I have no idea what's going to happen with my relationship with your father, and at this point, I wouldn't even try to guess. But the cold, hard reality that both of you must deal with is that children do not have the luxury of divorce."

Chapter Nineteen

Cutting a Gordian Knot

One week rolled into two, and early November sang with the rich, vibrant colors of autumn. Fiona never ceased to be amazed that life continued its forward trek, dragging innocent bystanders along by the scruff of the neck, no matter what obstacles were tossed onto the path.

Who was she kidding? She certainly wasn't blameless, and by no means a mere spectator in the tangled quagmire her family was involved in. However, she tried to push away her feelings of condemnation. She'd slipped outside to the front porch with a cup of chamomile tea to coax her body to calm and to wait for what she knew was coming.

The day's baking was finished, the kids were settling in for the night—Cassie finishing up a reading assignment, Sam studying for tomorrow's history quiz—and all Fiona wanted to do was relax. Although one quick glance at the fire-red sports car that had been sitting in the driveway for the past several hours placed grave doubts on a tranquil evening. But Fiona refused to go looking for trouble.

Herb-laced steam drifted from the mug as she took a sip.

True to his word, Stanley continued to practice patience with the kids. He called the house a couple of times a week and spoke with Sam. Although she was no longer blatantly disrespectful toward her father, Cassie diligently sustained her ironfisted hold on obstinate rejection. However, Stan continued to reach out.

Only once had he asked Fiona if she was ready to talk. Her face had flushed and her jaw had tightened, and her husband had looked a little worried before changing the subject entirely. She wasn't proud of her inability to forgive, wasn't proud that she couldn't even bring herself to discuss it. Every time she remembered the horror of thinking him hurt, maimed, dead, no amount of talk would whitewash it.

Fiona cupped the mug with both hands and took a slow, deep breath, grappling for some small measure of peace.

Several days after their Ocean City adventure, Fiona noticed that Di had left. Her car was gone from the driveway and the guesthouse windows remained dark. Fiona had sent Cassie over to pull the sheets off the bed, but her daughter had returned empty-handed, reporting that many of Di's things were still in the apartment. So Fiona decided to just leave it be. Di would show up for her belongings, eventually.

Cassie had commented on the apparent rift between the friends.

"We had an argument," was all Fiona had said.

"Must have been a helluva fight." One laser-eyed look from Fiona had Cassie waving her hands. "Okay, okay. Consider it dropped."

Fiona had been experimenting with a new recipe late this afternoon when Sam had come into the kitchen from school and announced that Di's car was sitting in the driveway. Curiosity had trounced her hostility a couple of times over the course of the evening, and Fiona had peeked out the window to see Di loading small boxes into her car.

Di's threat not to leave for good until they had talked made Fiona resigned to the notion that she'd be entertaining a visitor before the night was over.

It wasn't too long before notion became reality. From where she sat on the front porch, Fiona heard the door of the garage apartment close, then Di's shoes clicked down the long, wooden staircase. A sprawling red maple obscured Fiona's view from where she sat. The blonde appeared out of the darkness and paused at the base of the porch steps, carting a bottle of champagne in her good hand and awkwardly balancing two long-stemmed glasses in the other.

"There's going to be a celebration tonight." The brightness in Di's tone was fool's gold false. She tromped up the steps and set the glasses on the side table at Fiona's elbow. "But I fear that only one of us is going to end up making merry." She wrangled with the wire netting that covered the bottle's knobby cork. Her bum arm didn't seem to hinder her too much. "It all depends on the outcome of our conversation, you see."

Anxiety tightened the air, but Fiona couldn't say which of the two of them was more nervous.

Di set the wire on the wide porch railing and then began wiggling the cork back and forth. "You could wind up commemorating the end—" the bottle opened with a loud pop "—of a lousy friendship." She picked up a glass, tipped it at an angle to fill it with the bubbling wine, and handed it to Fiona.

Surprising even herself, Fiona silently set her mug on the porch railing and accepted the flute.

While pouring a glass for herself, Di continued, "Or I could toast its rebirth. Let's see where this thing goes, shall we?"

The heavy bottle thumped onto the side table.

"First off, let's drink to the girlfriends we were. What we had deserves that much, at least, don't you think?"

Fiona leaned forward. "Di, I—"

"I'm not talking about last week, or last month, or even five or ten years ago," Di hastily interrupted. "I'm talking about when we were girls. We were real friends then, Fiona. True friends, weren't we?"

Unable to say if it was due to Di's palpable desperation or the rush of warmth that hit her when she thought about their childhood friendship, Fiona nodded. She couldn't deny that it was impossible to reflect on her adolescence and not experience tender thoughts of Di.

"Okay, then. We're in agreement about that, at least." Di held her glass aloft. "To the girlfriends we were."

The sweet champagne fizzed on Fiona's tongue, and she lowered the glass, only to watch Di empty hers in a long series of swallows.

Di scooted the empty wicker chair forward so that, when she sat, her knees were nearly touching Fiona's. Then she promptly grabbed the champagne bottle and refilled her glass.

Her breath left her in a small rush. "Now what I've been trying to figure out for the past couple of weeks is why the hell you would spend so many years being friends with a dip-shit like me."

Di's self-deprecating statement disarmed Fiona. She had expected an apology—an apology she'd had no intention of accepting.

The base of her glass tipped as Di drank deeply again. "I mean, let's face it, I'm selfish. Egocentric. I'm underhanded and manipulative. There are times when I'm downright rude, and I cuss like a damn trucker." She slapped a hand over her mouth and shook her head. Her voice lowered. "I really did try hard to watch my language around the kids while I was staying here, Fiona. I swear I did."

The mention of Cassie and Sam made her brow pucker. "How are the kids, by the way? I've been worried sick."

Di's honest concern for her children moved Fiona. "They're fine."

"Do they know? About..." Her lips pressed together, as if speaking that name would set her tongue aflame. "Him?"

Fiona nodded. "He stopped by to pick up some of his things and he tried to talk to them."

Leaning forward, Di asked, "Were you okay?"

The trepidation in the question almost made Fiona smile. "You mean, did I attack him? Did I dislocate his shoulder? Stab him in the gut?" She smoothed her hand down the arm of the wicker chair. "I was able to keep my cool."

"So is he back in town for good? Or did he return to the beach?"

"He's here. He's living in an efficiency apartment in the city. He talks to Sam on the phone a couple of times a week. Cassie won't have anything to do with him. But Sam tells me his father has a new job, and that once the paperwork is finalized, Cassie and Sam will have insurance coverage again."

It felt good to talk to someone. There was only so much Fiona could tell the kids. She couldn't burden them with unnecessary worry.

"I know that's been a heavy load on your mind. What about you? Will you have coverage?"

Fiona lifted one shoulder. "As long as I'm his wife, I guess."

They fell quiet, the sound of tree frogs and crickets taking over.

Di drank another big swallow of champagne and then settled the base of the glass on her lap. "Are you going to leave him?"

"Can't do that when he's already left me."

"I guess what I meant was... are you going to divorce him?"

"I thought for sure that's what he wanted. I mean, he left out of the blue. Didn't tell a soul where he was. And when I found him, he confessed that he didn't want to be married to me anymore." Fiona looked across the lawn, studied the long shadows of the trees and bushes thrown by the silvery moonlight. "But he's been doing the strangest thing."

Di was silent, waiting.

"For the past two weeks, he's deposited money into our joint checking account."

Stan had always been generous to a fault. It had been one of the characteristics that had attracted Fiona in the beginning. Her father had been so stingy with his money, with his time, with his love. Stanley hadn't a selfish bone in his body. At least, she hadn't thought so until the day he'd up and walked out on them all.

"And it's a significant amount. He has to be keeping some of his paycheck for himself. He's got rent to pay, and he has to eat and keep gas in his car. But I think he's giving us the bulk of his earnings."

"Is he making any withdrawals? Writing any checks? Using the ATM machine?"

Fiona shook her head.

A puzzled look stole over Di's face. "Why would he do that? It makes no sense. He left you." She shrugged. "Unless he's changed his mind and wants to come home."

Fiona shook her head emphatically. "A man who wants to stay married doesn't walk out on his family."

The unmitigated truth killed the subject and they lapsed into silence once again.

"I sold my house in Philly," Di told her quietly.

Uncertain how she should respond, Fiona kept silent.

"I got a job. In Wilmington. It's just a small ad firm. But I think I can use some of the techniques I learned at Roche to help this business grow." Her inhalation was ragged with stress and her eyes filled with tears. "Fiona, I did an awful thing to you. I know you'll probably never be able to forgive me. And I came here to say... to tell you... that it's all right. If you need to cut the strings of our friendship, I understand. I won't like it, but I will understand." She shook her head, her wide mouth frowning. "I've been a lousy friend. A complete failure."

This wasn't the Di that Fiona was used to seeing. Where was the confidence? The bravado? This humble, self-effacing woman was a total stranger.

Something provoked Fiona to murmur, "You haven't been a complete failure, Di."

Di paused long enough to swallow. "Don't say nice things you don't mean, Fiona. You're the one person in the world who knows the real truth about the kind of person I am."

In an instant, Fiona felt as if she were riding a

merry-go-round of memories. She reached out, on a lark, and grabbed a golden ring.

"Remember when we were freshmen," she began, "and I had a crush on Adam Durkin? I tried for weeks to get his attention, and when I finally did, he acted obscene and insulting."

Di sat utterly still.

"You were more pissed than I was." Fiona lifted the champagne glass and sipped. "You started sticking wads of chewing gum to the door of his locker. Every time we passed you'd add another gooey gob. By the end of the week, the door was covered. Pink and gray and green and purple and blue globs. It was disgusting." The smile that curled Fiona's mouth was small, but it was a smile nonetheless.

"He was a real jerk. Someone had to do something to put him in his place."

Quietly, Fiona commented, "That someone wasn't a lousy friend."

Di suddenly looked small, her face brimming with emotion.

"And then there was the time," Fiona continued, "when we were at your aunt's house and I wanted to shave my legs. I cut a deep gash in my shin, carved a hunk of skin right off it. Viv didn't have

Band-Aids, so you walked all the way to the pharmacy and—" her lips twitched "—brought back antibiotic ointment and some gauze pads."

A groan ripped through the still air. "Don't use that example. I was a thief. I shoplifted that stuff."

The memory amused Fiona. "I know that. And I knew it then. You had no money, so you had no choice. It might not have been the wisest thing to do, but you wouldn't have done it if you'd been a lousy friend. You risked getting caught stealing... for me." With barely a pause, she said, "Then there was the time I inserted a tampon and the string came off right in my hand. We didn't know if it would work its way out or if I had to go fishing. So you phoned my doctor and pretended to be me because I was too embarrassed to call. A lousy friend wouldn't have done that, either.

"And what about all those times when I got in trouble or felt blue and Dad would get all hard-assed and refuse to let you sleep over? You'd stay on the phone with me literally all night long." Her eyes suddenly burned. "If I woke up, all I had to do was press a number, and soon you were right there with me again."

Tenderness softened Di's countenance. "You did the same for me lots of times."

They'd been two girls with little in common.

"You need another one?" Fiona asked. "How about the time our chorus teacher had us put on that performance after school and my father didn't show. I sat on the curb out in the parking lot afterward bawling my eyes out. You never said a word. Just held me tight and kept offering me tissues." Her voice was husky. "A lousy friend? I don't think so.

"And when you learned that Stan was missing, you didn't hesitate. You showed up on my doorstep with a box of Krispy Kremes."

Two girls who'd been deprived of their mothers. Two girls whose souls had hollow spaces that should have been saturated with maternal love. So each of them had done their best to fill the gaps suffered by the other. Fiona's pulse quickened. That's what they'd been doing all these years... mothering one another.

Di's voice grated when she asked, "So I may have had some redeeming qualities?"

Fiona knew the awesome power of being a mother. On a daily basis, she experienced the wonder of unconditional love radiating for her children, of the fierce protectiveness that could overwhelm her in a flash. She had no idea where all that love came from, she only knew it had no end.

If Sam were to come to her and admit to making some terrible mistake, would she shun him? Would she turn her back on him? Of course she wouldn't. She would take him in her arms and love all the bad away.

She would forgive.

Emotion swelled in her throat, and she tried to smile through the tears that blurred her vision as she reached for Di. "A few," she murmured, hugging her friend tightly.

Di held on for dear life, softly sobbing against her shoulder, and Fiona was left wondering if this was how the rebirth of a friendship was celebrated.

Later that week, Fiona arrived home from making her morning deliveries and her heart jerked in her chest when she saw Stan's Volvo pull into the driveway behind her. Something kept her hands glued to the steering wheel. She couldn't get out, couldn't even reach for the key to turn off the rumbling engine.

The kids were in school. What the heck was he doing here? What a crazy, stupid question that was. The only reason she could think of was that he wanted to talk to her. Without the buffer of the children, she panicked.

She wasn't ready. Damn it! It wasn't fair of him to spring this on her without so much as a phone call to announce his arrival.

He got out of his car and stood there. Then he stuffed his hands in the pockets of his suit pants.

His image reflected in the side mirror of her car. The splint was gone, and as far as she could tell, so were the bruises beneath his eyes. His hair had been trimmed recently. Apparent hesitation puckered his brow and had him looking like an uncertain little boy.

Well, she felt like a scared little girl.

With the kids gone, this would be a perfect time to ask him about the money. If he broached other subjects, she'd simply have to play it by ear. "It's time to grow up, Fiona," she muttered under her breath, glaring at her reflection in the rearview mirror.

One twist of her wrist cut off the ignition. A small tug on the door handle opened the door. Her feet felt leaden, but they succeeded in getting out into the cool open air.

"Sorry to just show up like this," he called from

several yards away. "I tried to call the house this morning, but you must have been out."

"I still have my cell phone."

He winced. "I know." After a moment, he said, "Sam told me about your new business." He nodded. "I think it's great, Fiona. That you're doing something for you."

Odd, conflicting emotions assaulted her. A small part of her burst with pleasure hearing that he approved. But a jab of irritation canceled out the warm fuzzies. She neither needed nor wanted his approval, damn it. When she didn't respond, he studied the ground for several seconds before meeting her gaze once again. Then he said, "I came for copies of the kids' birth certificates. I need them for—"

A battered red pickup sped up the driveway, its engine accelerating so high that Stan turned. The driver of the truck stomped on the brake and stones went flying as the vehicle skidded several feet before coming to a halt.

Fiona recognized Karen Snow when she jumped out of the passenger side of the pickup. "Don't hurt him, Daddy!" she yelled, racing around the vehicle. "You promised." Instinct alone urged Fiona to her husband's side.

A big man rolled out of the truck. Buck Snow's long-sleeved Harley T-shirt had seen better days. A red-and-black flame tattoo shot out from under the worn neckband licking at the curve of his jaw. He looked bull strong and just as dangerous.

"So you're the famous teacher man," he sneered, nailing Stan with a malicious look. "I've been watching for you. Day and night. I knew your ass would show up sooner or later." While Stan had freed his hands from his pockets, he appeared composed.

Buck slammed his truck door and stomped across the stones. "Why the fuck did you knock up my daughter and leave her high and dry?" Karen closed in on him, halting his forward progress. "Bein' married ain't no excuse, man," he said, craning to see around his daughter. "Somebody's gonna take care o' my girl here and it's the duty of that baby's daddy." Timid anticipation seemed to hum all around Karen. Her chin dipped slightly as she gazed at Stan.

Stan's focus steadily remained on what he saw as the threat. "I'm not the father of Karen's baby."

The declaration infuriated Buck. "You gutless sum' bitch. You did the dirty deed. She told me so. Stand up and take your medicine."

"I wouldn't hesitate to take responsibility—" Stan's voice hardened as he added "—if it were mine to accept."

Buck's greasy nostrils flared and he pressed forward, shoving Karen along a full foot with his burly chest. "You calling my girl a liar? I will kick your ass from here to Nigeria."

Although she doubted the man's knowledge of world geography, Fiona nevertheless tensed from head to toe. She'd witnessed one act of violence on her front lawn. She wasn't eager for another.

"How about if we all calm down?" she suggested.

Buck's too bright gaze raked over her. "Keep outta this. It's prolly all your fault, anyway. If you'd been keepin' your man happy, he wouldn't have been sniffing elsewhere."

The accusation jolted her. Stan's hand fisted and he pointed a warning finger at Buck. "Don't talk to her like that."

"And what are you gonna do about it, dude? Huh? What are you gonna do?"

"Daddy, stop. You said we'd only talk. You promised."

The testosterone levels rose, ear high. Fiona wanted to remind Stan that he was just recovering from a broken nose. Should he really risk a relapse?

"Yeah, well, that promise flew out the window. If this guy ain't got the guts to admit—"

"I told you I didn't have sex with your daughter."

Fiona glanced at Stan. When he read the silent questions in her eyes, he looked hurt. Then his blue gaze flashed with ire.

"But she told me..." Fiona let the sentence fade.

His jaw jutted the slightest fraction, an unwavering expression she'd seen a thousand times over the course of their marriage, and Fiona knew the truth. Never in her life had he lied to her. He might have walked out and left her for eight flipping weeks, but he'd never lied.

She directed her attention to the frail-looking young woman. Karen's belly was showing clear signs of her pregnancy now. Fiona held no suspicion that Karen had been deceptive about carrying a child, but she no longer believed her husband was involved in the young woman's predicament.

"Karen," Fiona began, "you weren't telling the truth when you came here, were you?"

"Was so! Everything I said was the truth."

"You said you were pregnant." Contemplation softened her tone as the events of that distressing day replayed through Fiona's mind. "But you never named the father." She tilted her head and lifted her hands to her hips, irritation poking her sharply. "You let me assume that my husband slept with you. Karen, do you have any idea of the anguish you've caused me and my children?"

The young woman's gaze slithered to the ground.

Buck Snow grabbed his daughter's arm and jerked her to face him. "What the hell are you saying, girl? It ain't him?" Karen's chin lifted in defiance. "You were the one who brought up his name to begin with," she told her father.

"Shit fire!" Buck's face went blood-red. "I said the name of every male you had anything to do with! When I mentioned the teacher man, you got all choked up. Naturally, I thought he was the one." He pointed at Stan. "If it ain't him, who is the daddy?"

Karen's mouth formed a firm line and her forehead puckered.

"You're not gonna say?" The young woman's bullish father backed up a step and he shoved her from him. "Well, I'm not takin' care of some bastard runt. When you want to tell me who the daddy is, then you can come home. Otherwise, I don't want to see your face." He stomped to his truck.

Fiona could only watch, astounded, as he turned the pickup around on her front lawn. "Watch my—" annoyance knocked the breath out of her as the man plowed right over the greenery "—peonies."

"Sorry," Karen said, clearly embarrassed. "He can be so stupid sometimes."

The nut doesn't fall far from the tree, Fiona wanted to say, but kept the opinion to herself.

"Karen, I don't understand all this." Stan took a few steps closer. "I spent a lot of my free time trying to help you. Why would you let everyone think you and I had...?"

She looked uncomfortable enough to squirm. "You're a nice guy. Anytime I needed to talk, you were there, listening and offering advice. I never had that before. Never had anyone who cared like you did. I felt safe when I was with you. And you always brought up your kids, what they were doing, the accomplishments they made. You're a good dad." She pressed her palms to her belly. "I'd like to have a daddy like that for my baby."

Fiona couldn't quite match up all the pieces of this puzzle, and couldn't help feeling the young woman's reasoning hadn't a bit of logic in it. But sometimes a person's motives simply didn't.

"Does your boyfriend know about the baby?" Without waiting for a response, Stan said, "Maybe the guy will be a good father, Karen." She refused to lift her gaze to his. "He doesn't know, does he?"

"Dan broke up with me months ago." Tears rolled down her face and her voice was raw. "I'm not sure who made me pregnant."

Fiona's heart wrenched. Karen was only a few years older than Cassie, much too young to be in a predicament this precarious.

"I'm sorry I hurt you," Karen said to Stan. Then she addressed Fiona. "I really am sorry. I almost told you the truth that day. But I... couldn't." She turned around and started walking down the drive.

Stan's troubled gaze connected with Fiona's, and she understood her husband well enough to know what was going to happen next.

"Karen," he called, "where are you going?"

The young woman paused and, with her back still to them, she shrugged.

"Do you need a ride?" He pulled his keys from his pocket.

Karen turned back. "My grandmother lives in Newark. Could you take me there?"

"Hop in." Stan looked at Fiona. "I'll pick up the birth certificates later, okay?"

"No problem," she told him.

As she watched Stan drive away with Karen Snow, all Fiona could do was shake her head. She wasn't surprised that he would offer to help someone who had tried to cause trouble for him. She would have been surprised, however, had he let the young woman walk away.

But that was Stan—generous to a fault.

Chapter Twenty

Sometimes You Win, Sometimes You Lose

Di felt as if she'd been reborn. As if a fire-and-brimstone preacher had shoved her under the cold, bubbling water of a stream and pulled out a new woman. New job, new apartment, and best of all, a whole new attitude.

She downshifted and eased her car around a curve in the road, amazed that these rural, rolling hills of Hockessin could be just minutes from the bustling city.

Having Fiona back in her life these past few months had changed Di. She no longer felt like the same person at all. The difference was wondrous and dramatic, and the revelations she'd experienced were nothing short of miraculous.

This transformation wasn't solely Fiona's doing, of course. The loss of Di's job had left her with something she hadn't had before. Time. And Jonni Jean's attack had given her a reason to think. Hard. Reevaluating her priorities wasn't an easy thing to do. Especially when she'd slowly come to the conclusion that the very ideals she'd been clinging to for most of her life had caused major flaws in her character—or had she held fast to the wrong ideals because of the flaws in her character? She was still working out that "chicken and egg" part of it. There was a lot she was still working out.

What mattered was that she was a changed woman, or on her way to becoming one, anyway. She wasn't yet the person she wanted to be (hell, a girl couldn't reconstruct herself overnight), but she sure wasn't the person she used to be. That was cause for celebration.

The most remarkable truths she'd discovered had to do with the most basic of principles. She'd spent years clawing her way to the top of her profession only to learn during these last few weeks of unemployment that making a living wasn't the same as making a life. That a title on an office door was just that—a thin strip of plastic that could be slipped from its holder and tossed in the trash bin in a nanosecond.

What really mattered was liking the person staring back at you in the mirror. For days after Fiona discovered her betrayal, Di had peed in the dark for fear of seeing her guilt-ridden reflection in the bathroom mirror. But she was figuring it out now, deciding the person she wanted to be, choosing the character traits she wanted to develop. Honesty. Integrity. Kindness. Contentment. Sincerity. Clean living (okay, she'd already admitted she was still working on some things).

Cultivating and enjoying relationships with people you loved, with people who loved you, soared high above material things—sports cars or city brownstones, gold bangles or Dolce & Gabbana. (Oh, hell, who was she kidding? Her addiction was Samson-strong, so she'd just have to learn to live with being a shoe whore.)

Her life examination had turned up some sad facts. She'd lost out on a lot over the years—a man, a marriage, children, to name a few. She'd been running away from them without ever realizing it, and she was still trying to understand why. There was the obvious, of course. She didn't want any man telling her what to do or where to go. She didn't want to be tied down. She liked keeping her entanglements as untangled as possible, so she'd spent her life dating men she didn't mind leaving (or losing). But now she realized that this mindset made for a superficial existence. She wanted meaning in her life, and that meant being willing to take some big risks.

Oh, yes, she had lost out. Living in Hockessin again, she'd discovered how much she'd missed her best friend these last twenty-odd years. Di's eyes watered and her throat itched when she remembered how forgiving Fiona had been. Di braked at the stop sign, wondering if she could have been as big-hearted had the tables been turned. She doubted it, not prior to this life-altering experience, anyway—losing her job, coming home to help Fiona, having her arm broken by her ex-lover's wife. But she really wasn't that person anymore, thank goodness. If Fiona took a notion to rip Di's heart out, Di wouldn't hesitate to forgive. When a person was pardoned of much, finding compassion for and making peace with others became easier. Fiona had lifted Di's heavy burden of guilt, peeled it right off her shoulders, and that made Di so happy. She went around grinning like a fool these days and did her best to make others smile, too. Very out of character for the old Di, but the new Di got a kick out of doing good deeds. And the good deed she'd performed today had her floating on air.

Glancing into her rearview mirror, she saw a brown-and-tan county cop car on her bumper. Eli. She waved at him and he lifted a hand in greeting. The road didn't have a shoulder, so she gunned the engine and took off like a bullet. He stayed with her and she grinned. She liked a man who determinedly remained in hot pursuit.

She pulled over the first chance she got, which happened to be in the parking lot of a small produce market. A large hand-painted sign stated the stand was open for business Friday through Sunday, and since it was Monday, the lot was deserted when she got out of her car.

"Hey, there." Eli shut his car door and strolled toward her. "I haven't seen you in weeks. How's it going?"

Something quivered between them, an energy that was almost palpable.

"It's going well, thanks."

"Judging from that smile, I'd say it's going great."

Giddiness gurgled into laughter. "I am feeling great, Eli. You'll never guess where I've been this afternoon. At the courthouse. Jonni Jean Bowers had to appear before the judge on her assault charge. I asked to speak and the judge agreed to hear what I had to say."

"I hope you asked to have the book tossed at her. The woman's dangerous."

"I did just the opposite."

Surprise slackened Eli's features.

"I asked the judge for leniency."

His confusion deepened to concern. "Why would you do that? That woman could have killed you, Di."

Shaking her head, she explained, "Jonni Jean might be a tad backward, but she wouldn't have crossed the line."

"Breaking a person's arm is crossing the line. The line of the law, anyway."

Chagrin crept in to steal some of the good feelings rushing through her. "Maybe. But I had to do this, Eli." Clearly, more explanation was necessary. "You see, I wronged Jonni Jean. Terribly. I did something just awful and didn't think twice about how my actions might affect her. I'll never be arrested or convicted for what I did. Jonni Jean was just looking for a little revenge. Some way to regain her self-respect."

Eli stared at her.

"It's okay if you don't understand. I did what I had to do. I feel good that I was able to show a little compassion. And I learned a valuable lesson, too. I have to think about the ramifications of my actions. The consequences of my behavior can be far-reaching. Like ripples in a pond." Her lightheartedness couldn't be held down for long. She lifted her cast and grinned. "And they can come back to haunt me, too."

Even without words, he made it quite plain that he didn't agree with her decision to attend Jonni Jean's hearing. The silence that settled between them was awkward.

They commented on the changing season and the glorious weather they'd been having, and then Di brought him up to speed with Fiona's situation and Stanley's return.

Eli rubbed the side of his neck, offering a silent whistle. "Sometimes you just never know about people."

A tall, wispy blade of grass swayed nearby and Di reached down and plucked it. "So how have you been?" Fully expecting an answer that was both cordial and quick, she was pleased when he surprised her with something real, something honest.

"If you really want to know, I've been taking a personal inventory."

Her curiosity was stirred, and at the same time she felt awed to learn that, just like her, he was doing some soul-searching. "Really?" she asked. "Why?"

"I think I told you that I'd applied for a job with the state police. Well, I was offered a position."

Di beamed. "That's great, Eli."

He shrugged his burly shoulders. "I thought I was going to take the job. It's what I'd been planning for myself. But I'm having second thoughts. The academy training would take six months, and then I'd have to participate in a ride-along program with a more experienced officer. Accepting the position would involve a lot of time and effort—" he lifted a hand "—which I wouldn't mind investing, but the sticking point was when I learned that I'd enter the job at a lower rank than I have now. I'm a patrolman first class. I earn a good income. A cop's pay is based on rank. Lower rank, smaller income."

"Ooo. I can see how that would cause a problem."

"I had a talk with my shift commander and he told me that I could make sergeant in the next few years."

Contemplating the notion made him smile. Something warm curled in Di's belly. Her voice was soft as she commented, "I can see you like that idea."

His smile widened. "I do, actually."

"So you're staying with the county?" She twirled the long blade of grass around her index finger.

"Not sure yet, but I think so. I don't have to make a decision for a few weeks. Sometimes you think the grass is greener when in reality it's not. Sometimes it's better to stay where you're at... where it feels like home."

Poignant emotion welled in Di. "Stay where it feels like home." She swallowed with difficulty. "I love the sound of that."

Although he didn't invade her space, he inched closer, the cocky set of his shoulders a stance she'd seen hundreds of times before on men who were about to make their move. Nerves danced in her stomach. She didn't want to have to turn him down again.

"Listen, Di," he began, "I know you told me you don't drink beer. But I was wondering if you might have a cup of coffee with me." He swiftly added, "Or a glass of wine, or a soda, or a lemonade. Whichever you prefer."

Old habits automatically kicked in and she said, "Thanks, Eli, but you're not really my type." She had to make a conscious effort to be honest. "What I should really say is... I'm not your type."

Humor lit his green gaze. "And how do you know what type is my type?"

She shredded the grass into tiny strips. "Well, I would think you're looking for a woman who's—" she shook her head, searching for words "—reliable and dependable and..."

He laughed. "That'd be great if I was buying a new car."

Flustered, she tossed the grass aside. "Quit it, now. You know what I mean."

Eli grew serious. "I think I do. But I'm not asking you to go in halfers with me on a speedboat. All I want is a date."

Fear played sharp, clashing chords in her head, and the resulting music scared her. She liked Eli. He was a good, solid man. He didn't deserve the likes of her. She didn't want to disappoint him.

Didn't want to hurt him. And she sure as hell didn't want to be hurt herself.

"In fact, I'd be willing to go out on a mini-date," he said. "No movie. No meal. Nothing involved but a drink of your choice at a location of your choice."

His interest in her was genuine; intuition told her that. He was the kind of man she imagined herself with, wasn't he? Reliable and dependable.

"Why are you smiling like that?" he asked, his tone honey-sweet.

"No reason." She took a deep breath, willing away the butterflies in her stomach.

He slipped his hands into his pockets. "So what do you say?"

Living a life of substance meant taking risks. She was changing, becoming a better person. But could she do this? *Should* she do this? Open the door to a person who had the potential of becoming someone important to her? Could she live up to what she suspected would be his high expectations? Could she gamble her heart, her happiness?

"I say... that sounds like a great idea."

Having dinner at the mall on a Friday night was

not Fiona's idea of a good time, especially when it seemed as though every other family in the county had the same idea. They'd taken a booth at their favorite Italian place because a table hadn't been available.

His head resting on his fist, Sam slouched over the plate of pizza crusts, sulking about having to forgo getting together with some of his friends in order to be here. Cassie had barely touched her salad, had barely said a word, and she ignored her father, stubbornly directing all dialogue to either her mother or her brother. Stan didn't look much happier than the kids. The entire meal had been oppressive and stressful.

The only reason Fiona was here at all was because Cassie had refused to come otherwise. And Fiona felt the need to do something to resolve the stalled situation between Stan and the children.

"Mom, how long do we have to sit here?" Contempt suffused every syllable of the teen's question. "There's a pair of jeans I've wanted to try on at The Gap." Cassie slipped out of the booth and stood by the table. "Can I go? It'll take me twenty minutes, tops."

Fiona eyed Stan, who offered a tiny, frustrated nod. "Okay," she said. "Twenty minutes."

"Do you need money, Cassie?" Stan leaned forward as if to reach for his wallet.

Without taking her gaze off her mother, the teenager cast a disparaging look. "I'm looking, not buying," she huffed at Fiona before flouncing away.

"Can I go to the arcade?" Evidently, Sam saw his chance to escape. "I'll be quick, too."

Throwing up his arms in frustrated surrender, Stan said, "What the hell." He stood and let his son slide out of the booth. "Here—" he pulled out his wallet this time "—take this. And have a good time."

Sam snatched the ten dollar bill with a grunt of thanks.

The instant Sam was out of earshot, Fiona said, "You shouldn't do that, Stan. You can't buy the kids' affection or their forgiveness. Sam doesn't need to be throwing quarters away at the arcade."

"When has anyone in this family ever worried about wasting money?"

She didn't like the sharp edge in his tone, but she ignored it and the question. Fighting with Stan had not been on her agenda tonight.

"I know it's frustrating, but you need to give

them more time." She slid her fingers over the condensation that had collected on the outside of her water glass. "They need to learn that they can trust you. In time their emotions will settle, and they'll open up and start talking."

"Why should they talk to me when you won't? You're setting the stage, don't you see that, Fiona?"

She jerked her hand into her lap. "You have no right to be angry with me."

The manner in which he clamped his jaw shut told her he disagreed. He set his white linen napkin on the table and leaned forward. "I don't want to argue. We're not going to get anywhere unless we can be civil to one another. I've waited weeks for you to be ready, Fiona. I just want us to talk. Is that too much to ask?"

Yes! Yes, it was. She wasn't prepared for this. She knew they'd have to discuss the whys and whos and whats and hows of what happened at some point. But not tonight. Not in the middle of a bustling restaurant.

"Come on, Fiona. The kids are busy. How about giving me twenty minutes?"

Logic reverberated in her head. She'd confronted a lot of scary things while he'd been gone: the prospect of being a widow, two anxious teens, an empty checking account, no inflow of income, public school for her kids, starting a new business. Fuzzy thoughts of lying half-clothed in Chad's bed riffled at the fringes of her brain, but now was not a good time for that memory so she slammed the lid on it.

If she could face all those terrifying situations and survive, how bad could it be to talk with her husband about what he'd done?

She sighed with resignation. "Fine. I'm up for it if you are."

He didn't quite smile, but he seemed openly relieved by her willingness.

When the waitress stopped at their table, Stan ordered two decaf coffees. The perky young woman promised to be right back.

"Where did the blood come from?" Of all the questions that had bombarded her over the past few months, she was surprised this one popped out first. Stan looked puzzled, so she explained. "The police found your blood on your briefcase and in the car. Where did it come from?"

He nodded. "From the cut." He reached up and smoothed his fingers over his clean-shaven jaw. "I'd cut myself shaving that morning. That was the proverbial straw that broke the camel's back."

"What do you mean? Why should a shaving nick even bother you? You have a styptic pencil. It's in the medicine cabinet in the bathroom."

He picked up the empty wrapper to the straw Sam had used to drink his soda. "You don't understand."

"So make me understand."

The waitress arrived with their coffee and a small pitcher of cream. "Anything else?" she asked.

Stan shook his head while Fiona concentrated on pouring cream into her cup. She picked up her spoon and stirred. And waited.

"Our lives had gotten so far out of control. You have to admit that much. You, the kids, me. We were running every single day and night. Every moment was filled with something, some meeting to attend, some obligation to perform. Heck, we had to plan a family dinner night. It was crazy, Fiona. Crazy."

Fiona thought about the evenings she'd spent watching movies or just talking with the kids or trying out a new recipe on them or playing a board game. Yes, the worry over Stan was like a steadfast sentinel standing off in one corner, but she hadn't failed to realize that a lot could be said about being home, being sedentary.

"Okay," she said softly, "I'll agree with that. Our lives were crazy. I'd thought it was all part of offering our kids a proper upbringing. I wanted them to have what I didn't have. I thought that's what you wanted, too. But it might have been too much." She tapped the spoon on the lip of the cup, then set it on the saucer. "It was too much."

"A piece of apple pie is good," he murmured. "Eating the whole thing isn't healthy."

"I said it was too much, didn't I?"

He lifted his cup, but then set it back down without taking a drink. "I feel bad about what I did. I feel like I tore our family apart."

Regret darkened his blue eyes, and Fiona sighed. "I was involved in just as many activities as the kids were. Granted, a lot of what I did revolved around the kids' schools, but I did plenty of things for me, too. I didn't have to be a member of—"

"Stop." Stan reached across the table and covered her hand with his. "I don't want to start placing blame. Pointing fingers isn't going to get us anywhere. I just want to know where we go from here. I want to know if we can move forward, if we can go on from here."

She wasn't sure what he was saying.

Moisture made his gaze glisten. "I am so proud

of the way you handled things. You held it together. You were there for our kids. I'm just..." He looked off toward a far corner of the crowded room. He sniffed and cleared his throat.

"I got dressed that Monday morning, grabbed my briefcase, and headed out the door." He drew both hands away from his coffee. "I was on I-95 when my chin felt funny. I'd forgotten about the cut. I reached up to scratch, and before I knew it, blood was everywhere. On my face, my hands, my shirt, the steering wheel. I pulled off to the side of the road to look for a tissue or something. And I just sat there. I asked myself what the hell I was doing. I was fighting traffic to get to a monotonous job that provided money that no one appreciated. I had to be at the college that night to tutor kids, most of whom weren't really interested in accounting. I remembered that when I'd accepted the teaching position, we were going to use the extra money for fun, to travel and see the world. But we haven't been anywhere or done anything as a family for... for I can't even remember how long. Every time we tried to plan a trip, someone had an obligation that prevented it. What about our obligation to our family? Little by little the extra money was no longer extra, and I was working two jobs just to keep us afloat. I felt like a rat in a maze with no way out. I couldn't do it anymore, Fiona. I didn't want to do it anymore."

He'd gone pale and looked spent.

"So you left me?"

"I didn't leave you." Frustration tightened his face. "I told you the truth. I left our marriage. I needed a change, Fiona. I went looking for a way out of the grind." His forehead furrowed. "But after a few days of being all alone, I realized my life wasn't so bad, after all. But... but how could I come home and face you? How could I face the kids? I couldn't come home, not after the way I left."

The reminder of how he'd deserted them stirred remnants of anger in her, and she tugged her hand from beneath his. But she couldn't deny that guilt swarmed in her, too.

"I don't like what you did, Stan." She inhaled deeply, uncertain about voicing her next thought. "But if you hadn't made such a drastic move, the chaos we were living would have only gotten worse, I suspect. None of us would have realized we were losing ourselves in all that... busyness. But with you gone, I was forced to step up. And what I discovered was... me. I found out what I'm capable of." Her smile was very small. "I also found out that I'm quite clever."

Stan returned her smile, but he didn't touch her.

"Do you think you can forgive me, Fiona? Do you think that we could start over? I'd like to come home. I want to be a family again."

Panic skimmed through her. "I don't know," she murmured. Then the new, sturdier spine she'd grown over the past three months made her sit up straight. "I won't be able to decide that," she said firmly, "until I hear the answers to some questions."

He tossed the wadded up straw casing aside and rested his forearms on the table. "Ask me anything, Fiona."

Her gaze was level and steady. "Tell me about your relationship with Shirley. I met her. Talked to her. The woman obviously has deep feelings for you."

Stan looked away only for an instant. "I had lunch with her fairly regularly for a while. And we had dinner twice." Judging from the sudden alarm on his face, Fiona recognized that she must have reacted physically to what he'd said. She breathed deeply, realizing she had a death grip on the napkin that had been draped across her lap.

"We were always in a public place," he rushed to clarify. "Always. And nothing inappropriate ever happened between us. I mean... there was no sex... no physical contact of any kind. We only talked."

"Talked? About what?" Had that high, frantic voice come from her throat?

"I don't know." He looked uncomfortable. "About my job. About my dissatisfaction."

"With me?"

"With everything, Fiona." A deep frown imbedded itself between his eyes. "Shirley was a sounding board for me. Period. I expressed my unhappiness, and she was willing to listen. If I want to be completely truthful—and I do—I have to admit that our conversations became quite... intimate."

He leaned forward. "But all we ever did was talk, Fiona. I swear to you. There was nothing physical in our relationship,"

Astronomical pain rolled over her. Tears scorched her eyes and she was damn determined they would not spill. Not here, at least, and not now.

"Nothing inappropriate, my ass." She scooted out of the booth and slammed the napkin onto the padded seat. The diners at the tables closest to them glanced her way, but she gave them no notice. "You are the biggest jerk on the face of the earth, Stanley Rowland."

"But... I don't understand."

Neither did she. All she knew was that she had an ache that hurt badly enough to make her contemplate murder, and if she didn't get out of here soon, she was going to embarrass herself by sobbing or shouting or both.

"Drop the kids off at the house." She barked the order, then spun around and stormed out of the restaurant and out of the mall.

She could hardly see to drive. It wasn't safe, but she had to get as far away from him—as far away from this pain—as she could. Finding out that her husband hadn't slept with that gorgeous woman from his work should have made her happy, should have relieved her angst.

So why was she bawling her eyes out and driving as if the hounds of hell were on her heels?

Chapter Twenty-One

Reflections

Full-blown autumn had completely chased away the stifling mid-Atlantic humidity. The air held a cool crispness, and the sun blazed in the sky above fat, cotton ball clouds. Fiona had made the last of her Saturday morning deliveries, but rather than heading home to make the pancake breakfast she'd promised her kids, she found herself pulling into the state police barracks' parking lot. She crawled past Chad's parked car, and then steered her van into an empty spot nearby.

After what had happened between them, she didn't feel comfortable going to his apartment.

She'd pulled into this parking lot twice since that embarrassing night. His car hadn't been here on her first visit. And although she'd parked and cut the engine on her second, she had lost the courage to actually go inside the building to speak to him.

An apology was certainly in order. Hell's bells, she'd been in the man's bed, ready and willing, and then she'd started yammering on about Stan. How insulting was that?

There would be no excuses today. She was going to see him, and she intended to express her regret, no matter how much it might make her cringe.

Her shoes scraped across the gritty asphalt when she got out of her car and locked the door. When she looked up, she saw Chad exiting the back door of the brick building with a couple of other men. He saw her immediately and loped over. Although the greetings they exchanged were benign, the honeybee buzz of underlying tension was unmistakable.

"Do you have a few minutes?" She consciously loosened her grip on the strap of her purse.

"Sure," he told her. "We could go inside to my office, but it's so nice out, why don't we go sit over there?"

He pointed to a picnic table sitting on a grassy

spot under a shade tree covered with flame-red leaves. Fiona nodded and followed him. She settled on one wooden bench and he sat down across from her. He set down the envelope he was carrying and folded his hands on top of it.

She needed to get this out into the open before she chickened out again. "I came to tell you I'm sorry." When he didn't respond right away, she explained, "For what happened at your apartment that night—"

"Fiona, don't." His soft tone held no hint of animosity. "There's no need for that. Really."

"Oh, yes, there is." She could feel blood rushing to her face. She'd wanted him that night, plain and simple. She'd acted like a reckless trollop, so desperate for him that she'd practically attacked him. He'd suggested then that what she'd wanted was revenge. Even after all this time she hadn't been able to decide which of them had gotten it right.

"I shouldn't have come that night. I shouldn't have..."

His fingers slid over hers, cutting off the rest of her thought.

"Stop, now. I mean it." His expression was tender as he withdrew his hand. "You were going through a lot. I understand that now. And I understood it then. If anything, I should be the one apologizing. I was the one who should have had a clear head. I shouldn't have allowed things to go that far." She got the impression he wanted to touch her, but instead he tucked his hands beneath the table.

"I came to thank you, too," she said. "You helped me more than you'll ever know, and I appreciate it. You helped me find my husband, but you helped me in other ways, too. You made me feel things, Chad. You made me feel... attractive. At a time when all I wanted to do was crawl in a hole and hide. You have no idea what you did for my self-esteem." For a long time, he said nothing. Finally, he asked, "How are things with you? How've you been?"

"Miserable," she told him. She hesitated. The subject of Stanley should be taboo between them, but knowing Chad had a sympathetic ear, she caved to her desire to talk. "Stan wants to come home."

Chad nodded, seeming to gauge her reaction. "I'm glad the two of you are talking, at least." His vibrant brown eyes told her he was lying.

"We've only really talked once. Last night, in

fact. And I left the mall in tears." She muttered, "The bastard." She heaved a sigh. "I haven't been able to come to terms with what he did to us. Leaving like that." After a moment, she said, "Karen Snow admitted that Stan's not the father of her baby."

"That's got to be good news."

She shrugged. "He did admit to having a relationship with the woman from his work."

Chad slipped into his deadpan detective face.

"No sex, he assured me. But there were meals together." The pain that knifed through her chest surprised her. "And they had conversations that were apparently very... private." She closed her eyes as she struggled to get a grip on her stormy emotions. Two fat tears squeezed from beneath her lashes. Mortified, she roughly wiped them away.

"And that hurts you."

It wasn't a question. Her anger sputtered. "He should have been sharing his thoughts and feelings with me!" She read nothing in the detective's expression, and frustration had her wailing, "Damn it, Chad. You should play poker."

"I do. And I'm good at it."

"Don't you agree that he's a bastard? An ass of the highest order?"

A small, sad smile thinned Chad's mouth. "Fiona, I shouldn't even be discussing this with you. I shouldn't have to remind you that I've been trying to come to terms with how I feel about you, about this whole situation."

Shame forced her to glance down at her laced fingers where they rested on the raw table boards. "I know I'm not being fair to you. I shouldn't be here talking about this. I'm sorry."

"I like you, Fiona. You know that. And it's because I like you that I have to point out that your reactions—the magnitude of your hurt and anger—are very telling."

Her gaze swung to his. "What are you saying?"

There it was again, that damn stolid mask.

"Come on, Fiona," he murmured. "It doesn't take a rocket scientist. You wouldn't be overwhelmed if your husband didn't mean something to you. Sooner or later, you're going to have to examine just how intense those feelings are. Until you do a little soul-searching, you're going to be hanging in limbo." He stood up, picked up the envelope from the table. "I have to get back to work. I was on my way to an interview. But would you please tell your husband something for me? Tell him I think he's one hell of a lucky man."

She frowned, her thoughts in turmoil.

"Have a great life, Fiona. I mean it."

She watched him stride across the grass, get into his car, and drive away, and still she sat there under the blazing tree. Five minutes passed. Then ten. The longer she sat, the more she stewed.

Of course she was hurt. Of course she was angry. Marriage took commitment, faithfulness, the giving of one's self to another. Fiona had taken that commitment seriously. She'd been dedicated to Stan for more than half her life. To be unfaithful or disloyal had never entered her head. Stan had been dead wrong to give pieces of himself to someone—*anyone*—else but her. She'd been betrayed. She felt betrayed. The mere thought of Stan confiding in another woman clawed her to bloody shreds.

Your reactions are very telling.

You wouldn't be overwhelmed if your husband didn't mean something to you.

Chad had advised her to do some soul-searching or risk remaining in limbo. But did she have the guts to really scrutinize her life? Did she have it in her to take off her blinders and really see? Ignoring it certainly wasn't working.

There had been a time when she'd been devoted

to her husband. Her love had been passionate, the kind of love that made her hanker—yes, *hanker*—to be with him every moment of every day. And he'd felt the same. She remembered a time, years ago, when they'd call each other two, three, sometimes four times a day to check in, or relate a funny story, or simply to hear the other's voice.

A crushing sadness surged through her and fresh tears burned her eyes. She missed those days. Fiona pressed her palm to her chest in some vain attempt to alleviate the ache in her heart.

Why did she hurt this badly? Why?

The question withered in her mind as she glanced up through the colorful leaves to study the blue sky beyond.

She hurt because she cared about Stan. Because she'd devoted herself to him. Because they'd built a life together.

She hurt because she loved him.

Desperately.

The revelation made her feel utterly wretched. It also annoyed the hell out of her. She pushed herself up off the picnic bench, absently brushed at her bottom and trudged toward her car, a single anxious question rolling through her mind.

Did she *want* to love Stan?

"I guess that sounds stupid to you."

After Fiona spoke, Di watched her friend slowly swirl the fancy stirrer around in the Blackberry Mojito.

"Not stupid." Di shook her head. "But I am a little confused. You'd feel less hurt if Stan and that woman had had sex?"

"Meaningless sex, I said. Because it would have been... meaningless."

Di sipped her Scotch. "I had meaningless sex—" she lifted her cast "—and look what it got me. I saw that punch you threw at Stan. If you discovered he'd had sex, I could see you swinging one of Sam's baseball bats."

She'd been trying to make Fiona smile, but it was a wasted effort.

When Di had arrived at Fiona's this evening, she'd immediately launched into a bout of excited babbling about her pending date with Eli. He was like no other man she'd ever gone out with. So far, he'd even refused to kiss her good night, which was baffling, to say the least. And he asked her so many questions. He seemed intently interested in her thoughts and opinions on a wide range of topics. However, after prattling off those few short facts regarding her budding relationship with Eli, she'd realized that Fiona was barely listening because she was preoccupied. Di had sat down at the kitchen table and ordered Fiona to start talking.

After hearing about Stan's wish to return home, Di had wanted to tell Fiona to screw that idea altogether. But a small, still voice in her cautioned her to speak with care. Fiona had to do what was right for Fiona. Di decided then and there that she needed to be a friend who was willing to listen and not pass judgment. Fiona had to work things out in her own head before listening to the drastic recommendations of others.

It had taken some doing, but Di had finally convinced her friend she needed to get out of the house. Di had offered to take her anywhere she'd like to go, and had been totally surprised when Fiona suggested Maxwell's. Di hadn't asked any questions; she'd just agreed. While Fiona changed clothes, Di had called Eli to see if he minded a change in plans, and he hadn't. The guy was truly amazing.

When the three of them had arrived at the establishment, they'd been stunned by the differences. Years ago, Maxwell's had been a loud, smoky pool hall famous for its drunken brawls. Fiona confessed that Stan had brought her here when they'd been dating and that they'd had fun playing pool. She said coming to Maxwell's had made her feel like a rebel because she'd known her father would never have approved.

However, the sleek black sign now announced the place as Nuance, and it was a stark and contemporary upscale billiards room complete with a wine tasting bar. When Di had called out to the bartender to order drinks, the man behind the counter had informed her he was Senior Mixologist and Liquor Chef. She and Fiona had shared a chuckle over his pretentious attitude, while poor Eli had nearly choked when he received the bill. Di had plucked it from his fingers and sent him off to find someone with whom to play a game of pool, so she and Fiona could talk.

"Look, honey—" she set her glass down on the cocktail napkin "—I think the bottom line is forgiveness. Can you forgive Stan? Everything rests on the answer to that one question, don't you think? If you can, then maybe the two of you could work things out. If not—" she lifted her hands "—I think you'll have no choice but to kick him to the curb."

"But the kids—"

"This has nothing to do with Cassie and Sam," Di said. "This is all about you. You and Stan. If you can't forgive him, you'll end up unhappy and bitter. So will he. That's no way to live."

Di had meant to keep her opinions to herself, but here she was, running off at the mouth. Personally, Di felt that Fiona should file for divorce and be done with it. Not because of some woman Stan hadn't even slept with. If their privates hadn't touched, then adultery hadn't taken place, but that was just her. Why Fiona kept harping on a few chatty lunches was beyond Di's understanding. The real snag in Di's mind was the way Stanley had abandoned them.

To her, that was unforgivable. But she'd bite her tongue clean off before she told Fiona that. Fiona had to make up her own mind.

"She does have a point, Fiona."

Both Di and Fiona looked up to see Stan standing by their table.

"But I think an even bigger issue is trust. Can you learn to trust me again?"

"What are you doing here?" Fiona's expression

was an odd mixture of amazement and irritation, and Di had to press her lips together to keep from smiling at how she'd blatantly ignored his question.

"Our daughter called me."

"Cassie? Called you?"

For an instant, it was clear that amazement visibly overrode Fiona's irritation.

"She said her mother was going to a pool hall," he said. "That her mother was going to end up drunk and arrested." His eyes widened. "And that it was all my fault."

Di had to hand it to Stan, he had Cassie's drama down to a T.

"She ordered me to find you and bring you home. Then she promptly slammed the phone in my ear."

Ah, teenagers. The bane of every parent's existence. A grin crept over Di's mouth.

"And what are you smiling about?"

Uh-oh. Fiona's ire had once again superseded all other emotion.

"If you want to know, Fiona," Di told her calmly, "I was mentally patting myself on the back for being childless."

Di couldn't decide what message her friend's

silence conveyed, but Fiona was definitely either sizing her up as a bitch or a lucky dog.

"You've wasted your time," Fiona snapped at Stan. "If I want to get drunk and disorderly while I chalk a pool cue, it's nobody's business but mine, damn it."

He pressed his knuckles on the tabletop. "True. It's none of my business."

"How the hell did you find me?"

Stan shrugged. "It wasn't hard. We have a history here, you know." Then his voice went quiet. "I probably shouldn't have come. But I was concerned about you, Fiona. After the way you left the mall last night..."

Oh, boy. This was turning into a private conversation. One that Di could see quickly becoming awkward for her to sit through.

She reached over and touched Fiona's sleeve. "Honey, do you want me to stay? Or should I go see what Eli's up to?"

Fiona hesitated, but then there was a clear dismissal in her small nod.

Although she was concerned and would have stayed with Fiona no matter how awkward she'd felt, Di would have been lying if she'd said she wasn't relieved for the opportunity to pick up her drink and go find her man.

"I'm surprised to hear you were concerned about me." Fiona eyed Stan as he eased down into the chair Di had just vacated. "Where was your concern all those weeks you were gone and I was going out of my head with worry?"

"Touché. I deserve that."

She glared. "You bet you do."

"Look, Fiona, your anger is warranted. We both know that. So rail at me. Hit me again if you have to. Ask me questions about Shirley, about Ocean City. I'm open to anything here. Just stop isolating yourself from me. Stop running away."

She seethed for a moment.

"What's with the money?" she asked. "Why are you depositing money into our account?"

"Because I'm serious about us working this out. I don't want a divorce, and to prove that to you, I'm willing to give you everything I've got." He splayed his hands on the table. "I need a little, of course, but I've been depositing the rest. I don't want us risking the house."

She didn't want him making plans to come

home. He had no right. She wanted to tell him she didn't need his money. But that would be a lie. The fact that he'd given her his money even before she'd been willing to speak to him was a worthy gesture.

"Why, Stan? Why would you go to another woman? I lived in the same house with you. Slept in the same bed. If you were unhappy with the way your life was turning out, you should have talked to me. Not some woman you worked with." She took the plastic stir stick from her drink and placed it on the napkin. "If you didn't like what was happening in our marriage, you should have done something to change it."

"I tried. It's next to impossible to get you alone in that house without teenagers interrupting, so I tried planning a night out. I made three different reservations at the Back Burner this past summer, and I had to cancel each one because things couldn't be arranged properly for the kids."

The restaurant was a favorite of hers. She vaguely remembered a couple of times where he'd suggested they go to dinner, but she didn't see what the big deal was. She'd made and cancelled reservations, too. One particular night that came to mind had been their anniversary. She'd made arrangements for her and Stan to celebrate, but then Sam's teacher had announced a need for adult chaperones to attend the class's three-day field trip. What could she do but call off her anniversary plans?

"And this past Christmas I bought us a three-day stay at the Elk Forge B and B. I thought if I could just get you away from the house we could talk. The trip was set for mid-January, but—"

Her breath left her in an audible rush. She'd forgotten all about it. "Stan, why didn't you remind me?"

He sighed. "You were inundated with those fundraisers. I'd never realized that January was such a busy month for you."

She closed her eyes, cradled her face in her outspread fingers and breathed, "Oh, my gosh. I'm so sorry." January had been a nightmare. Many of the cases of pizzas that had arrived for the fundraiser to benefit Sam's school had been damaged. And the company they'd used for the St. Anne's benefit had announced bankruptcy halfway into the event. As head chairperson, Fiona had been responsible for finding another company to use, posthaste.

"I wasn't angry," he said. "How could I be? You

were doing your job. You were taking care of the two things in this world that are most precious to me—Cassie and Sam. But I was sad. And disappointed. And that's when I started doubting that I could ever stop the whirlwind our lives were in. It was... depressing."

A frown marred his brow. "Shirley was just... there. She was someone to talk to. Someone who was willing to listen to me."

His gray-blue eyes were intent. "It was wrong, Fiona. I do know that. And I'm ashamed of the fact that her attention made me feel... good. But my gut ached every time I was with her." His chin lowered. "You can trust me when I say I didn't sleep with her. And I only met her in public. But even that started getting to me. I was stunned when I realized why." He pursed his lips for an instant and then admitted, "Because she wasn't you. I love you, Fiona. And I've missed you."

She stilled, unable to figure out the quagmire of emotions raging through her. She felt guilty that she'd allowed her role as a mother to occupy her so completely. She should have been available to Stan. But he couldn't patch up his betrayal with a couple of feeble endearments.

"But walking away like that?" She pinned him

with narrow-eyed accusation. "Do you have *any* idea what we went through? Stan, you let us think you were dead!"

His face paled. "Fiona—" he swallowed with difficulty "—I felt dead."

The defeat in his voice floored her, and her anger dissolved. She didn't speak for a long time as she thought about how far out of reach she'd been to her husband. Her throat felt raw as she said, "There seems to be time now. Downtime, I mean. The kids have cut way back on their activities. And I've cut mine down to nothing."

"Fiona, I'm not suggesting you should—"

"I know you're not." She hushed him with a slight wave of her hand. "I've found something more exciting to occupy my time."

He nodded. "Fiona's Fabulous Confections."

The admiration in his tone gave her delicious chills. "I can pretty much make my own hours. I have specific delivery times, but I can do my baking whenever it suits me."

The pride glowing in his gaze warmed her heart. But she felt suddenly uneasy. If Stan were to learn about some of her behavior—that she'd been kissing another man, rolling around in bed with him—surely her husband's respect for her would wither. All of Stan's dirty little secrets had been laid bare, and he'd offered to answer any questions she might have about the things he'd done and what drove him to it. How fair was it for her to keep her secrets to herself?

"Stan," she slowly began, "there's something you should know."

Her overwhelming guilt was enough to stir his concern.

"I had a—" She stopped and swallowed. How did she describe Chad and her relationship with him? He certainly hadn't been her lover, and labeling him a "gentleman caller" would make her feel ancient. She took a steely inhalation. "I had an admirer."

She watched sadness flatten Stan's mouth. He said, "I'm not surprised."

"Nothing happened," she quickly assured him. She recalled the swift, but passionate kiss she and Chad had shared, and she muttered, "Nothing much, anyway." The image of herself half-clothed in Chad's bed had embarrassment flushing her face. She forced herself to look Stan in the eyes. "I can honestly say that you were right there with us."

The statement evidently amused Stan. He tried

to hide his smile by shifting his hand, but she saw it.

"Sounds crowded," he murmured.

"And awkward as hell."

His grin broke into a chuckle. "One thing is certain. You've still got it."

His reaction surprised her. "You're not angry?"

"After all I've done? Fiona, how fair would that be?"

She sighed, the tension in her shoulders relaxing. Powerful emotions swept through her. "Making that admission was one of the most difficult things I've ever done." A lump rose in her throat. She studied the ice cubes floating in her glass. "I can understand why you kept quiet all those years about what happened between you and Di."

Stan leaned forward and took her hand in his. "I was a fool. And that was a mistake. There was excessive alcohol involved. But I know that's no excuse."

When she didn't look at him, he released his hold on her and sat back. "God, Fiona, I'm so sorry. About everything." Then he asked, "Will we ever be able to untangle this mess?"

She lifted her gaze, saw the regret etched in his features. "I don't know. I honestly don't know."

Di's laughter drew her attention and she glanced over to see her friend leaning over a pool table, lining up a shot. Eli stood nearby smiling. She envied their lighthearted fun. She turned back to Stan. "Should you find a counselor?"

He looked stricken.

"For all of us," she hurried to add, and he relaxed. "The kids need help to deal with all of this. And it wouldn't hurt for you and me to have a little help, too."

"I'll agree with that."

The hope emanating from him urged her to warn, "I can't make any promises, Stan."

"I know you can't. But I have faith—"

She hadn't seen that warm twinkle in his steel-blue eyes in a very long time.

"—in what we had."

That knocked the breath out of her and brought back a flood of tender memories. Early in their marriage, when they had lived on next to nothing, Stan had never failed to profess his belief that they would make it because, he said, they had what it took. The declaration had always made her feel safe and secure, and best of all, it had made her feel loved.

She was scared, though. There seemed to be so much to work through. And she felt like a different person. More a leader, less a follower. She'd had to be. He might not like the woman she'd become, and she had no desire to go back to the woman she'd been.

"We'll have to go slow." The shyness that came over her felt strange, but also exciting.

"Fast or slow, makes no difference to me. I know where we're going." He checked himself. "I mean, I know where I'd like for us to go."

The fear that flashed through her dissipated just that quickly. He would give her room to find her own way. But hadn't he always?

She took a sip of her rum-laced cocktail. "Well, I came here to have a little fun. You want to go rack up a few balls?"

He grinned and slid out of his chair. "Yeah." He nodded. "Yeah, I do."

Stan held out his hand to her, and she took it.

A loud, repetitive beep roused Fiona from sleep.

She groaned and looked over at the clock before thumping on her pillow and settling back down under the comforter. It sounded as if a truck was backing into the driveway of one of her neighbors. But what company made deliveries at seven in the morning? Lord, the sun had barely peeked over the horizon.

A large engine revved, and even with the window closed, she could tell the beeping grew steadily louder. Her eyes snapped open and she rolled out of bed. Snatching her robe from where it lay draped on the chair, she glanced out the window. Sure enough, a flatbed truck was backing onto her property.

Fiona flew down the stairs, stuffing her arms into her robe and loosely tying the sash before jerking open the front door and racing outside.

She approached the truck, waving her arms to get the driver's attention. "Stop!"

The man behind the wheel braked and lifted a hand in greeting. "Morning! I've got your drywall," he called from the open window.

"But I didn't order drywall."

The driver frowned.

"It's okay," Stan called. "Keep it coming."

Fiona turned, and the scene before her made her eyes widen.

She hadn't seen the Volvo parked next to her van in front of the open garage door. Nor had she noticed the kids' bicycles, both mowers, the wheeled tool chest, the rakes and shovels and various lawn equipment that Stan had cleared from inside the garage. Her husband looked quite pleased with himself.

"You must have been working in the dark this morning," she commented. Confusion made her frown. "What are you doing, Stan?" Without waiting for an answer, she pointed at the truck. "And what's the drywall for?"

Stan lifted his hands. "Surprise."

The pucker in her brow only deepened.

"I'm going to build you a state-of-the-art kitchen. Complete with stainless steel appliances, commercial-size ovens, and marble countertops." He pulled a roll of white paper from his back pocket. "I've met with an architect, Fiona. Come look at the plans."

His excitement was palpable as he unrolled the blueprints, but all Fiona felt was panic.

"Wait." Her feet remained planted on the lawn. "Please don't be offended, Stan, because I appreciate the thought. But—" She shook her head. "We can't afford this."

Her reaction dampened his enthusiasm. He lowered his hands. "Sure we can. I've worked out the figures. I took a loan against my retirement plan. I wanted to show you, you know—" doubt crept into his tone "—how much I believe in you."

The deliveryman had turned off the truck and was now using a small crane to unload the drywall.

Something knotted her stomach, and she identified it as dread. The only word she'd heard was loan. How long would it take them to pay back the money this venture would cost? What if her business failed? What if their marriage failed? Did they need this huge debt hanging over them? To Fiona, it sounded as if Stan was adding one more twist to the tangled mess of their lives. Didn't they have enough to deal with?

He wasn't normally a presumptive person. How could he expect her to happily jump onboard with this idea? Yes, their relationship was improving. Stan had come to the house for dinner several times over the past two weeks. Even the children were warming up to the idea of having their dad back in their lives. But who knew what the future had in store for her and Stan as a couple?

Fiona felt terribly guilty for her negativity. "We've only been to one counseling session. Do you really think this is…"

The understanding smile he offered made the rest of her thought go unspoken.

"You didn't hear me." His voice was soft as he moved closer to her. "I said *I* took out a loan. *I* borrowed the money. My name is the only one on the paperwork. I'm the only one responsible. This isn't supposed to be a burden. It's a gift. From me to you. Free and clear. No matter what happens between us."

The fact that he'd figured out she was feeling obligated embarrassed her. It also made her realize just how well he knew her.

"You're right," he said. "We've been to counseling once. But I got so much out of what the therapist had to say."

Fiona had liked Dr. Prues immediately. The woman had been quick to identify that the lives of the entire Rowland family had become out of balance, and she'd complimented them on wanting to do something about it.

"I had a revelation," Stan continued, "when she said that I should wake up every morning and ask myself what I can do to make you happy. I realized it's been a very long time since I've done anything to make you happy. Something special, I mean. Just for you."

Moisture gathered in her eyes, forcing her to blink, and her heart swelled to the point that it ached. God, this was so like Stan. He'd always been kind. Always been caring. Always been giving.

Those traits were what had drawn her to him all those years ago—and they were what drove home the notion that he was the person she wanted to spend the rest of her life with.

A tear slipped down her cheek as she closed the gap between them and wrapped her arms around his neck. The warmth of him felt good against the November chill.

"How could I have ever forgotten," she whispered, "how much I love you?"

He studied her face, his gaze filled with devotion, adoration. He didn't have to say it. She felt it. *Knew it.* Just as she knew, with every fiber of her being, that they were going to be okay. They were going to make it.

True passion and a heart-wrenching familiarity heated the kiss they shared.

When they parted, she asked, "Are you sure we can afford this?"

He nodded, hugging her closer. "Absolutely. I'll go over everything with you this morning."

Excitement skittered through her, setting her heart racing. There was so much to be excited about.

She kissed him again, but the applause behind her interrupted their intimate moment. With Stan's arms still around her, she twisted to see a small group of men standing nearby.

Stan grinned. "That would be the drywall crew."

She waved. "Good morning," she called. Then she looked up into her husband's face. "Guess I should get dressed, make a big pot of coffee, and whip up a batch of muffins, huh?"

"Wouldn't be a bad idea."

They nearly got wrapped up in another tender moment, but she tore herself away finally, hurrying across the dew-damp lawn with light and joyous steps.

And life continued on.

* * *

Thank you for reading FINDING FIONA. If you enjoyed the book, please consider leaving a review. A good review will help other readers choose this book. Also consider telling a friend about the book. Word-of-mouth recommendations are the best advertisement for authors! Donna Fasano appreciates your support.

Book Club Discussion Questions

A book club is a great way to get together with old friends and make new ones. The perfect gathering has three ingredients: 1. a good book 2. delicious snacks 3. a lively discussion. The following questions have been suggested as a means of kick-starting the discussion. Whoever leads the discussion should try to get everyone involved by making sure each person has a chance to offer an opinion. It's okay to discuss, dissect, and disagree about any aspect of the book: plot twists, character flaws, alternative endings, etc. The most important thing is to have a good time!

As a stay-at-home mom, Fiona became lost in the job of raising her children. Could you relate to this idea? Have you ever become so wrapped up in one aspect of your life (kids, job, church, volunteering, etc.) that you've neglected others? How important is balance in living a successful life? Is "balance" the same for everyone? Is it possible to live an "unbalanced" life and still be happy?

Did you find Fiona's stay-at-home mom situation current or dated? Do you know any women or men who have chosen to remain at home to raise the children over being gainfully employed? In this age of equality, should a person—no matter their gender—have the right to make such a choice?

How did you react to Stan's emotional affair with his co-worker? Would you have been more disturbed if the affair had been physical? Do you feel marriage can withstand an extra-marital affair? If your spouse cheated, but then ended the affair, would you want to know? Is it possible to truly "get over" infidelity and rebuild a trusting relationship? What are some ways to "affair-proof" a marriage?

Did Fiona and Di's friendship add an engaging aspect to the story? How old is your oldest friendship? Have you ever been friends with someone who is very different from you? What do you think held Fiona and Di together so closely? How did you feel when Fiona ultimately forgave Di for her betrayal with Stan? Was the situation believable? Could you forgive a friend who betrayed you?

What did you think about Di's unconventional handling of Sam, Fiona's son, and the teen who was bullying him? Do you agree with Di's decision not to tell Fiona about the situation?

Many novels, movies, and TV shows portray "older man/younger woman" relationships as quite normal. How did you feel about Fiona's attraction to Chad? Did she come off as a cougar? Or did you root for the two to become involved? Why are older woman who date younger men seen as predatory while older men get away with the same type of behavior? How can the double standard be broken?

In the original manuscript, Fiona ended up leaving Stan; however, the editor felt this wasn't how a true "romance heroine" would act. Would you have rather seen Fiona end her marriage and start a relationship with Chad? Why or why not? How sacred is the marriage pact?

A Note From The Author

Things moms say:

"Sometimes my "mom voice" is so loud, even the neighbors put on their pajamas and brush their teeth."

"I used to think I was patient, but then my kid got out of bed for the 67th time to ask why ducks don't have arms."

"We have officially reached the you're-on-your-own portion of the day! I've clocked out. Good luck!"

"I look so peaceful when my kids are sleeping."

Dear Reader,

I feel for Fiona. I'm a mom; I've been there, done that. Parenting (for moms *and* dads) can be an overwhelming job, a 24/7 task that can sometimes seem thankless, unappreciated, and woefully under-valued. However, (thank the good Lord!) raising children can also bring some of the most enriching, gratifying, and beautiful experiences imaginable.

Do we, as parents, make mistakes? Oh, my, yes! But we also sometimes hit it out of the freakin' park! The most important thing, I think, is loving our kids, listening to them, and offering them a soft place to fall, so to speak. Children are resilient, and they're very smart. If we open our hearts to them, they'll forgive us our faults and foibles. They'll come to understand that, although we aren't perfect, we're doing the best job we can.

Once, when my children were very young, I was leaving my mom's house, both my boys were crying in the backseat of the car because, naturally, they wanted to stay with Mom-mom. I felt harried and frustrated and unloved. My aunt, who was visiting, shouted out, "They'll grow up! I promise!" Those two short sentences woke me up like a smack to the cheek, and I laughed. That incident taught me not to take motherhood so seriously. Hold on to those precious moments. Let go of the awful ones. And make lots of memories because there is one

promise I can guarantee—your kids will grow up...
and they'll grow up way too fast.

All my love,

Donna

Other Books By Donna Fasano

Ocean City Boardwalk Series:
Following His Heart, Book 1
Two Hearts In Winter, Book 2
Wild Hearts of Summer, Book 3
An Almost Perfect Christmas, Book 4
Grown-Up Christmas List, Book 5
The Wedding Planner's Son, Book 6

~ ~ ~

Reclaim My Heart
The Merry-Go-Round
Her Fake Romance
Take Me, I'm Yours
His Wife for a While
Mountain Laurel

~ ~ ~

The Single Daddy Club Series:
Derrick, Book 1

Other Books By Donna Fasano

Jason, Book 2
Reece, Book 3

~ ~ ~

A Family Forever Series:
A Beautiful Stranger, Book 1
Made in Paradise, Book 2
A Reason to Believe, Book 3
An Accidental Family, Book 4
Nanny and the Professor, Book 5

~ ~ ~

Non-fiction Books
Cooking In All Directions
Prayer of Quiet
Favorite Christmas Cookies
Recipes of Love
Guy Food

About The Author

Donna Fasano is a USA TODAY Bestselling Author whose books have sold 4 million copies worldwide and have been translated into two dozen languages. She lives on Maryland's Eastern Shore with her husband.